UNIVERSE WITHIN

A NOVEL

GENNA PFISTER

xoxo
GWP

RIVER GROVE
BOOKS

Published by River Grove Books
Austin, TX
www.rivergrovebooks.com

Distributed by River Grove Books

Design and composition by Greenleaf Book Group
Cover design by Kirk Fuson and Greenleaf Book Group

Publisher's Cataloging-in-Publication data is available.

Print ISBN: 978-1-63299-727-2

eBook ISBN: 978-1-63299-728-9

First Edition

For my shining stars,
Jason, Jackson, Savannah, and George.
I love you endlessly, forever, and always.

STELLA

How could the universe take away such a positive light, and leave so much darkness around me? I can't shake the feeling my dead husband isn't dead at all, and that he is lying right next to me, looking into my eyes, telling me all the sweet words I need to hear to escape my anxieties. I need him more than ever.

I feel something lurking behind me; a dark intensity that could devour me. Deep down, I know nothing is there, but I can't help turning my head to look. I roll over to face my fears, to prove to myself I'm alone in my room. There is nothing, but the darkness hides in the cracks of the walls and behind the curtains, waiting for my doubts to return and strengthen its presence. I close my eyes and refuse to cry. I try to be strong while I remember my loving husband, who always made me feel safe.

Anger settles within the pit of my stomach. I spiral into remembering every mistake, every heartache, every disappointment from my past. I'm sure it's some form of evolution that causes our brains to remember negative moments far more than positive ones. It's a defense mechanism to ensure we don't experience it twice. I am responsible for my own life and what I learn from it. The constant question of why is what keeps me up at night.

Why did I say that so long ago? Why does it still bother me? Why are we here? Why is this happening? *Why* couldn't it have been some evil, twisted freak who died instead of my perfect James?

Nights are particularly difficult. My brain doesn't shut off. I have to force myself to forget the agonizing emptiness of my bed, which turns into tearful remembering of his gentle hands in my hair and his calming voice. The exhausting internal battle plagues me. Each morning is a relief to some extent.

The sun shines on my face through the edges of the curtains, and the darkness is gone. I wake up relieved to have gotten through the night. I'm optimistic and hopeful. I can't stay depressed forever. Coffee in its blackest, most potent form surely expedites this state of mind.

I quickly scramble eggs and jelly some toast, pack my leftover Mediterranean wrap and French macaron for lunch with extra coffee, then smack a kiss on our wedding photo as I leave.

I race over to my therapy appointment with Dr. Murray, the new guy, before my workday. Susan, my previous therapist who retired, highly recommended him and assured me we would mesh well. I never liked the idea of having a male therapist, and I have my doubts, but I trust her. I've been dreading opening up to someone new, but what have I got to lose? My friends can't visit me without a pity face and tone that make me physically ill. I can't blame them, but I need a break. That's where my therapist comes in.

His office is even closer to my house than Susan's, and I like the fact that it's inside an actual house instead of a bland office building. It seems much more personal and comfortable. When I park my car and lean over to grab my purse, I see a sticky note has fallen onto the passenger seat floor. It was a grocery list he made when we wanted to try a new Bolognese recipe. It's ridiculous how much this little note means now that he's gone. I kiss it, stuff it in my pocket, and run inside.

The whole house smells like freshly baked cookies. The living room is the waiting room, and instead of magazines, the coffee table is filled with beautiful art and photography books. Susan, things are looking good so far.

I pour myself a mug of coffee and sit down on a couch that looks like it came straight from my grandma's house. It's got the vintage-cool aesthetic that is so trendy right now. I appreciate how clean and inviting the house feels. A catalog of Richard Avedon's most famous photographs is on the table, and immediately I feel a connection. I'm more comfortable than I anticipated. Are there actually cookies somewhere, or is this some sick trick candle scent meant to torture people?

The door across from me creaks open, and a man steps into the threshold.

"You must be Stella! Hi, I'm Nathaniel Murray. I'm so happy to finally meet you. Please come in!" He waves me in. I simply smile and follow. I feel shy and a little nervous. I see a plate of cookies on the table next to the couch. What a relief!

"So, Susan gave me your previous case files, but I haven't looked at them. I wanted to get to know you first and see if you'd want me to read up on your past, or if you want to start fresh?"

My gaze skims over his dark grey hair and light, scruffy beard. His tortoiseshell glasses frame his round face well, and his corduroy pants match his plaid shirt. His cozy appearance is comforting, and I suppress the urge to hug him. That would be very embarrassing.

"Please, help yourself to the cookies."

I must have been eyeing them.

"Thank you. I think the stories will stay the same, and I'd rather not have to retell my entire history. Please feel free to read up on me."

"Perfect. I will definitely do that," he says as he crosses his legs and prepares his pen and paper. "Now, how are you today? What's on your mind?"

I smile and break eye contact. Not sure where to begin, I fumble with my cookie. Even with years of therapy, I find it difficult to process my feelings. My eyes dart all over the room, searching for something to talk about. I hope I'm not coming off as awkward as I feel. My gaze stops at a framed black-and-white photo of Pablo Picasso feeding birds.

"Did you decorate this place? I really like the art you've chosen."

He glances over his shoulder at the picture. "Yes, I found that print at a garage sale. It's not an original, but I'd never seen it before."

"It's refreshing to see the artist as opposed to just his work. It's easy to forget he was a regular person."

"Exactly. Perspective."

"Right." My enthusiasm fades, knowing we're done talking about the photograph. What else do I say? Can he sense my panic?

"Stella, if you were here with Susan, what would you be talking about?"

So, yes, he knows I'm uncomfortable. "That's a good question." I shift in my chair. "Probably how I'm adjusting to my life without my husband around anymore. He passed away just a few months ago."

"That is terrible to hear. I'm so, so sorry. Was it an illness?"

"He had appendicitis but neglected his symptoms. He thought it was a stomachache. By the time we got to the hospital, it had already burst, and he had sepsis. It was too late to save him, apparently."

"That is tragic. It must still be a shock since it happened so suddenly," he says, jotting something down. "What's the hardest part of living without him?"

"Falling asleep, waking up, coming home to an empty house. There is a constant void without him. He knew how much I loved him, but I didn't get closure. He was there, and then he wasn't."

"Did you have a service for him?"

"Yes, of course. It's all a blur. I was physically there, but my mind wasn't. I was in denial. Couldn't mentally absorb what was happening. Our families and friends were there. It was a beautiful service, but nothing feels right about burying your husband."

"Of course. Do you find yourself carrying on with your life, or do you feel like it's too hard to function?"

"I'd say it's a good mixture. I go to work and pretend things are normal. Put my head down and focus on the job. And I go to ballet. Since I'm not very close with my classmates, I don't have to worry about anyone bringing it up. But I can't see my friends right now. It's too awkward."

"So, you don't like talking about it with people you know?"

"Not at all. I have nothing good to say right now. Nothing positive. Why would I want to hang out with my friends and be a Debbie Downer the whole time? I don't want that. I can tell it's too soon for them to act normal around me, so I'm fine avoiding them for now."

"And when you're not working or going to ballet?"

"I'm moping around, desperately missing him, crying, or distracting myself with TV. It's pathetic, I know."

"It's not pathetic at all. It's completely normal. Everyone copes differently with death. You're young, and you have your whole life ahead of you, but it's important for you to keep your husband in your daily life. Eventually, you'll need to store his things and start focusing on your future as just Stella, but that could be months or years. You need time to heal. You can take as long as you need. I'd encourage you to reach out to your friends, though, even if it makes you uncomfortable."

I stick my hand in my pocket and grip the sticky note. "His name is James, by the way. Over eight years of marriage is a lot of time to get over. I feel like we grew up together. I married him when I was twenty-two."

"Did you ever plan on starting a family?"

"It was definitely on our list." I don't bother to go into the details about our miscarriages. We were trying to conceive for over a year.

"Do you ever feel consumed with darkness?"

"Whoa, getting straight to the point, aren't we?" I give a nervous laugh. "Um, yes, but not in like a horror movie type of way." I wiggle my fingers, portraying the spookiness, giving away my uneasiness about the topic.

"In like what type of way?" he asks with furrowed brows, his eyes slightly squinted.

"I don't know. Sometimes, when I'm alone in the dark, I feel like there's someone watching me. I know there's no one there, but I can feel them creeping closer like they're about to steal my soul. If I close my eyes, I see stars slowly stream across my eyelids. They go faster and faster until there's a bright light, and then it's over. The creepy feeling is gone, and I feel fine. I think it's just me being scared at night without James."

"And that doesn't sound like a horror film to you?"

I don't give him an answer.

"Stella, that would be scary for anyone. It sounds like a big deal to me, and you shouldn't have to suffer like that. How often does this happen?"

"At least once a day."

"And, when it's over, do you feel better about life or worse?"

I let out another laugh even though I don't find this funny at all. "I typically feel pretty scared, but relieved that at least I got through it."

"Do you think there will be a time when you can't get through it?"

I never thought of that before. "I hope not. James was my bright light, and I was his. We were so goofy and happy together. Our energy bounced off each other, and we lifted each other up. Now that he's gone, I just feel like I'm not safe, not meant to be happy."

"Don't let his absence keep you from shining your light. You can be just as positive and uplifting as before. Let him live through you. It's up to you."

I let those words sink in. "You're right. I guess I knew that deep down."

"I'd like to offer you something for your troubles. It's an all-natural supplement that has been studied for decades and is now grown in a lab to limit contamination. It has a bit of a stigma to it, but I've seen such positive results. I absolutely recommend you try it. It's a capsule containing an extremely small dose of psilocybin. Are you familiar with it?"

"Shrooms?"

"Yes. Mushrooms. It will not make you hallucinate, but most of my patients feel uplifted, more optimistic, more artistic. Relaxed, less stressed, less tired. It's got potential to help you get through this difficult time. This, and, of course, continuing to talk things through with me."

"Wow, I'm shocked. I will definitely try them. Is it something

I will notice after taking just one? Or will I only notice a difference after a few weeks?"

"You will be able to tell whether you like it or not after one capsule. I will give you a prescription for fourteen for now, so you have enough to get through next week before we meet again. If you don't like it, stop taking them." He hands me the prescription with the name and address of the pharmacy around the corner.

"So, morning? Noon? Night? When do I take it?"

"Let's start with you taking one capsule after work and see how that goes. I look forward to talking with you next week."

"Yes, thank you. See you then."

I realize my cookie is still sitting on my lap and take it to-go. He walks me out, and I wave from my car. "Wow, Susan. So, you send me straight to a drug dealer? Was I that bad of a patient? No hope for me? Sheesh!"

The cookie is gone in three bites, tops. I set the prescription down in the passenger seat and question if I'm really going to go through with that assignment. With my hands on the steering wheel, I try to reset my mind into teaching mode. I put the car in drive and head to Portland Shores High School.

Teaching is my great escape from reality. I crave deep conversations and meaningful moments. While my students are slightly immature for such undertakings, I often resort to Hemingway, Ellison, Steinbeck, Fitzgerald, and Thoreau. These are my favorites to discuss with my students, knowing very well only a small percentage actually listen to anything I say. I might as well enjoy myself with topics I'm passionate about. My classes consist of me mostly having conversations with myself about *why* the authors chose to do things a certain way or wondering what inspired them. It's all very exciting to me, and my students *must* absorb some of my enthusiasm and curiosity. That's my hope, anyway.

I pull into the parking lot and take a deep, cleansing breath. On my way inside, I admire the sun shining through the massive ash trees and breathe in the morning breeze as it wafts up through the wet soil.

"Good morning to my beautiful class of soon-to-be deep thinkers!" I say as I enter my room. My kids love how overly positive I am, and they genuinely don't want to let me down. It's a great feeling.

"Did everyone do their reading?"

"Unfortunately, I did," snorts Conrad from the back. I jerk my head in his direction, showing my disappointment in his tone.

"I loved it, Ms. Frasier!" calls Stephanie, my favorite.

"Lovely. And anyone else?" The class moans and groans. "Oh, come on! *The Maine Woods* was written on your stomping grounds! Thoreau didn't leave out a single detail about the beauty of our forests. What did you learn?" I sit on the edge of my desk.

"I learned that I don't want to go camping," Kim says, and everyone giggles.

"I can understand that. In our journey through transcendentalism, is there anything you can relate to? For example, I get butterflies in my stomach every time he gushes over the scenery."

"I liked the history he included," Stephanie says.

I point my finger at her. "That's right. Excellent! He was very educated on the history of the land." I look around, waiting for someone else to share, but the room stays silent.

"Do you think he felt sorry for the Native Americans?"

Ethan raises his hand. "Yes . . . but he also really respected them and their way of life. He related more with them than the loggers and industrial people."

"Absolutely. You guys are making me so happy. You're really seeing the big picture. Isn't it strange to think that these essays were simply bits from his journal? Can you imagine having so many opinions, thoughts, and ideas during a trip?"

They all give me shy smiles.

"Well, get ready!" They moan again and cover their eyes. I love every second of their discomfort. This is what shapes them into freethinkers.

"Your assignment is to walk from this class to the far end of the football field with your notebook. You are to pretend to be Henry David Thoreau. You will document everything you see along the way, how it made you feel, and your thoughts. Be creative. Get into character. You have twenty-five minutes remaining. Go!"

The kids all jump out of their seats and find a partner. I follow along, smiling and listening to their sarcastic comments. I love their enthusiasm.

When my off period comes and I am eating lunch while I grade papers, I sit back in my chair, stretch my arms above my head, and think about all the students I've taught in the past. I wonder if I've had a lasting impact. As much as I love these kids, I still feel like there's something missing. Like I haven't found my true purpose in life. What else am I meant to do? Does my job have a purpose? Of course. Does it nourish my soul? No, but is that the responsibility of my job? I need to get my soul fixed; I think.

I am a functioning, broken human who needs fuel. But what is my fuel? Before, it was cooking and baking, discussing and traveling—anything with James was perfection. We were married for eight years and closer than we had ever been before. Now, nothing feels quite right.

It's too quiet to read books alone in my apartment. Cooking for one is cruel, but baking for one should be illegal. Should I get a cat? James was allergic, so we never had pets.

I check my calendar for my upcoming ballet class. I forgot my instructor emailed me about the new time change. I still have three classes, but five p.m. is doable.

—∿∿∿WWWW∿—

After ballet class, I am drenched in sweat, and my calves are aching. The floors were extra sticky from the fresh Marley flooring, and I might have broken one of my toes mid-piqué.

Ballet was something James wanted me to keep up with. He knew it filled my cup. Nothing makes me feel more beautiful and feminine than putting on my ballet attire and lengthening my body to classical music, stretching this way, reaching that way, turning and leaping. It's the epitome of *seemingly* effortless beauty. I'm not nearly as coordinated as I was when I danced as a teen, but at my age, it's less about perfection and more about the continuation of learning and trying my best. My teacher is still hard on me, but she knows how much I love a good challenge.

At least I can go to ballet without getting any sappy sympathy. The dancers change often. Only a few remain constant, but our conversations are always short and casual, mostly pertaining to ballet. Dancing is something I cherish, and James would be proud to know I stuck with it.

I say my goodbyes, find my keys, and make my way past the lingering parents who are watching their girls in the other studios. I choke up seeing how impressed the parents are and how proud they are of their children. They hardly notice me squeeze by as they whisper compliments on their daughters' improvements. I feel proud to be a part of this studio. It's a smaller one run by a local mom who started it all from scratch. It has come a long way in the past year.

When I get in my decade-old Prius, I notice I have a missed call from my mom. I tap the call button.

"Hey, Mom. Did you call?"

"Yes, honey, I was trying to catch you before I started making this recipe you gave me. I was wondering if I could substitute almond flour for flour since I have a guest over who—"

"Yes, that's totally fine. I actually prefer almond meal in mine, but just add a bit more salt."

"Oh, okay, great! About to pull it out of the oven. I went ahead and added the almond flour. I'll have to call you tomorrow. Moshe just surprised me from Israel. He's working on a project in Texas, of all places!" I pictured her with her cordless phone kinked over one shoulder with her ruffled oven mitts on in Sedona.

"Wow, that sounds interesting. Can't wait to hear about it. Enjoy your evening."

"Wait," she shouts. "Your friends have been calling me to check on you. They say you won't answer their calls or texts. Pamela is especially worried."

"I'm sorry they call you." I sigh. "I will reach out to them."

"You're not getting together with your friends, honey?" Concern echoes in her tone.

"No. It's too soon," I answer and hear my voice crack.

"I get it." She pauses, probably not sure what else to say. "I'm here for you, ladybug."

"I know. Thank you."

"Okay. Love you, honey. Bye."

I hang up with a lump in my stomach. This whole grieving process is so complicated. At least, I'm happy my mom is enjoying her life with her new beau.

With James gone, she calls me all the time with fake questions, just so she has an excuse to check on me. We have remained close over the years, and she's always searching for new hobbies. Art is her constant passion, but right now, it's Judaism. She signed up for an ancestry website and found out she's Jewish. She went to Israel to do her Birthright tour and fell in love with her Jewish tour guide, Moshe. His life's work is in preserving religious artifacts. I'm very protective of my mother, and I'm not really sure about this guy. When I meet him, I will feel him out. I'm a very good judge of character.

My tire pressure light turns on just as I pull into my neighborhood. I try to think of the last time I changed the tires, or got them rotated, or aligned, and I've got nothing. James usually took care of the cars. The steering wheel jerks in my hands. It must be totally flat now. I park in my designated spot behind the apartment complex, knowing I can get it fixed over the weekend, but dreading driving James's car to work tomorrow. I step out and kick the tire, then turn and kick James's tire, imagining it was his shin.

"Damn it, James!" I whisper. If he were here, he'd make me laugh. We were always so good about laughing when things went wrong. We'd quote a funny movie line and cackle until we had tears streaming down our faces.

If he were here now, he'd say, "Stella, that's what happens when you don't change your tires regularly," and I'd jokingly elbow his ribs. Then he'd say, "I'll take care of it." But he's gone, and everything seems so serious and dull.

Thunder claps. It begins to sprinkle, and I snap back into reality. The rain pours, and I run to my apartment and unlock the door. I smack a kiss on our wedding photo and drop my bags on the kitchen floor. In the living room, I find my way around the sofa and plop into my squeaky wooden desk chair. Pushing aside my stack of bills, I find my soft, leather-bound journal. Its luscious lined paper doesn't bleed through. I flip through all the crinkled papers stiff with my handwriting and find the next clean page.

I used to come home and tell James about my day. In a way, I still do when I journal. I imagine him floating in space as some bright aura, mingling with other souls and spirits, time being nonexistent, listening and simply being. The universe absorbs his energy and makes him the most beautiful star; his soul stretches far as rays of light.

I fidget with my wedding band and find comfort in its familiarity. With a glass of wine, I write until my handwriting becomes illegible and I'm numb to the pain of being alone.

When my mind trails off and writing becomes a nuisance, I feel the weight of the silence in my empty apartment. I step outside onto my tiny porch for some fresh air and search the sky for answers.

My problems don't seem overwhelming, considering there are billions of stars in the Milky Way alone and galaxies in every direction. It's frightening to think how massive the universe is, and how insignificant human life must really be.

Why are we here? Are we just a random concoction of chemical reactions, or were we created? Or are those two things mutually exclusive?

Life has never been easy for humans, but for so long, it was simple—survive. Now, we have surpassed simply surviving, and we require more if we really want to thrive. We all have a desire to feel connected, somehow.

I keep the porch light off as I soak in the awe-inspiring view of the moon and stars. I wonder who else is looking up and away. We can't possibly be the only intelligent creatures in this immense universe. I close my eyes, remembering those nights in the woods so long ago, my drawings that I was so proud of, and the way—

I refuse to let myself go there. It was probably all a dream.

ANDREW

I've got to get out of this city. I'm a thirty-five-year-old man, living in Manhattan. I learned a long time ago not to waste my time and to spend it wisely. My mom taught my sisters and me to constantly try to be the best, work the hardest, be the strongest. She'd say, "Life is too short to be lazy, and there are far too many lazy people on this planet." For me, that meant getting a good job that pays well and making time for my passions.

Tonight, I am on a date. I think for sure it will be different. Dating has to be the most awkward part of life. Even when there is a ton of chemistry, it can be a chore to get to know each other. Ask the same questions, give the same answers, fumble through conversations until you decide if you want to see this person again.

I have been set up on a few blind dates by my sisters before, and they went fine. But this woman was recommended by a friend from work. We're close, so I have high hopes.

This woman chose a trendy bistro nearby that I love, so things are looking good. When we sit down, she mentions I remind her of someone from her childhood; that I even have the same personality. It turns out the resemblance is uncanny, and she calls him while we are eating to discuss our similarities. Eventually, they are on the date, and I am watching. I politely excuse myself and pay the bill on the way out.

—∿∿∿∿∿∿∿—

At home, Chester greets me by running full speed and skidding to a stop at my feet. He whines and yelps and howls until I scratch his back and gush over him for a minimum of three minutes.

I rescued Chester from my old neighbors when he was a puppy. They were younger and had a wild party one night and overdosed on heroin. I never saw them as the type to use the hard stuff, but maybe that's why it ended badly for them . . . or maybe they didn't know it was heroin.

When their families cleared out the house, I offered to take the dog. My neighbors named him Chester, not me, but I liked the name enough to keep it. He's a lavish breed, a golden labradoodle. But, as pretty as he is, I keep him humble with long, shaggy hair.

The rest of the night will be me, Chester, Franz Liszt, and a giant bowl of weed. Nothing melts away the stresses of life like Mary Jane, and it enhances my piano playing. I take pride in my blunt rolling skills and keep my stash on top of the upright someone in my building sold me. To muffle the sound a bit, I placed the piano behind my couch and keep a piece of felt down behind the hammers.

I keep things simple inside my apartment to make up for its location. Though it's small, being so close to the park makes it ridiculously expensive. Why spend money on decor to enhance aesthetics when I could put it toward enhancing myself? As expensive as it has become over the years, weed is a far better investment than designer couches and hand-made rugs.

I sit down at my piano and open my Tupperware of blunts. I take one hit, savoring the smoke inside my lungs until I exhale. Smoking weed helps me feel the music more intensely, and it keeps distractions at bay. I don't think about my emails or busy work calendar. I think about each note as I play "Un Sospiro" by Franz Liszt. Much slower than Liszt intended, of course, but I convince myself it sounds better this way.

Liszt is easily the greatest composer to have ever lived. Okay, Liszt and Rachmaninoff, but I've been learning "Un Sospiro" recently. Their music transcends time and space, propelling through my skin and bones into my gut. It literally pains me to think about the beauty of their work.

When my fingers and my back beg to slouch on the couch, I search for my favorite pianist's concert performance on YouTube and listen to the professional. How could anyone write this? *How?*

———∿∿∿∿MMMM∿∿———

Chester is early to rise on this chilly Wednesday morning. He whines at the foot of my bed until I'm awake, then scratches at the front door. Having a dog in Manhattan is a lot of work. I don't have the luxury of a backyard. I mean, when he's got to go outside, it's a good while before he's in a spot where he can relieve himself.

I get dressed, get his leash, go outside and around the block, and then he's finally free to pee. Oh shit. He's pooping, and I don't have a bag. He never poops before I feed him. When I turn around, I hear someone cuss me out for not cleaning up after my dog, and I ignore them. They don't care that I'm getting a bag from behind the potted plant on my stoop. After cleaning up, I decide to take Chester down to the park for a while before work. The air is crisp, and we need to stretch our lungs.

The Upper West Side is close to Central Park, which is the only part of Manhattan I really enjoy. Even still, it's filled with homeless people and trash, and I can't stand how far it is to our little secret pocket of woods where we can play fetch.

It's illegal to have a dog off the leash, but it seems like his God-given right to chase a damn tennis ball without having to fight other dogs for it at a dog park. I keep a lookout and get in as many throws as I can in ten minutes.

I'll buy us a house with a backyard in a beautiful neighborhood, eventually. I could retire now and live off my savings for the rest of my life if I really wanted to. My sisters have been begging me to come back home. My parents' house is sitting vacant near the rocky cliffs along the shore my dad and I used to climb. I could teach math at the university if I got bored. I need to stop dreaming about leaving the city and work up the nerve to actually do it.

As Chester and I head home, we pass a girl wearing a t-shirt with Dr. Filippenko's face on it and the words "Dark Energy." He's one of the scientists responsible for discovering the accelerated expansion of the universe. I catch myself laughing and wonder what Dr. Filippenko would think to see his smiling face on her ruffled shirt. I've seen strange things in the city, but I never thought about physics and fashion having a moment.

In college, I double majored in math and physics. Math ended up being my strong suit, although physics was fun, and I excelled at both. They go hand-in-hand and were extremely thought-provoking.

The most beautiful part of math is its omnipresence in nature. From the mesmerizing spirals in shells to the intricate fractals of a snowflake, the perfectly symmetrical patterns adorning butterfly wings, and concentric circles like the rings inside a tree trunk, math seems to be woven into every nook and cranny of nature and the universe, beckoning us to explore its hidden secrets. Physics focuses on how the universe behaves like it does, which happens to rely heavily on math for its findings.

You have to be a deep thinker and have a strong sense of curiosity to maintain a constant motivation for learning. That's the key—learning more. Will we ever have it all figured out? Dark matter and dark energy, for example . . . we know they are there making up ninety-five percent of space, but they are still among the greatest mysteries of the universe.

—⁓⋁⋀⋁⋀⋁⋀⋁⋀⋁⋀⁓—

When I arrive at work, Cynthia is eager to hear about how my date went with her friend.

"Honestly, it's too early for this. I haven't even had coffee yet," I say on my way to the office Keurig.

"Okay, but, Andrew, I *told* you she was perfect for you! She's gorgeous, funny, and she lives in your neighborhood." I see her reflection in the office windows, gesticulating dramatically as she follows me.

"It turns out she is perfect for someone who is exactly like me, but not me," I say, squeezing through the line waiting for the coffee machine.

"What do you mean?"

"She said I reminded her of someone she grew up with and literally called him. I left. That was the extent of our date. It's okay, though. I'm happy she found what she was looking for." I grab a clean coffee mug and go to the end of the line.

"I just don't understand you. You've been on so many dates, and you don't seem to care about following up with anyone. Have you any desire to fall in love?"

"Of course, I do." I turn toward her to talk. "It's no one's fault but my own. Look, I think deep down I don't want to get too attached to anyone in New York because my heart isn't in it. I know I'm not going to stay here. In fact, I think it's time to get out of here and move back home. I appreciate your efforts, Cynthia, but I promise, Chester and I are doing just fine for now."

"You literally referred to Chester like he's your friend. I'm worried about you."

"He is my friend!"

"Andrew, you need a girlfriend. This is getting scary." She emphasizes scary with a deeper tone, dramatizing her feelings. She knows exactly how to make me laugh.

I finally get my cup of coffee and make my way to my office. Cynthia is being awfully quiet, and that's out of character for her. I face her, and it becomes clear she finally registered what I said.

"Oh please, don't cry," I beg. "I'm so sorry."

She points her finger at me in a very mom-like fashion. "I knew you were too good for this city, but damn it, I didn't think you'd actually leave!"

I grab her shoulders and say, "No matter what happens, you are going to continue to kick corporate ass. Clearly, it's what you were meant to do. You don't need me. We'd both be competing for chief actuary in a few years, anyway."

Right out of college, we started at this company together, and we sort of helped each other through the hurdles of climbing the corporate ladder. We always had each other's backs, talked each other up to other colleagues and bosses, and referred each other for projects. We remained friends and decided to never make things complicated by adding romance to the equation.

"Come on, you're better off without me. You wouldn't handle it well if I became your boss, would you?" I anticipate a sucker punch, but she laughs and exaggerates her finger-pointing, clearly holding back her sarcastic anger.

"I'd be your boss, and you know it. But I'll still miss you."

"I'll miss you too."

—∿∿∿∿∿∿∿—

As much as I dislike living in the city, it does have some high points. I love the fast-paced liveliness and the diversity. There's always some event going on, and it's easy to stay busy. I was invited to attend a charity event for Kids with Anxiety. It's an important event for our time. Mental health has never had so much attention.

This event is being held to steer families away from pharmaceuticals and use methods of addressing anxiety at its root with deep meditation, therapy, and yoga.

I enjoy attending events I believe in and put on my best suit for the occasion. As I enter the venue, I'm surprised by how many people there are. Most are congregating near the bar. I check my tie and make my way to where the lights are dim and probably fifty round tables are set up for dinner to be served.

I'm a firm believer that we humans are more powerful than we think. Everyone gets anxiety, but it's important to overcome fears and push to be strong. Humans will not be able to face the problems of our world when we are consumed with our own. The charity focuses on mental health as a daily exercise for the brain, which makes perfect sense to me.

I ask the bartender for a double Macallan, so I won't have to come back later for a second drink. I take it with me to the entry table and find my table number. I would have come to support this charity even if it wasn't created by my boss, Heather. She funds the workshops and events held for the local public schools, and it is important to present myself with enthusiasm. I'm lucky to have her as my superior. She's easy to respect. That's rare these days.

Among the other invitees are wealthy New Yorkers who thrive off the sociability and networking aspects of these events; there are the doctors who donated their thoughts and feedback on potential cures or activities to diminish the side effects of anxiety; and then there are people like me: the fillers.

We, the fillers, attend these events out of obligation. We provide our minuscule monetary contribution that we know matters little in the scheme of things, yet we feel a small sense of pride being part of the event.

The fillers congregate in the empty spots of the venue where nothing of real importance happens. We unite and form a drunk frenzy of common folk that eventually turns into a messy afterparty.

I find myself upstairs at someone's wildly over-decorated apartment. The walls have a heinous black-and-white wallpaper print that is trying to look like Rorschach inkblots, and a shiny cobalt blue chandelier with feathers above the bulbs hangs over the kitchen table. Strange, trippy art looms from shelves and hall tables, casting mysterious shadows upon the walls. The music is constant throughout every room and hallway—grunge bands from the nineties mixed with new-age indie pop.

We're all dancing and singing to the old hits we love. Then a bong gets passed to me. I inhale the smoke, and when I release my air, shit gets weird. Damn it, Manhattan.

Boom. Lights out. I'm still aware I'm sitting on the couch in a strange living room, but my brain cannot escape the visuals I'm seeing to move any part of my body. The marijuana is probably laced with LSD.

My eyes are open so wide I think they might pop out of their sockets. Regardless of my fears, I surrender to the drug. My grip on reality slips further away. I hear my heartbeat like loud drums. I feel each lub-dub in my eyes and fingertips. Its hold on me is taking over, and if I don't relax, I'll be stuck in a bad trip. I focus on my breath.

I'm intelligent enough to know this is temporary, and I should try to enjoy this other-worldly experience, even though I didn't ask for it.

Auras are over everyone's heads. Some cover their whole bodies. Some shoot straight into the air. All the neon colors warp into a stone path on the floor, with frogs eating each other and giant mushrooms that glow with intensity and appear to radiate heat.

An overwhelming ohm buzzes through my body, low, deep, and penetrating. Someone is in my head. Someone else is here. A figure emitting the most beautiful light brings up emotions I didn't realize I'd carried. I try to move, get up, and get closer to this figure I'm drawn to. I find myself on the balcony peering into the dark sky, seeing past the city lights into the depth of the starry universe.

I feel a jolt, and fly through space and time, leaving Manhattan, then Earth, then the solar system, then the galaxy, and I see her. Her bright, luminescent face stares straight back at me, eyes sparkling, white hair flowing all around, her neck shining bright. It's painfully quiet.

Without her saying anything, I hear her. *"Come find me."*

I feel the jolt again. I'm rushing backward, being pulled away against my will. I reach out to her to hold myself still, hoping she will speak one more time. Tearing through the vacuum of space, my blurry vision disorients me.

I fall to my knees and grab on to the railing outside at the stranger's apartment. I'm sober and stunned. Someone helps me up.

"Hey man, sorry. Some people can't handle weed after drinking."

"You're Brett, right? I don't think that was just weed." I hold my arm over my mouth, unsure of whether I'll be sick or not.

"I picked that up in Colorado. It's called Third Eye. Fucks you up, right?"

"It's not laced with anything?"

"It has a micro-dose of synthetic LSD. Same effect, but shorter trip," he says as he takes a bag out of his coat pocket.

"How long was I tripping?"

"Not long. You're good, right? I have to order some pizzas."

"Yeah, thanks."

The party suddenly seems dull. I have to get out. I thank the hosts and head home, unable to shake the intensity of the experience. I felt like I was hallucinating for an hour at least, but apparently, I was only out of it for a few minutes.

My friends in college took LSD and hallucinated for an entire day. It was a weekend drug, for sure. I'm so relieved that bowl wasn't spiked with the old-school LSD.

Walking home, I can't help but wish I could see the stars again. The lights of the city deflect the natural beauty of the night sky. If I could just see the stars again, it might make me believe what I experienced was real.

Who was that in my trip? It wasn't anyone at the party, that's for sure.

When I was with her, it was as if she could see into the depths of my soul. Her words echoed in my head and struck the pit of my stomach.

Come find me.

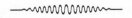

Chester's tail is whacking me in the face at two beats per second, and my phone is ringing on the empty pillow next to me. I drag it to my ear to answer.

"Hello?"

"Andrew," Heather whispers. "Is everything okay? You're late for the meeting."

I bolt up in bed. "I'm so sorry! I slept right through my alarm. I'm very, very sick. I shouldn't be around anyone today. Please, if you don't mind, I can send out an email with my plans for the new policy. Or we can reschedule."

"I understand. This doesn't have anything to do with that wild after-party, does it?"

I pause to debate my answer. "I certainly don't think that helped my situation, no."

"Well, I'm glad you were able to make it to the event. It was a great turnout. It meant a lot to have you there. I hope you feel better by tomorrow, buddy."

"You should be very proud. It was a huge success. And thank you. I'll keep up with my emails from home."

"Sounds good."

I roll over in bed and it hits me: A book . . . from the top of my bed frame. I rub my aching head. I forgot I had set it up there in the middle of the night. She came to me in my dream, the girl from my LSD trip. The drugs must have been lingering in my system.

She led me to a view of my childhood home on the water. It was a memory of mine, fishing off the docks alone before dinner. I looked down at my ten-year-old self and the bright light shining from underneath the ocean. It came racing toward the shore, making a wake as though there was an invisible ship above it. I dropped my pole and ran. I suddenly saw the scene from the perspective of the light and watched my younger self run away. The glowing goddess snapped me out of the memory, touched my heart, and with an all-encompassing blow, I woke up.

I remember now. In the middle of the night, I had the urge to re-read some old college books about theories that consumed my adolescent brain: other spatial dimensions, the multiverse, dark energy, and quantum theory. I read until sleep took hold of me.

I grab the books and flip through the pages, trying to see where I left off. I wrote something in the margin. "Third Eye. Slip."

My head is spinning. Was she telling me to get back to the shore? Was she trying to say she was under the water that night looking up at me?

I honestly don't know what to think, but I've never felt more determined to follow through with something. I know for sure she's at least urging me to follow my heart. And my heart has been telling me to get the hell out of this city. There's a good chance I'm having a mid-life crisis, or I am having some sort of spiritual awakening with the dead, but I don't care. The answer is clear. I push the covers off and call my sister.

"Hey, Claire. Is Mom and Dad's house ready to move into?"

"Andrew!" she squeals. "My baby brother is finally going to move back home!" I hold the phone away from my ear. "Have you called Syd yet? She's going to freak! Oh my gosh, the kids are going to flip. This is amazing news. I knew you'd come around. Mom and Dad would want you to live there. It's begging to be your home."

I can't help but smile at hearing how exhilarated she is at the thought of my return. She's just as enthusiastic as Chester is when I come home.

"It's begging? Or you are?"

I can't deny my own excitement. It's time.

STELLA

I feel a little groggy. I would never admit I had too much wine, but I did. Exercise and alcohol don't work well together. My muscles are achy and tight. I chug a lemon water on the drive to school. Work goes quickly, and I head to the pharmacy after. In the parking lot, I contemplate my situation. Is this for real? Am I about to go in there and buy shrooms?

The pharmacist is very professional and courteous, putting some of my nervousness at ease. As if concealing a handgun, I look around and stash them in my purse. I lean over the counter awkwardly and raise my sunglasses above my head.

"Am I a complete idiot for trusting my therapist with this recommendation?"

He gives me a shy smile. "Well, if it makes you feel any better, we fill that type of prescription about twice as often as antidepressants. So, they must be good for something."

"Right, at least there's that," I say slowly. "Thank you."

As I turn to leave, I wonder whether I should do any research on the pills, or if that would deter me, give me false expectations. It's like going to see a movie when I've never seen a preview, but it's won a lot of awards. They're usually better that way. I should just try them, without any expectations. I close my car door and pop my first pill. It will kick in by the time I get home.

—✲✲✲✲✲✲✲—

When I get to my subdivision, I stop at the neighborhood nature garden. The flowers look so beautiful. With fall approaching, they won't stay for long.

I sit on a bench along a gravel path that leads to the koi fishpond and check my bag to see if I have any fish food. I usually carry a bag of little pellets for them, but it must be in my other purse. I find a crunched-up granola bar and save half for the fish and eat the rest.

It settles well in my stomach, and I feel a warming sensation on the back of my neck from the setting sun. The sky turns to a golden peach, illuminating the clouds and even the birds. Bees dig their little faces into the flowers next to me, and I swear I hear them sniffing around, like little puppies. They are so precious I can't take my eyes off them.

I get closer and lie on the ground with my face resting on my hands, just like a little kid. The grass has a soft glow, and the leftover water droplets from the sprinkler system shine like diamonds. I can't believe my eyes. Thousands of tiny bugs fly around the leaves of grass, and I feel terrible for ever having walked on them. The grass is filled with so much life and beauty.

I stand and follow the gravel path to visit the koi fish, who seem frisky with excitement to see a human who might feed them. I drop crumbs of granola, amazed at how fast they snatch it up. I sit and admire their extra colorful scales as they take turns tasting an acorn and spitting it out.

Nature is sharing its magnificence, and I can't help but feel a sense of calm and connection. My therapist was right when he said I'd know after one pill if I liked them. The answer is yes. I'm so happy and peaceful by myself for the first time in a long time. Life is everywhere all the time.

The wind blows, and I feel James wrapping his arms around me. I breathe him in and close my eyes. He will always be a part of who I am.

The sun is almost fully set when I get home. I turn on Billie Holiday on my Bluetooth speakers while I get ingredients out for dinner.

When I don't have any plans for dinner, I usually cook a shakshuka with chickpeas and eggs. It's hearty, delicious, and refreshing. Today, I add kale for some extra greens. I pour a glass of wine and sit on the couch to eat and watch reruns of *The Big Bang Theory*. When I'm full and satisfied, I lean my head back and look around my apartment.

I remember us buying each piece of furniture with so much enthusiasm at how much it would add to the character of our home. I stop and stare at the artwork James bought me for our fifth wedding anniversary and the teacups we collected from all the hotels we visited overseas. They hang neatly from little hooks under the cabinets in the kitchen.

It's quieter than I'm used to, but it's the home I made with my favorite person, and as much as I'd love to hear the clatter of James doing dishes, I have to start accepting the silence.

I close my eyes and focus on something that makes me happy:

books. I picture my favorite used bookstore with a view of the coast and make a mental note to visit after school tomorrow since it's a half-day.

———~ww\\\\\\\\\wwww~———

After school, I follow doctor's orders and take another shroom capsule, then head straight to The Curious Thinker. I walk to the store and pause to stare at the open sea, admiring the small islands scattered about. The sailboats are out displaying their silent journeys, speckling the horizon as far as the eye can see. The ocean. We know so much, yet so little. That's part of what makes it so intriguing. It holds a power over us—sparks curiosity and wonder. It might as well be an entirely different world. Perhaps that's why it's so refreshing to be near it, to watch it. I breathe in the fresh, salty air and go inside.

The Curious Thinker has a very large floor plan considering the size of the store. It's three stories squeezed into a two-story building. I'm greeted with the choice of descending into the back (which turns into the bottom floor), staying on the entry-level floor, or climbing the winding staircase to the top, which is like a balcony. It couldn't possibly be any more visually appealing. I'm filled with an overwhelming urge to wander, as if there are particular books quietly calling my name.

The effects of the pill are soothing, warming me from the inside out. I go straight for the winding staircase. I always go to American Literature first, and then I work my way down.

The magical smell of the aged pages gives me goosebumps as I rub my fingers along the spines. The first book that catches my eye is *Invisible Man*, by Ralph Ellison, printed in 1959. I've read it before, of course, but I skim the pages and remember the powerful emotions it brought about.

Someone rushes past me and places a note on my open page. I turn to see who it is, but all I catch is long blond hair whipping around the bookshelf. I unfold the piece of paper. It's a drawing. I drop the book and back into the railing behind me.

How could this be? All my drawings were taken away. I lean over the rail to catch another glimpse of the person; the bell that hangs over the front door rings, so I know I'm too late.

With my hand over my mouth, I stare at the paper on the floor. I smooth my hair out of my face. My hands are shaking. Perhaps the shrooms are making me hallucinate after all. . . . No, I'm not. This is real. It's one of the drawings I made when I was seven years old—an image I drew hundreds of times that ended up getting me into a lot of trouble. It's of the little girl I met in the woods. We were close in age and good friends until my parents found out. I thought the drawings were all confiscated when the police came, yet here I am holding one.

I turn my drawing over, and there's a note. "Remember me? Meet me at 7 p.m. next Friday at the corner café. Please, keep it our secret."

Completely shaken, I fall to my knees. I thought it was all my imagination. Is it still?

—⁓⁓⁓〰〰〰〰⁓⁓—

I race home. I'm nervous as hell and refuse to believe I've been swept up in this again. Why is she back? So much time has passed. I haven't allowed myself to think about those nights for so long, but the memories come flooding back.

When I was seven years old, we lived on some heavily wooded acreage near Oakland, right on the edge of a small lake. At night, I'd hear the owls and try to spot them with my flashlight from the porch. Sometimes, I'd catch their eyes glowing in the dark. One night, there was something else. Someone, in fact.

She was around my same height with eyes that glowed, just like the owls, and although she was clearly not human, I was too curious to be afraid. The hair stood up on the back of my neck, but she peered around a tree as though afraid of me. When I spoke gentle words to try to explain I meant no harm, she emitted pulses of vibrations.

I stopped talking and inched sideways to get a better look. She leaned with her back against the tree, staring as intensely as I was. We stood for nearly ten minutes without moving, frozen in shock and disbelief. Her light hair flowed as if it were underwater, and her eyes were very large for the size of her head. She had a human-looking body, but her skin was pale and rubbery. Somehow, she was beautiful.

It was as if she could hear my thoughts, and she replied inside my head. She said I was beautiful, too. No words were spoken, but we were communicating. I moved closer to see her face more clearly, and she ran between two trees and disappeared.

I dropped my flashlight and walked in circles around the trees, searching for trap doors or ropes. I wondered where she'd gone. I raced back inside and sketched a picture, so I'd remember.

The next night, I couldn't sleep and went out to see if she'd meet me again. I took a blanket and a flashlight. When I found the same tree, I sat and turned off my light so my eyes could adjust to the darkness. The quiet was haunting, and it felt like forever until my eyes caught movement in the distance.

She was near the shore, peering from a crouched position. I held my breath and waited for her to come closer. I could sense, or possibly hear, she was feeling the same as she cautiously approached me.

"Hello," I whispered, and she echoed the word inside my head before she sat on the blanket with me.

We continued meeting outside in the dark for twenty nights. We used basic vocabulary to exchange pleasantries, which at such a young age included complimenting each other's appearance and how cold the air felt. But she could only speak inside my head. When she opened her mouth, I could only feel vibrations. After a while, the question was too hard to ignore. I looked up at the sky and asked, "Did you come from out there?" She looked at me and then at the water as if she had more to say. Ultimately, her gaze met mine again, and she projected, "*Yes.*"

Our time together was thrilling, but I became too comfortable. She was no longer a curious-looking creature who lived outside. She was simply my friend.

My parents found my pile of sketches, and they first thought I had a very vivid imagination. Being seven years old made it hard to hide my excitement and enthusiasm. I told them I had been meeting a stranger in the woods every night, and things went south. The police were called, the woods were searched, and I very innocently explained she wasn't human. They sympathized with my "vivid imagination" and displayed their concern fervently.

The police told my mom they had been on the lookout for child predators who manipulate children in these unusual ways, like claiming to be from space, and the FBI had a lot more information.

When the FBI came to our home, they made sure I knew they were special police officers who were going to help me stay safe. No matter how special they tried to appear, it was frustrating for me to answer all the same questions again. They confiscated my drawings and warned my family not to speak of this ongoing investigation. I would have kept one, but they told me how important it was to keep this secret. Even at seven years old, I could sense they were the ones keeping secrets from us.

My experience took a toll on my parents. My mom was scared, and my dad locked all the doors at night with dead bolts operated by keys on both sides. He installed nails on the window frame to keep the window from rising more than a few inches.

I couldn't go out and look for her to apologize for my absence, and it killed me. I felt horrible for telling my parents. Even so young, I should have known they wouldn't understand. I knew my friend was special, and I was confused and bothered that everyone thought she was dangerous.

One night, out of a desperate desire not to forget my friend's face, I tried to make another drawing. My mom walked in with shock and disappointment on her face. She ripped the paper out of my hands, tore it to shreds, and burst into tears. She hugged me tightly and sobbed. I knew not to draw anymore.

The months turned into years, and we moved to the coast. We lived as normally as we could. I pushed the memories away and tried to focus on being a normal kid who never had contact with a possible alien.

I never even told James about it. I would feel strange bringing it up to my mom again. We hardly ever talk about the days when my parents were still married, let alone that wild time. Sometimes, I wonder if it was the catalyst for their separation.

Nearly thirty years later, she's here. She remembers me and wants to talk. What does she want after all these years? How could she meet me in public? She's an alien. Is this some sick joke?

The questions flood my brain as I hurry inside my apartment and pour myself a glass of wine. I am absolutely going to meet her: There's no doubt. I just need to gather my composure and try not to freak out.

I refuse to believe I'm dreaming this all up. I am actually a week away from having dinner with an alien. This will be the longest week of my life.

ANDREW

As Chester and I drive the U-Haul into the driveway of our new home in Vinalhaven, my hometown, both my sisters are lined up on the porch with their families. The house looks like it needs some work, but nothing I can't handle.

We jump out, and I'm pulled to the ground from every direction. All my nieces and nephews are screaming, "Unca Andwew! We love you!"

"I've missed you guys," I say, then pretend to be a big scary monster. The kids have grown so much that they no longer run away in giggly fear but whip out their imaginary swords, guns, and fairy wands and fight me until I'm defeated.

"Kids, back off! We need a turn."

Claire and Sydney help me up and give me big hugs, followed by their husbands.

Kyle shakes my shoulders. "Hey, man, great to have you back."

"It's about time. Someone in the family should live in this house," Josh says, pointing behind him.

Claire crosses her arms. "I knew he'd finally cave."

"Yeah, well, it seems like destiny to me," Sydney says. "We'll all be together again. Claire and I bring the kids here to rock climb in the back every once in a while, but it's so sad coming to an empty house."

"It will be much more fun to visit Uncle Andrew instead of Mom and Dad's old house."

"It does have a better ring to it." I grab Chester and put my arm around him, "What do you think, bud? Your own yard." He whines and takes off running, sniffing everything and dodging the kids chasing him.

It's been a few years since my last visit, but as we walk in through the front door, I'm immediately struck by the amazing view. It's such a relief coming from the city where concrete is around every corner.

The house has a cabin feel to it, but it's got high-end wood floors, granite countertops, and upgraded appliances. My sisters call it cabin-chic, which sounds fancier than it is. It's rustic but meant for entertaining with the large, open living and dining rooms.

As excited as I am about the house, I'm drawn straight to the floor-to-ceiling windows by the back porch. The trees look taller and fuller than when I was here last. The backyard stretches about a quarter mile, scattered with spruces and maples.

Chester runs toward the shore, and I follow. The rocky shoreline is met with crystal-clear blue water. A smaller island sits about two hundred yards in the distance, and another to the southeast, maybe five hundred yards away. I call him over and lean against the cliff, touching the rough edges, remembering so many climbs from my childhood.

Sydney wraps her arms around me from the side, and I wish Mom and Dad were here to see us all together again. They'd be happy I moved back home.

"You thinking about Mom and Dad?"

"Yeah, actually," I answer with surprise in my voice. "I wish I could climb with him again."

"Every route you made with him is still here. You will climb with him again."

"Remember how much he loved telling us the beta for every single tiny move?" I chuckle.

"Oh my gosh, he never stopped!"

"It was so annoying, but he couldn't help it."

"He loved it so much, though."

"Yeah," I say, giving the stone one last grip. "I miss him."

She takes my arm, and we head back toward the house. "Mom would have brought ridiculous modern decorating magazines over and have this entire house planned out by now, and Dad would be asking you to get the canoe out so you two could go fishing."

"That's *exactly* what would be happening right now."

"I still have Dad's old canoe. You can have it. Man, I miss them. We'll have to keep up their yearly tradition of planting a tree, you know."

"I know." I sigh. "We will." I've already found the perfect spot in the front yard.

"You know, you could get a nice sectional sofa for the living room that leaves room for a large coffee table for all those space books you like," Claire yells from the porch as we walk up the stairs.

Sydney giggles. "Looks like Mom is here, after all."

We were closer as kids, but Claire and I are closer as adults. I'm the middle child, Claire is the oldest, and Syd is the youngest. Our parents were total soulmates, madly in love with each other for their whole marriage. They were amazing parents who made sure we all knew how to be decent humans. I can't imagine too many people find a love as compatible as theirs, but they set the bar high.

Staring out my new back windows, I can't help but think of the woman I met during my LSD trip: that beautiful glowing goddess. *Come find me.* Was this a metaphor? I've been playing back the moment we shared over and over. I saw her with LSD in my system, so, before leaving New York, I asked Brett if he wouldn't mind parting ways with a bag of the Third Eye.

—~vvvv\/\/\/\/\vvvv~—

Josh and Kyle helped me with the heavy lifting of bringing things in from the U-Haul. My apartment was small, so my furniture won't fill the house. My sisters took a few things after my dad passed and cleared out all the clutter. For now, I'll get good use out of the kitchen table and couch that have remained.

Where I am lacking in furniture, I make up for in artwork. I finally have lots of wall space. My Hubble telescope image of what I like to call "the edge of the galaxy" shows the dense collection of colorful stars of the Milky Way. I bought it in the city because I missed seeing the stars. Here, on my small island of a town, I can see the entire sky lit up on clear nights. Tonight is a perfect night to try to connect with the woman again.

The sky is bright with stars. The moon is nearly full. I get my pipe and fill it with the Third Eye marijuana-LSD concoction. Outside, on my porch, I make a silent plea to the universe to let this work and take a rip. I stare at the stars as I exhale, hoping to connect somehow.

The drug hits me hard, and the weight of it pushes me down into the chair behind me.

She is waiting for me. She's as bright as a star, but I can't look away. Her long, flowing hair dances behind her, and she walks down from the sky. Stars follow in her footsteps and ripple as if she was walking on water. She stops in front of me and reaches for my hand.

We go to the same place as last time, through the atmosphere, far away from Earth, up and away until the entire galaxy is in my view. She touches my forehead and shows me pockets of dark energy spread throughout the universe like a woven net.

Somehow, with her eyes, she communicates feelings and information. I am connected to her, connected to the universe.

She turns. I follow her gaze and know it's her solar system in the distance on the opposite side of our shared galaxy. Then, she touches my third eye, and the dark energy reveals itself as a river of eyes, kaleidoscoping across the empty space. She tells me to relax and let go.

We are engulfed in an eye, and she communicates for me to think about her solar system. Within a blink, we are directly above it. She inches closer to my face and stares into my soul, and I know how important it is for me to trust her. She takes my hands and pushes me back to reality. This time, I hear a voice as I'm falling. *"Are you ready? It's time we meet on Earth. My name is Ali."*

Back in my chair, I catch my breath and begin to connect the dots. I've never given up hope there may be other intelligent life somewhere in the universe, but I never thought I'd meet any. Even traveling at the speed of light, the next closest solar system is 4.3 light years away. It would take too long for humans to get anywhere. Our bodies don't handle space well, and we don't have the technology to support long trips.

There's too much space between us.

I stare at the sky. "You knew I'd have doubts, didn't you?"

My head is spinning with theories, but with some major vagaries that seem to imply the dark energy is some sort of portal; it doesn't make sense.

Maybe that strange invisible boat scenario that happened to me as a kid was Ali, and when she found out her approach was frightening, she decided to wait until I was older. An older, more curious person searching for answers. Now that I've shown her I'm not afraid, she has so much to tell me. Has she been waiting all this time in the other realm for me to be ready to listen? I don't know why she chose me, but my gut tells me this is very real and very important.

—〰〰〰〰〰—

I rub my hands over my face and through my hair as the sun rises. I stayed up all night writing down everything I could remember, drawing sketches, and making sure to include my strange thoughts about dark energy. My mind is still racing in every direction.

This is huge. This is bigger than what I am capable of acting upon. All I can think to do is go for a drive. It's still early, but I grab the keys to my dad's old Bronco and head for the ferry.

On the short trip inland, I get out of the Bronco and lean over the edge of the ferry. Watching the water below, I wonder if this is all part of some larger plan. The timing seems too perfect.

Space and science are huge passions in my life, and I regret not pursuing a career in those fields. Making huge amounts of money working for The Man came too easily right out of college. Later, I figured switching careers would do more harm than good. But working for corporate America has left a void in my life. My life lacks purpose, to me anyway.

One moment, I'm a lost soul living in the city, cranking through the daily grind with an itch for a change when I'm bombarded with an encounter that shakes me to my core. Now, I have no job to distract me, I'm finally able to focus on my passions, and I'm considering a new theory of space travel because an alien contacted me on a micro-dose LSD trip. As unbelievable as it sounds, my entire body and being are aching to learn more. I desperately want to talk this through with one of my old physics buddies from college. I take out my phone and make plans to meet him in his lab.

As I leave the ferry, I have a warming sensation on the back of my neck, and I turn on the A/C. It's a ten-minute drive to the lab. Although there is coffee there, I don't expect to be fed as well. I pull over at the nearest bakery and grab a spicy breakfast sandwich with eggs, bacon, cheese, and jalapeño on a toasted muffin. At the table facing the windows, I get the warming sensation again. I rub my neck and think I see Ali. I drop my sandwich and stand, knocking my chair down in the process. She turns and opens her car door. She's just a random girl. She's very similar looking, but definitely not Ali. It's ridiculous for me to think I'll randomly find her walking down the street. That would be too easy.

The customers and workers are staring at me. I apologize, pick up my chair, and continue eating. The muffin and the OJ hit the spot. Rubbing my face, I remember how sleep-deprived I am and try to prepare myself for seeing my buddy, Zain. I throw my wrapper and cup away, pull myself together, and head down to the lab.

Entering the parking garage makes me warm with reminiscence. I learned so much at this lab. It was a great group of people. Good memories. Zain and I both went to Carnegie and interned here during the summers. The ten-story building stands alone along a busy highway, and the lab is on the middle two floors. I take the stairs, and Zain buzzes me inside.

"Zain, what's up, man? It's been way too long."

"Holy shit, Andrew. Wow, yes, it has." He leans in for a handshake.

It's as if no time has passed. His dark, curly hair is wild and untamed, not quite long enough to be tied back. His Pakistani accent is less noticeable than I remember, but it lingers for sure. He never liked shaving, but his beard is nicely manicured.

He's the same old Zain I remember from college—super positive and friendly. I can see why he's running this place now. Everyone loves him.

Other familiar faces trickle in from the surrounding rooms. Colleagues who interned here with us during college. We catch up and shoot the shit for a while, swapping corporate work-life stories. Eventually, everyone returns to their projects, and I hang out in Zain's office.

He's got every classic desk tinker toy available: Newton's cradle, Orion's perpetual motion, Galileo's thermometer, magnetic ball sculptures, a Zen garden, and of course, the Rubik's cube. A procrastinator's paradise.

"So, are you looking for work?"

"Working here would be a dream. I'd love the opportunity, but you probably won't want to hire me after I tell you what's going on," I say, solving the first layer of the Rubik's cube.

"Okay, my interest has been piqued. Go on."

"You should first know everything I'm about to say needs to stay between you and me. I'm assuming you've already explored the matter in great depth, but I'd still like to introduce my new thoughts on . . ." I finish the middle layer of the cube.

"On what? Man, you're killing me. What is going on?"

With the third layer finished, I toss the Rubik's cube on his desk. "Dark energy."

"Dark energy? What about it?" He leans against his windowsill as if to brace himself for a deep discussion and pushes up his glasses inquisitively. Nothing gets science geeks going like talking about unsolved mysteries of the universe.

"Have you ever thought about how it might possibly be a type of wormhole?"

He rests his chin in one hand and stares at the floor. "I have never considered that, no. But I'm listening."

"I had this dream," I say, noticing my dry mouth, "and it gave me this idea that wormholes are all around us, and they're all connected using dark energy like a vessel."

"Hmm." He paces around his office. "Dark energy and dark matter have never been directly detected. But with the accelerating expansion of the universe, our calculations show us they must exist and work together with gravity and regular matter to form galaxies."

"Right," I say, tracking with him. "Maybe there's no way to prove it, but what if dark energy is the key to connecting us to the entire universe? A deeper connection than we can comprehend right now. And we have to harness the awareness somehow?"

"You mean for traveling?"

"Yes. It's like—" I pause, popping my knuckles. "It's like we need to open up our minds to see the wormholes."

"So, you think we need other forms of detection. Not just mathematical calculations, but an advancement in human perception?" His eyes narrow.

"Yeah," I exhale and lean forward. "It sounds . . . have I lost it?"

"Hey man, we've all been there. I mean, it sounds like you're onto something. I'm just not sure how I could help. Humans are definitely missing a major factor that would enable us to travel through space fast enough to get anywhere distant. Even traveling at the speed of light is too slow to get anywhere."

"Exactly. As intelligent as humans can be, I don't think we're capable of understanding the connectedness of it all. To me, it seems almost spiritual."

Zain sits in the chair next to me and says, "The spirit is not an easy subject to understand, but I find it hard to ignore the idea that we are all connected somehow."

"But maybe it's more than that. I guess I need to sort through my ideas better before I bring them up in real conversations." I laugh.

"I would expect nothing less from my old friend." He grabs my shoulder. "You're an old soul, Andrew. This world needs more people like you."

"Likewise, buddy. Tell me what you guys are working on these days. Fill me in. My mind obviously needs some distraction."

"You bet." He jumps up and leads the way through the lab he's so proud of. I try to listen as he shows me around, but my mind is elsewhere.

After a couple hours of catching up, I climb into my warm car. The weight of today's events and the lack of sleep hits me. I lie down on the front seat and watch the clouds slowly crawl across the sky.

STELLA

My week of anticipation was cruel to my psyche. I had to lie to my therapist, pretending everything was fine. I had to hide my fears at school, putting on a happy face. I forced myself to go to ballet, expecting it to relieve some of my stress. My state of worry was constant, but thankfully, the time has finally come.

My heart is beating out of my chest when I pull up to the restaurant. My mouth is dry, and I'm shaking. She chose a public spot possibly to keep me from totally losing it. She must trust me not to be hysterical, so I must resist the urge. I open the car door, walk into the restaurant, and tell the hostess I'm meeting my friend. She leads me outside to the terrace, where I see her sitting, staring into the night sky.

I stop, and my hand flies to my mouth. She is as beautiful as I remember. The same striking face, but a more human skin tone, and much longer blond hair.

I slowly walk to the table, thank the hostess, and sit. With both hands covering my mouth, I sob, releasing my anticipation, but I wipe my face with my napkin and apologize.

"I thought you were a dream," I say through my tears. She reaches over to take my hands in hers. I jerk back, unsure of her intentions.

"I am so happy to see you again, Stella."

I glance up, see the tears in her eyes, and admire her new appearance. "How are you here? How is this happening? And you speak English!"

"I have never left. I have been here all this time, watching from afar," she says. "I have taken many years to adapt, to mimic your kind."

"This can't be real. Is this a dream?" I cover my eyes in embarrassment.

"No, Stella. You are filled with a beautiful, kind spirit, and that is how you were able to see me so many years ago. I can explain everything to you in detail when you are ready, but right now, I need you to trust me again and listen." She reaches for my hands, slowly this time, and I hear her in my mind.

"You gave me a name so many years ago. Do you remember?"

I look down and fiddle with my napkin, trying to reply telepathically like I did when we were little. *"Ali."*

"Stella, what else do you remember from when we were younger?"

I laugh awkwardly and cover my mouth with my shaking hand. "It took me years to try to forget what happened. But I remember communicating with you through our minds and trying to explain our differences. . . . It was the highlight of my childhood, meeting with you."

"Mine too, Stella."

My cheeks get hot with guilt. "I hope you know I didn't reveal your existence to my parents on purpose. They found my drawings and started asking questions. I was too young to understand the importance of keeping you a secret. They got scared and locked me inside and even called the authorities."

"Oh, Stella, I knew the moment it happened. My family and I fled the area before we were noticed by anyone else. I got my fair share of punishment from my parents back then as well. The authorities who came, did they believe you?"

"It's hard to know exactly." I sigh. "They asked questions that made it appear that I was being manipulated by an adult or dreaming it all. Regardless, they confiscated all of my drawings and kept close surveillance on our house for a few months. They were very persistent in their efforts to make sure we never spoke about it again."

Ali's expression turns serious. "We have tried to communicate peacefully with the government, and they are not interested in helping us."

"You mean other people know you exist?"

"Yes. Your government has known about us for decades," she whispers. "But they refuse to communicate with us. They prefer to pretend we don't exist."

My stomach sinks. The police possibly knew Ali was an alien so long ago.

"What do you need help with? How could I possibly help?" I can see a glimmer of hope in her eyes, and she scoots her chair in a little closer.

"Firstly, I want to say how sorry I am for your loss. I know this hasn't been easy for you lately. Losing loved ones is universally painful and monumental."

I tuck my hair behind my ears. It's been decades, yet somehow it feels like an instant ago we found each other in the woods. "Thank you for saying that. I miss him every moment of every day. I think he would have loved to meet you."

"I hope it brings you comfort to hear that I have met him. Well,

my spirit has." She closes her eyes. "He said you'd appreciate me saying that Rose lived a full life without Jack, and it's okay to let go."

I cry and laugh at the same time, blot my eyes with my napkin,
and try to say something, but keep laughing, and then crying.

"He would bring up *Titanic* . . . a symbol of my life right now."
I take a breath and smooth my hair down. "That honestly does make
me feel so, so good. Thank you, Ali."

"You will see him again. I promise."

"Ali." I scoot my chair closer and readjust my silverware. "I
thought I'd never see you again. I thought you—" I glance to the
street. "I thought you probably went back home . . . to your other . . .
planet," I whisper, but her expression shows no humor or discomfort
in my statement.

"We've been sort of stuck here. It's a long story that is important for you to hear alongside my friend. I'd like to introduce you to
him." She sips a bit of water, and I'm relieved to have a break from
her intense stare. "The truth is we've waited as long as we can, and we
need your help to get back to our planet."

"My help?"

She smiles as if she knows something I don't.

"Yes." She leans close to me. "There's no one else I trust more in
this world."

"Ali, I'm flattered. That's so nice of you to say, but it's been like
twenty-something years. I don't know you anymore. I could be a
completely different person, too. A psychopath!"

She throws her head back and laughs, holding her cheeks.
"Humans think they change as they age. You're still the same person, Stella."

I'm relieved to see her smile. Her joy is contagious, and relief
sweeps over me. "I know what you mean."

"When we met so long ago, we instantly connected. Our souls, our spirits, are connected. You'll see. You have to trust me. Can you trust me?"

I want to say yes. I've connected more with Ali in ten minutes than I have with any human in the past few months. Am I up for this? Can I even do anything? My breathing is rapid, and I don't know where to look, then Ali takes my hand in hers.

"Stella," she projects, smiling. *"It's me."*

I feel tears well up, and I nod. *"I trust you."*

She squeezes my hands. We stand and hug, and I sense she needs to go.

"Can I come over tomorrow? With my friend?" she asks.

My eyes shoot wide. "Wait, an alien friend?"

She laughs. "Human. Promise."

I take a deep breath. "See you tomorrow."

She nods and leaves.

I sit back down, alone. I remain at the table, frozen in disbelief and worry, until I order a glass of wine and some bruschetta. Staring into the void of the ocean, I only see proof of its existence where the moon reflects off the flittering waves. I rub my wedding ring between my fingers.

How can I go home and act normal, as if this weren't the wildest day of my life? Will I even be able to sleep? There is a buzzy static inside my head, and butterflies in my stomach. I bite my lip, dig around my purse, and take a shroom capsule.

ANDREW

I wake up in a daze and see the setting sun. I've got to get home to Chester. Hopefully, the last ferry hasn't left. I start the car and head through town to fill up.

Putting the nozzle in, I try to tune out the gas station news blaring out of the kiosk. I look down the street and take a mental note to come here again. The street has really come together over the years. It's filled with nice restaurants and bars, even a new music lounge. It's right on the water, so I'm sure they have outdoor seating.

I notice one restaurant has a terrace with stringed lights hanging around the perimeter. I rub away the warming sensation on my neck and see the most striking woman sitting at a table with another person. My gut is ripped apart by her beauty, and I freeze. Could it be Ali?

The nozzle clicks. I close the gas cap, jump in the Bronco, and park on the other side of the street near the restaurant door. Will I seem strange meeting her outside when she leaves? What will I say?

I can't sit still, so I jump out and pace back and forth, silently going over heroic things I could say. No matter what, I will sound bizarre and possibly frightening. *I have found you* even sounds creepy. My neck tingles again, and I stop pacing. She is on the sidewalk, her hands clasped together, smirking with a side-eye glance.

"Ali?" My voice quivers. I hope I haven't dreamed all of this up.

"Andrew," she says softly, with her eyes wide open. "I am so pleased to finally meet you."

I don't blink, fearing she might disappear if I do. "I can't believe it's really you," I stutter. "I can't believe you're real." She smiles and sweeps her hair to one shoulder.

"I have so many questions. Where can we talk?" I ask. If we stay on the street too much longer, I will cause a scene.

"Take me near the shore. We can talk there."

"Okay, then should we just go to my house? My dog is waiting for me, and my house is on the water."

"Sure. Yes."

"We need to hurry to catch the last ferry." I jog over to the Bronco, open the door for her, and hop in the other side. We start off, and I'm shocked by my loss for words. Could I be any more awkward? Come on, just be genuine.

"Well, Ali, it's easy to say you've turned my world upside down. How did this happen? How have we met before?"

"Before?"

"You know, the, um, well, the time before whe—"

"I'm kidding! I'm joking!" She elbows my arm. "I have learned many things from humans, and humor is one of my favorites. Of course, Andrew. We have met because our souls are connected to someone who . . ."

"Who, what?"

"To someone who will help us."

"So, you can see into the future?"

"Yes, but not in the narrowminded way humans have created such ideas. I cannot see exactly what happens, but my spirit guides me and provides helpful insight."

"So, did I interpret things right? Did you really come from another planet?"

"I was born here," she says, pointing to herself. "But my parents are from another planet. They have been here on Earth for thirty-five years and came together during that time."

"There have been aliens on Earth for thirty-five years? And you haven't been found? How is that possible?" I feel clammy and crack the windows. I'm surprised we're already on the ferry.

"We have remained in hiding on the ocean floor with our location never being detected. Although, we have attempted communicating with humans. We know that if we become visible to too many humans at one time, it could cause fear or unintended consequences, like war."

"What do you mean become visible? You can be invisible?"

"Not exactly. Our ships have the ability to reflect their surroundings and move silently through the air. Our species has been evolving for ten thousand more years than humans, and although we are more technologically advanced, we remain dependent on natural organisms like plants and animals to survive just like humans." She wraps her hair up in a hair tie. I turn on the air-conditioning in case she is hot.

"I don't understand. How do you look so much like a human?"

"We've been on land and gathered data in order to manipulate some of our DNA to make us appear more human. That has been my job the past few decades."

"To become human. By altering your DNA?" I ask as the ferry docks.

"Not all of us have changed. My parents remain in their original form," she adds. "In our earliest efforts, we realized how frightening it was for humans to see us. Then we resorted to making our appearance known from our ships, but that hasn't worked out well either. So, we figured it'd be easier to talk to humans if we looked the part. It's just getting them to believe us."

I pop my knuckles and let it all sink in. "I'm not sure I'll be able to sleep at night ever again."

"We've discovered most humans aren't in touch with their spirits enough for us to communicate with them like we did with you. You're special in that way. When you tapped into your consciousness, your soul opened up. Your soul met mine. You could sense the depth of the experience, and it stayed with you. It shook you awake, and now you're here, talking with me in the real world."

"It felt too real to ignore or pass off as a hallucination."

The ferry gates open, and I drive, sneaking glances at her when I can. "I felt like it brought out my life's ambitions, made me remember what really matters in life, and helped me start being myself. I mean, I knew there was a bigger message, something major happening, but I couldn't quite put my finger on it."

I continue down the road and turn onto my street. "After our first meeting, I finally got the courage to move back home." In my driveway, I open her car door for her.

She steps into the dark. Her beautiful pale skin ever so slightly glows in the moonlight. I'm insecure bringing her to my house, but I'm sure she appreciates having a private place to speak as much as I do. I open the front door, and Chester runs full speed through the hall, then skids to a stop. He smells the air, as though unsure of whether to approach Ali or not.

She bends and sticks her hand out. He smells it for a long while, and then his tail wags.

"Hey, buddy!" I say and scratch his ears. "I'm sorry, I'm sure he's not used to meeting . . ." I look down at her, unsure if calling her an alien again would be rude.

"Aliens?" She gives me a huge smile.

"Yes. Aliens."

"Don't worry, Andrew. You are an alien to me, too. We're experiencing the same unease. But we're doing it for the good of our people. Do you want to show me around your home?"

"Yeah, please come in," I say, leading her through. "It won't take long. Here's the living room, kitchen, and the bedrooms are down that hall. Bathroom right around the corner." I lean against my Bösendorfer upright.

She gasps and rubs her fingers along the keys. "I love your piano. Do you play?" she asks.

"Oh, I love playing." I scratch my head. "I wouldn't say I'm very good, but I do enjoy it. I didn't have room for a baby grand in my New York apartment, but I think I can make room for one here." I look around, picturing where I'd place it.

"Baby grand?"

"Oh, it's a bigger piano." I pull a picture up on my phone. "It sounds better than what I've got. That's all. I would also feel pretty cool having one in my house."

"Will you play for me?"

I rub my hands around my neck and scalp. I'm so physically and mentally exhausted and have so many questions reeling through my head.

"I can definitely try, although it won't be my best performance." Insecure, I sit and warm up my fingers. I feel like going back to the first piece I learned by Rachmaninoff, Piano Concerto #2, which normally accompanies an orchestra. Instead of leaving that out, I pull up the music video that excludes the piano. I connect it to speakers so she can hear the orchestra while I play the piano. Ali sits on the couch with an eager smile.

I start playing and slowly readjust my seated position, letting the music lead the way. I finish the introduction and hear the strings of the orchestra, which always gives me goosebumps. Nearing the piano solo, I get nervous, hoping the notes come back to me. The clarinets, flutes, and horns—it all goes together with such intensity and perfection. I finish the first movement and stretch my hands out. My arms and fingers are throbbing.

"That's all I can play right now, but the piece is much longer." When I turn around to see her reaction, she is wiping away tears. "It makes me emotional, too," I say. "Especially when I hear the whole orchestra. It's a beautiful piece."

"It's more than beautiful. It's unbelievable. Humans are truly amazing creatures. We do not have pianos. But I hope we will find a way to make them when we return. You are extremely talented. When did you learn?"

"Well, my mom tried to get me lessons when I was a kid, but I wasn't interested then. I ended up teaching myself when I was in my twenties."

She smiles. "You are special, Andrew."

I stop the music on the speakers. I got a lot of nervous energy out while playing, so I move to the opposite side of the couch.

"So are you. I have so many questions for you. Why have you made contact with me?"

"Our planet has a great freeze every few millennia, so we gathered our ships and sailed the currents of the sky to give it time to reset without our presence. Generations go by between the freezes, so our methods of travel change. It's a new puzzle each time. Our records indicated this would be the biggest freeze our planet had ever seen before, which meant a longer time away in space."

She took a deep breath and settled into the couch. "As I'm sure you know, time slows as you get closer to a black hole. We estimated ten years in limbo would amount to two hundred years on our planet, time for it to thaw enough ice to sustain life again. But ten years living in space is not easy."

"Right, nearly impossible." My mouth is dry, and I jump up to get us some glasses from the cabinet. The fridge water filter is broken, so I fill them up in the sink.

"Thank you," she says, before taking big gulps. "We have gravity chambers on our ships, but it's better to stop on nearby planets or moons to let our bodies feel true gravity. Along the way, we discovered Earth, a beautiful blue planet filled with life, warmth, and air. We determined it was inhabited by an intelligent species and couldn't miss this opportunity to meet you." She finishes her glass of water. "We had to plan a way of communicating with you without inflicting fear."

"Wow, that's incredible. I can't imagine where you'd even begin."

Ali nods. I can tell she is relieved to get this information out. "It has taken longer than we anticipated, and while our attempts at communication were quite blatant in the beginning, we changed our methods rather quickly."

"What changed?"

"When we learned you have weapons capable of destroying your own planet, we became wary of broadcasting our existence. We do not want to fight with anyone."

"So, that's when you decided to manipulate your DNA?"

"Yes, and it was a huge decision for our people. It turns out that manipulating DNA uses up a lot of our energy resources. We were willing to make the sacrifice to try to communicate with humans, to finally reveal ourselves in a way that wouldn't frighten you."

"Of course, because any right-minded intelligent civilization would want to communicate with another intelligent species in the universe."

"That was our hope. But, through our efforts, we have learned that humans are not ready. Unfortunately for us, we don't have enough energy resources to return home. We need your help."

I lean back on the couch and rub my face. "What do you need?"

"We need an abundance of organic minerals."

"Why not just take it? You want permission to take what you need?"

"Yes. While we can reluctantly understand that your leaders do not want to acknowledge our existence, we do not want to cause any more scenes. We try to stay remote, but in the past, when the jets have seen our ships in the air, they lock us in their radar for missile launches."

"I wonder if you were in no-fly zones."

"You have parts of the sky where flying is forbidden?"

"Totally." I snort. "Otherwise, anyone could fly over and drop a bomb. They took your presence as a threat."

"Do you see why we need your help?"

I stand up to look out of the windows. "I see what you mean, but I'm not sure I have the connections to be useful."

"I know much about humans, yet there are plenty of things I don't know. If we're going to make progress, we need some humans to be on our side. You could be our middlemen." She stands and follows me, but I stare into the dark night.

I can see her standing behind me in the reflection of the glass. Her arms are folded, and she's looking down.

"I have someone I'd like you to meet," she says. My interest is piqued, and I turn to face her. "She is very special to me. She's kind-hearted like yourself. I met her when I was very young, and I know she is honest and good. Ideally, the two of you could be on our side."

I hear her, but my mind is busy running scenarios.

"If it's okay with you, I'll come back in the morning."

I'm shocked and disappointed she wants to leave already. I still have so many questions. "Oh, sure," I say, patting all my pockets for my keys.

She smirks. "It's okay. I'll walk."

"What?"

She points to the water.

"Oh, that's right. Ocean floor," I say quickly, embarrassed I didn't remember. "So, you said you all are living in the water? Like mermaids, or what?" I immediately regret my nervous banter.

"We live inside our ships most days, and sometimes we venture into the sky for solar energy."

I cover my eyes with my hand, unwilling to expose how excited this makes me. "I wonder if all those weird UFO stories are true. Did you guys ever try to write messages in crop fields?"

"Most definitely. In fact, we were inspired by the message humans wrote on the craft you sent out into space."

My heart sinks, and then, my brain splits into a million pieces, metaphorically speaking.

"Are you talking about the Pioneer plaques? Or the Arecibo message?"

"I'm not sure, but the signal from the craft was received by one of our ships while we were traveling through the galaxy. We never interfered with it but took many notes. We tried to mimic the same sort of message in the fields, hoping it would make an impression."

"Oh, it made an impression, all right. Although, the ones that were released for public view were not translatable. I wonder if the government kept any a secret." I stare off, pondering this thought.

"I think you're onto something. It caused panic for some time, which we regret. That's when we decided to try going onto land so that we may learn the language and common behaviors. Meeting Stella was the first step in that process."

She stares off to the side as if she is thinking of her friend. I lean on the window frame and take in her subtle, messy appearance. Her long, wavy blond, almost white, hair, her baggy jeans and knit sweater, and sneakers that look like they've seen better days.

I can't deny I'm drawn to her, longing to know more. Images flash back to me from my LSD trip, reminding me of the depth of this situation.

"Stella? Is she who you want to introduce me to?"

"Yes," she says and smiles.

"I know you said you want to leave," I hold my hands up, "and you totally can. I'm sorry I keep asking questions. Let me walk you out." I open my back door. She bends and scratches Chester's ears, then she follows me. Holding the door open for her, I ask, "Do you have many human friends?"

She pauses on my porch. "I have met people here and there, but no one stands out like you and Stella." She shifts her weight. "I also have questions for you. I have spent most of my days on land watching humans from afar. How do you guys connect to the universe?"

"Honestly," I rub the back of my neck, "not many people know how to do that. I mean, there's religion and meditation, but most people are too self-centered to worry about more than their daily life."

She looks down and fiddles with her fingers.

"How do you connect to the universe?"

Her eyes meet mine only for a moment.

"It's funny that I realize how personal that question is now," she says. "The universe is a part of us. Deep inside, we are connected. My people and I, we have this dream state where we can communicate with our spirit. Not in terms like we are speaking now, but more fluid. I don't know how to explain. Our spirits are our guides."

"And it was your spirit I met, right?"

"Yes," she whispers. "You see, Andrew, something inside of you was calling out to her, to me."

I nod. I can't deny my soul searching, contemplating my future, and what I really want out of life. It's hard for me to wrap my head around all the spiritual stuff.

"You think this is all part of some big plan? You think the universe wanted us to meet?"

She smiles and sighs. "I think we will make a great team, Andrew."

She waves and walks down the steps, and I watch her silhouette slowly disappear into the trees.

STELLA

When the sun hits my face, I jerk up in bed. I jump in the shower to wash away all my worry. Whatever may come, let it come. I will be strong and brave. What good could come out of me being scared and weak?

I open my laptop to check on emails. A few students sent me questions, and I reply to them. There's a picture from my mom of her and Moshe kissing in a hot air balloon. She is living her best life. Grinning, I close my computer with a fuzzy feeling I hope I can hang on to throughout my day.

I giggle to myself. I have an important meeting with an alien today. No, an alien and her accomplice. My giggles turn into full-out laughter, but no one is here to share the hilarity of the moment. I quiet myself and try to focus on being productive. I need to clean this place before they get here.

I start unloading dishes and notice how good it feels to have gotten a full night's rest. The shrooms must help me sleep.

I hadn't really considered the fact my night terrors and evil darkness episodes were anxiety, but both were a result of my mind losing control. The shrooms help me relax and focus on what's in front of me, not behind. I'm not sure I need to take them every night, but I'll hold on to them as a reminder of what it feels like to be without the debilitating fear of something lurking behind me.

Looking at my face in the mirror, I smooth out my hair and add a layer of lipstick. When I sit on the couch, wondering what else I can do to pass the time, I notice water is spilling out from the air vent on my sidewall. I hastily grab some towels and smash them on the puddle, then go outside and run upstairs.

"Hello? Herold, are you there?" I yell, banging on my neighbor's door.

There's no answer. I pound on his door again.

"Turn your water off!"

Should I try to get in? I jiggle the handle, but it's locked.

The neighbor across the way calls out, "What's going on?"

"Is he home? There's water spilling into my living room!"

Her brow furrows. "I'm not sure."

"Can you call someone?"

"Who?"

"I don't know! The fire department!" I run back down the stairs and into my apartment.

Inside, water is leaking through the ceiling fan and light fixtures. I cover my mouth and turn off the lights in case there would be sparks. Running through the hallway to get more towels from my bathroom, I miss the rug and slip. My knee hits the floor, and I get up as fast as I can.

There's a leak in my bathroom. The ceiling is bowing like a heavy water balloon. At least it's tile in here. I pull the towels off the rack and take them to the living room.

All the pocket lights are dripping. My chest tightens, but I throw the towels down and frantically find my phone to dial the landlord. Maybe there's a water shut-off outside. The phone rings, and I race to the door, hoping to get a head start. A thunderous crash sounds behind me.

My hands fly over my head, and I turn to see my entire ceiling collapsed. There is insulation and water-soaked wood piled in my dining room. My heart is pounding. I could have been crushed. With one hand on my front door handle and one covering my mouth, my breath comes faster. The walls spew water over my shelves, my artwork, my furniture. Everything is ruined. I've lost everything.

The door handle turns under my hand. I hear a voice from the other side but can't understand what they're saying. The door opens, and I fall into someone's arms and sob.

I lean into a man's strong body and feel tiny against his broad chest. He must be a firefighter.

He pulls me away from the door and into the parking lot. I lift my head slightly. Through my tears, I think I see Ali directing the firefighters to the upstairs apartment. My perception of reality slows. I can't catch my breath, and I'm dizzy.

The man cradles my head and says, "Breathe in through your nose, and out through your mouth." I follow his instruction and become very aware of how handsome he is.

"That's it. Nice and slow." He breathes with me. When we exhale together, my mind calms.

I realize I'm still in his arms and separate myself a little.

"I'm so sorry for falling on you like that." My voice fades as I'm caught off guard by his height and stature. His striking eyes show a hint of concern. Heat rises to my cheeks, but I can't break my stare.

"Don't even worry about it. I feel lucky we got here when we did."

"It all happened so fast. I wasn't sure the fire department would come, but I'm glad you came so quickly."

He puts his hand on my shoulder. "Are you hurt?"

I step back and look at myself. My hands are shaking, but I don't feel physical pain.

"No, I think I'm okay. I just can't believe my entire ceiling collapsed." I wave my hands at my ruined home.

Firefighters break the door of my neighbor's apartment. A few moments pass, and the paramedics take up a stretcher.

I jog to the paramedic leading the way and ask, "Is he alive? Is he okay?"

He looks somber, and over his radio, I hear someone say, "It's confirmed. He's deceased."

I shriek, and my chest tightens. Herold was such a sweet old man. He was our neighbor for as long as we've lived here. I bury my face in my hands.

"Stella, I'm so sorry!" Ali says from beside me and hugs me. "I heard them say he must have had a heart attack."

The man puts his hand on my shoulder again and says he's going to check on the damage.

I fan my face with my hands. "I hate that this happened while you're here, Ali. This is miserable."

"Why don't we help you clean up the mess and dry what we can. We'll get you set up somewhere."

I nod with my hand on my throat, hoping that helps hold down my emotions.

"I see you've met my friend Andrew."

"Who?"

She points to the man who was so nice to keep me upright while I cried. He is talking with the real firemen about how to sort things out.

"Him?" I point.

She smiles and nods.

He walks toward us, and my face heats. Admittedly, I'm relieved I have an excuse to talk to him.

"I'm Stella, I'm so sorry about—"

"I'm Andrew." He smiles. We shake hands, and I avoid eye contact for fear I might stare again.

We stand by as the firefighters remove the large plywood and insulation piles. They tell us mold will start growing pretty quickly, and that the apartment maintenance should strip the walls as soon as possible.

"We'll go straight to a laundromat to wash your clothes," Ali says. "Go pack those, and I'll take your pictures. Andrew, you pick through the books that can be saved and anything from the desk area."

She must have heard my mental checklist, and her calmness holds me together.

I enter my apartment, take my laundry basket, and start throwing clothes in. I reach for James's clothes but stop, close my eyes, and tell him how much I love him. I leave his clothes to be cleared out. The damp towels and toiletries, I put into a wet suitcase. Lifting it is harder than I anticipated, and I guess my grunting is loud, because Andrew comes in.

"Here, let me take that. I've filled up the trunk of my Bronco. Do you have a car I can start adding to?"

I catch myself staring at his muscular build. "I have two cars parked in the back. Although, one has a flat tire," I say, half lucid. He must be six-four and close to two hundred pounds of muscle.

"I'll check for a spare while I'm out there."

As he turns the corner, I let out a deep breath. Why am I so shy around him? Staring, blubbering. What a mess. He is wildly attractive.

"*He does exude very strong human qualities,*" I hear Ali say in my head, and I nearly jump out of my skin.

"Hey! You scared me. You can't read my mind unless I let you!" I smile, but my face gets hot.

"Sorry. I was on my way in here to check on you." She gives me a big grin. "Next time, I'll ask."

I lift my eyebrow and wonder if I'll be able to tell when she is in my head. "*Can you talk to everyone telepathically?*"

"No, people are too closed off to hear me. Your open spirit is special."

"I'm so happy you're here. Thank you for helping me." I take her hand and give it a squeeze.

Andrew walks in and looks around. "Unfortunately, I think we've taken all we can salvage. I can call a moving company to dry off your wooden shelves and chests, and your bed frame and move it to storage if you'd like."

"Wow, yes, that would be great. Thank you so much." I turn to Ali. "You guys are lifesavers."

———~~vvv\/\/\/\/vvv~~———

As we're sitting in front of six washing machines at the laundromat, I finally get a chance to talk with Andrew and Ali.

"Well, so much for inviting you in for tea." I exaggerate, wiping away imaginary forehead sweat. Andrew smiles.

"It really shows your true characters," I say. "I wouldn't have blamed you if you saw what happened and rescheduled."

Ali sighs. "Helping your friends in need is a universal quality that brings positivity to both parties. How could we have left you alone after that?"

"Yeah, it was a messy situation no one should have to handle alone. I was happy to help," Andrew says.

"It's a strange feeling. Not having a house anymore."

"Do you have family nearby?"

My mom will completely lose it and freak out when I tell her what happened. I'm not looking forward to that phone call. I think of my friends, but I don't want to be a burden.

"No, I don't, actually. I'll have to stay in a hotel until I find a new place."

Andrew pops his knuckles and looks nervous. "Okay, I know you just met me, but I live on the island not too far from here. You're more than welcome to stay at my house. My sisters are basically neighbors, and Ali lives not too far off the coast."

This guy must feel really sorry for me. Sympathy is something I avoid at all costs. "Oh, that is incredibly nice of you, but I can't possibly intrude. I would feel better in a hotel for now. Thank you, though."

"It's a nice house, Stella. You would feel very comfortable there. I've been. And Andrew plays the piano. You could dance to the music he plays."

My eyes widen. I can't believe she would say that. "*Sorry!*" I hear her say.

"You dance?" he asks, sounding impressed.

"Oh my gosh, just barely." I'm mortified and reposition myself on the uncomfortable bench.

He's smiling, seeming to enjoy embarrassing me. "Ballet?"

"Yes, classical ballet, but I don't perform or anything. It's just for fun. And you play the piano?"

"Yes, mostly classical. I tend to learn pieces that are way too hard for me, but I enjoy the challenge. I'm sure I could benefit from having a lesson or two."

"I mostly danced when I was younger, so my technique is terrible, but it still makes me happy. I love it. I'd love to hear you play sometime. The piano is such a beautiful instrument. Very impressive."

"Thank you. I just moved from an apartment in the city. Now that I have more space, I'd love to get a better piano."

"*Ali, does he know you're an alien?*"

"*Yes, he does.*"

I stand up to see if anyone else is nearby. There's an older couple at the vending machine, but I think they're sitting on the other side. The washers and dryers will drown out our conversation.

"How did you guys meet?" I look back and forth at them. Andrew seems to be at a loss for words and glances at Ali.

"Andrew's spirit came to me in an alternate dimension. I was able to communicate our dire need for a human collaborator in our plan to leave planet Earth."

"Right . . . what she said."

"Wow, that sounds intense."

"Very," he says, the color gone from his face.

"So," I look around once more, "the goal here is to help you leave Earth, right?"

"Yes, we never intended to stay this long. We have probes around our planet now. Our data indicates it will be habitable once we disperse new vital minerals. We also need to replenish our supplies for the voyage home. It has been our mission to stay hidden so as to not disturb the evolution of your species. Which reminds me, I would like to introduce you to my family."

My heart nearly jumps out of my chest. "What?"

The beam of light the movies portrayed for me pops into my head. I admit, I am relieved not to be the only human here. Andrew may be a stranger to me, but he's human, and right now, that's a very strong bond to have, when considering being introduced to an alien species.

Andrew's eyes are wide, but he sounds calm. "I think it's a good idea to meet the people we will be representing, as long as you think it's safe."

"I would never put you in danger. They would like to thank you personally."

I lean over and whisper, "No pressure" in Andrew's ear. He looks at me and smiles.

This is my first time really looking at him. I've noticed his large stature, but now I can study his features. His sandy brown hair, long enough on top to see his natural highlights, reminds me of my first movie star crush, Leo DiCaprio in *Romeo + Juliet*. His facial hair is showing its shadow, just the way I like it. His light brown eyes match his hair, and I stare a little too long, lost in his handsomeness. His smile is warm and inviting, with good teeth and large lips that beg to be—

"What do you think?" he asks.

I jerk into the moment. "Wait, I missed the question. I must have been daydreaming." I notice my leg is leaning against his, and I yank it back.

"Do you think you could meet Ali's family tonight?"

Oh, that's right. This is real. I fidget with my shirt. "With you?"

With his elbows leaning on his knees, he nods. He nudges my leg with his and says, "We've got this."

"Where could we do this?"

"The shore."

ANDREW

I offer up my garage as a storage place for Stella's things. I only just met her, but I have a strong sense of protection for her. She must feel completely alone, having just recently lost her husband, and now her home. She doesn't deserve this.

"You were right, Ali. Andrew's house is incredible. Check out that view!"

Chester is barking at her, begging for attention. She kneels and lets him jump onto her shoulders. He licks her face and almost pushes her over. "That's Chester."

"Chester is the sweetest dog. I have fallen in love with him. Chester, show me your backyard. Is it okay if we go outside?" she asks. "I have got to check out that view."

"Absolutely. Yeah, take him. He'll retrieve a stick for hours."

"Oh, fun!"

She opens the back door and lets Chester lead the way. He acts like he's met her before.

Stella has a way about her that is very welcoming and kind. She pulls me in with every glance. Her beauty shines from within, and I'm aching for a connection.

I stare at her through the back windows. Her long brown hair is effortlessly elegant. She throws it from one side to another, never really getting a part in it. Her strong ballet figure shows her competitiveness. She's a natural beauty with bright blue eyes and dark lashes.

Ali comes and stands next to me, breaking my concentration.

"When we were little and she found me in the woods, Stella was not afraid," she says. "She could have run away screaming and told her parents she found a monster in her backyard, but she stayed. She knew I was afraid, too. She fully accepted me for what I was and showed me kindness and patience. She is strong. Suffered great losses, but she is not broken. You and Stella will form a great bond. Your spirits are connected, as I'm sure you can tell."

I continue watching Stella and Chester, and I nod. "I think you're right. I can't wait to get to know her better, yet I feel so comfortable with her, like I've known her all my life."

"Me too," she says, and we share a smile.

Stella is heading inside, and I walk away from the window to clear the books off the table and pick up dog toys.

She opens the back door and wipes her feet. "I'm glad you don't have very good service out here. It was a good excuse to get off the phone with my mom. I got the news to her, but not much else. She's totally freaking out, just as I expected, but at least she knows I'm okay."

"Feel free to try calling her again if you want. Service is better inside."

"Oh, no. That's not necessary. I'm not in the mood." She looks around at the house and hangs her sweater on the hook by the door. "This house is amazing."

"Thanks. It was my parents'. This is where I grew up."

"Have they passed? I'm so sorry," she whispers.

I wave my hand. "It was a while ago. They had a good life. Luckily, we kept this house. I'd hate to see someone else living here."

"I can imagine. Your property is huge." She spreads her arms toward the windows. "It looks like the yard angles out as you go to the shore."

"Yeah, the shoreline is probably four times longer than my front yard."

"And there's so many trees!"

"We've got some great climbing walls down there, too."

Her eyes widen, and her mouth hangs slightly open.

I question if using "we" was appropriate. My subconscious will probably always view this house as my family's home. I live here, but it's not only mine.

I can't help but smile at her reaction. "I'll have to show you sometime," I say, hoping she's interested.

She looks at Ali, who is still standing near the windows. Stella holds her hands up in front of her. "I'm interested, but one thing at a time, guys. We already have big plans ahead. Right, Ali?"

"My ship is located not too far from here. I can call them to the shore."

"Right now? Like, right now, right now?" Stella asks.

"They can meet us here in two hours. You will board our ship outside." She grabs Stella's hands and asks her not to worry. "Would you feel comfortable introducing me to your family?" Stella appears to be at a loss for words and looks at me.

"Well, there's a big difference," I say gently.

"If I introduced you as a human, I would be thrilled to introduce you to my family."

"Right," I agree.

"But this is . . . slightly terrifying for me."

"It goes both ways. My family is trusting me to bring humans into their home on an alien planet."

Stella meets my gaze, and I say, "She has a point."

"Why aren't you scared?" she asks me. "You're not worried? Even a little?"

I cross my arms and think I'd be much more comfortable on the couch. I motion for them to sit.

"I'm glad you brought this up. Am I nervous? Yes. But I've been thinking a lot about this. Ali knows how lost I've been lately. I was in the city with a nice career, but I wasn't happy. I couldn't shake the feeling I had a bigger purpose. You know?" Stella nods, and I feel like she understands what I mean.

"When I found Ali in the sky that night, and she showed me that there is, in fact, more to this life, I knew I had to do something about it. I needed to remove myself from what society had made me believe was meaningful. A corporate job, living in a big city, and money do not satisfy my soul. But this new purpose Ali has provided does." I look into Stella's eyes. "And this new friendship I have with you does." She leans her head to the side and smiles. "So, yes, when you think about the fact we're about to meet intelligent life from another planet, it's hard to believe. But I've never been so sure of something in my life. This is monumental, and someone has to be the first. It might as well be us."

I turn to Ali, then back to Stella. I hope my speech made an impact on her.

"That was beautiful. Your honesty is refreshing." She looks down and brushes her hair out of her face. "You seem so sure, so genuine. You're a lot braver than I am."

"I wouldn't say that."

"It's true, but I'm still taken aback by your sincerity." Her eyes meet mine, and I beam. "I know I can be dramatic. Now that I think about it, I guess I'm mostly scared because that's what Hollywood has brainwashed me to be."

"Exactly. This should be celebrated. There's life out there, and that life wants to meet us." In my excitement, I clutch Ali's shoulders.

Chester jumps on Stella's lap, matching my enthusiasm, and she hugs him.

"Well," I look at my watch, "two hours gives us enough time to eat. I'm starving. You hungry?" Stella nods. I point to Ali and ask, "You hungry?"

"Yes."

"How about I make us some dinner, then?"

"Cooking. A great distraction." Stella stands. "What can I help with?" She seems to feel a little better.

I grab a cutting board and knife and toss her an onion to chop. I give Ali some carrots to peel, take some chicken out of the fridge, and season it before I place it in the skillet. All the veggies get tossed into a pan to sauté.

"Chicken soup?"

"Even better. Chicken and dumplings. Here, mince this parsley, and I'll make some cornbread batter."

"My mouth is watering. You'll let the batter cook in the broth?" Stella asks.

"Oh yeah, they'll be so tender and fluffy." I stir the vegetables and add a pinch of sugar to the cornbread.

"Who taught you to cook, Andrew?"

"Growing up, my mom would always ask my sisters and me to

help with dinner. She put together all my favorite recipes in a binder for me to take to college, and I've kept up with it ever since." I open a cabinet and hand the old, worn-out book to Ali. "Of course, these aren't the only recipes I use, but they are the most special."

"This is so thoughtful," Ali says as she thumbs through the pages. "She sounds like a caring person."

"She really was. She'd be thrilled to know we're cooking one of her recipes together."

"It's going to be delicious," Stella says, mixing the batter.

I see the chicken is cooked and shred it with two forks, then put the chicken with the vegetables and add broth.

"So, now we just scoop the batter into small bite-size pieces and let them cook in the broth with the lid closed."

"Beautiful." Stella claps.

Ali opens a few drawers. "Shall I set the table?"

"I can't get over how human you act. You know so many common phrases and have proper etiquette." Stella sounds amused.

"It's easy to learn about being human when you broadcast television signals in every direction and then portray the life of humans in dramas and comedies." She practically giggles. "Not to mention, I had thirty years of braving the lands and practicing my language with anyone who would talk to me, short conversations here and there. Some people thought I was homeless and gave me money, which I would use to buy books. Stella, do you remember that book you gave me?"

"Oh." She squints. "The noisy one that made the words glow as you read along."

"Yes, that introduced us to your written language. My DNA had to alter quite a bit before I could pronounce anything because I am not built with a tongue like yours. Ours is not so flexible. We use telepathy and vibrations to communicate, and our tongues are used for swallowing food."

"I remember those vibrations."

"Andrew, in case you didn't know, Stella and I can communicate telepathically."

"Seriously?" I ask, verifying with Stella.

"Yes, apparently I'm a freak of nature."

"No, Stella," Ali politely refutes. "Your spirit has always known this day would come, and you were born open and free."

Stella rocks from one foot to the other and lifts her shoulder, seeming to accept Ali's compliment. How many women could so easily take a comment about their spirit to heart?

"So, that's how you two communicated when you were younger?"

"It wasn't really words I was hearing as much as a feeling, if that makes sense."

"It does, actually." She smiles, and I'm reminded of being in the stars with Ali.

"Everyone we see tonight will still be in their natural form, which you shouldn't let bother you. We're all in this together. The universe created so much life, and we're part of it too."

"On that note." I hold one finger up, lift the lid, and poke the cornbread dumplings. "Dinner is ready!"

STELLA

All comfortably full from dinner, I take a moment by myself on the porch. Staring into the sky, the chilly breeze hits me, and I cross my arms. The leaves rustle in the wind, and the gentle ocean laps the shore in the distance. The setting sun has never looked so beautiful and alive.

The magnitude of today weighs on me. A small part of me wonders if James is watching all this from afar, relieved I was forced to abandon his belongings, forced to get out of my comfort zone and take this leap of faith. He would want me to be brave.

"Hey," says Andrew gently, peeking through the glass door. "I don't want to bother you."

"Oh, no, you're not a bother. I'm just getting some fresh air."

He makes his way beside me and offers me a chair. We sit looking at the colorful sky while Ali washes dishes.

"I, uh, grabbed this earlier and didn't want to pack it away in storage. I thought it might be special or something." He hands me something wrapped in a kitchen towel. Inside are my wedding picture that hung by my front door and my journal. My breath escapes me, and tears well up. I cover my eyes and try to speak, but my throat tightens. We stand, and I hug him tight, silently thanking him. My head rests on his chest, and he rubs my back. His warmth is hard to pull away from, but I take a step back, clutching my treasures to my heart.

"Thank you. You have no idea how much this means to me." I wipe away my tears and sit, admiring my wedding photo. I touch James's face on the glass as if to send him a message. I hope he can feel how much I miss him.

"You look beautiful," Andrew says, and my heart skips a beat. For a moment, I think he's referring to now, but I see his eyes on the picture.

"Gosh, we were so young. I look at this picture and see teenagers. Although, we were twenty-two."

"Hey, when you know, you know, right?"

"Right." I meet his gaze and take a deep breath. Flipping through the pages of my journal, I lean back into the chair.

"Can you believe this is really happening? Do you know I've been suppressing these memories of an alien encounter for as long as I can remember? And now it turns out it was all real, and we have to magically help them escape Earth." I wave my arms for effect.

"I can't believe it either. My brain has been boggled ever since my first encounter with her. They are light years ahead of us technologically, and they don't want to cause a frenzy among us. They want to politely leave without disturbing anyone. It's not how I pictured an alien invasion. They have great respect for us and where we are in our evolutionary process."

I stand and pace the length of the porch. "And what if we can't help them? What if they're all depending on us, and we can't do anything? The government made damn sure my family and I never spoke of Ali again and even tried to convince us she was some kind of pedophile who was trying to kidnap me. I don't know how we could possibly get through to them."

"*I have a plan.*"

I stop to stare through the window. "Ali, have you been listening this whole time? Quit that."

"What?" Andrew turns, looking back and forth between us.

"She's inside my head. It's hard to get used to." I glare at her and smirk.

She comes to the door. "*It's time.*"

"It's time?" I look up at Andrew. I feel naked, ill-prepared, like I'm forgetting something.

Ali gives us each a flashlight, and we make our way down to the shore. The wind is picking up, and I desperately wish I had brought a sweater. My body trembles and shivers. We're nearly to the coastline when Ali turns toward us.

"You should know that I will be the interpreter, and we won't stay long, so don't stress out." She straightens her clothes and brushes dog hair off my shirt as if I was a child. "And don't touch anything." She steps toward the shore and waits.

I lean over to Andrew and whisper, "Do you suddenly feel like a little kid?"

"She definitely made me question whether I am appropriately dressed."

A light shines under the water, and it slowly approaches us, getting brighter as it gets closer. Andrew inhales deeply with an expression not of fear, but as if he'd seen this before.

There is a small wake behind the light as it ascends. A small metallic orb, about the size of a car, rolls onto the shore, and a hatch lowers with steps that lead to a brightly lit room. There are no buttons or switches, no pilot, nothing mechanical. It's very simply designed, with seats in a circle around the perimeter.

We find seats, the hatch closes, and the orb descends. I sit with my hands folded in my lap, trying not to completely lose my senses. Andrew looks like a kid in a candy store. He's following orders by not touching, but I see in his eyes he is using all of his self-control.

"Okay, this is super advanced. Where are the pressure gauges? How deep are we going? Where is the ship? Are there windows? How will we get into the ship? Did the edges to the hatch door disappear?"

Ali smiles and giggles. I smile, pretending to be comfortable.

I can feel the orb lowering from the sensation in my stomach, but I have no idea which way we are going. It's probably better this way. If I could see the depth and how far we are from breathable oxygen, I'd probably have a heart attack and die right here, right now.

We slow to a stop. I hear loud gushing, like a waterfall, and the hatch door opens. Ali steps outside, and an abundance of vibrations comes from the room outside. Ali settles me and asks us to come out. Andrew grabs my hand and helps me step into the mother ship. It's enormous and bright, and when my eyes finally adjust, maybe a hundred figures face me.

I can hear Ali introducing us telepathically in their language, which my brain interprets as humming, singing almost. She sounds profoundly angelic, and I cover my mouth. These are real creatures who deserve their shot at life just as much as we do.

Andrew has tears in his eyes. He feels it too. We look at each other, and I silently acknowledge a deep sense of responsibility to help them.

Two step closer to Ali, keeping their eyes on us.

"We welcome you to our home away from home, and we thank you for coming to our aid," Ali interprets.

They stand at about my height and have similar features to Ali when I first found her in the woods. Humanoid figures with smooth, light features, both with long flowing blond hair and large eyes. Their pupils are big, with slivers of white showing around them. They wear tight beige fabric clothing that looks like silk. As they stare at us, their necks glow with a soft white light, similar to the shade of their hair.

"This is my mother and father," Ali says.

I try speaking, but my voice cracks, and I'm afraid I might cry. I ask Ali if I can get closer, and I hear a small uproar among the people.

"Yes, yes, of course. Please come." She waves me forward. "You may call them Nova and Elio," she says, pointing to each of them.

I approach and stick out my hand for her to shake, but remember not to touch anything, so I wave. They look to Ali, then do the same.

Andrew steps beside me and waves as well. He clears his throat and looks to Ali.

"Thank you for allowing Ali to bring us here to meet you and for giving us the opportunity to try to help you. We are humbled and honored that you would seek help from our kind and exhibit civility in response to other humans' inability to see past their fears and thirst for power. Our kind could obviously learn a lot from you."

Ali looks at Nova, then back to us, and says, "Through our efforts in communicating with your kind, we have concluded that, although you have come a long way evolutionarily, you lack the capacity to appreciate life beyond Earth. We understand how frightening it must be for us to intrude upon your planet and use technology that you cannot fully understand yet. We do not want to inflict fear or panic among your people."

"There has been an uptick in the general population's interest in other life within the universe, so maybe you've had a subtle impact," mentions Andrew.

"We had given up hope of safely communicating, but Ali insisted she could find the help we need. She believes you two could speak to your government on our behalf," Ali interprets.

Andrew and I glance at each other. I feel the pressure of the situation and nod to acknowledge this idea has potential.

"We can absolutely help with that," I say, "but, it might take some time. Our government has a hierarchy that would prevent average people like us from talking to someone of high ranking."

Nova takes a few steps closer to Ali. "I urge you to work your way up the hierarchy to represent us. You must find a way to trust us, as we trust you. During our time here on Earth, we have learned that there is a lot of secrecy held within the power of the government. We know they have seen us, yet the general population is unaware of our existence. We want you to know that we will not keep secrets from you. You can trust us. Any questions you have, we will answer honestly. There are ways we can reveal our presence covertly for the sake of your credibility."

"Right, we need to find a way to be taken seriously, and proof will be necessary," Andrew says.

Elio looks at Ali, who interprets, "Perhaps someone of importance will come to you if you lead them."

That reminds me of my experience with government intervention. "That's brilliant." I look at Andrew. "When I first met Ali, and my parents found out, government officials came to my house to confiscate my drawings, so they obviously took us seriously."

"We will position our ship near the shore of your house and allow it to be visible to your type of radar. When you decide you need proof, their satellites will see us, and they'll believe you."

Andrew rubs his hands through his hair. "But how will we know they won't just blow you up or take it as a signal to start a war?"

"You have to find a way to work your way up the hierarchy, and reveal the truth when it matters," Nova explains through Ali. "This ship is one of many. We hope to gather minerals and leave. We would never steal what we need and will only accept help if it is given. These minerals will not impact Earth life in any way, as they are readily available and renewable. Earth is the only living planet we have found thus far in our journey, and we plan to explore more on the way home. We are willing to have a working relationship with humans, and will happily share locations of other livable planets, as well as methods to extend Earth's life."

Andrew shakes his head and shuffles his feet. "Wow, this is an incredible opportunity for humankind. We'll have to get really creative, but we might be able to get someone's attention. Regardless of what my government decides to do, I sincerely hope we can remain in contact somehow," he says. "I have so many questions to ask you, and so much to learn. My science buddies would give anything to be here right now. Humans have only just discovered the accelerated expansion of the universe, and—"

I tuck my hand inside the crook of Andrew's arm. "Maybe we should take this one step at a time." He looks disappointed, but ultimately puts his hand over mine.

"You're right," he replies and looks back at Nova and Elio. "The most important task at hand is making sure you all get what you need to return safely home."

Nova's neck glows, and the entire room of onlookers also glow.

"When we glow, it is meant to convey our humble gratitude. We thank you," Ali says. She motions for us to get back into the orb.

As we sit in the orb with Ali, I feel a wave of relief and hug her tightly. "This is incredible. This whole experience is amazing. I'm so glad I found you in my backyard so long ago," I say almost in a whisper, my throat tight. I'm overjoyed at the success of the visit, worried about how we'll follow through, and sad for all her people to be in this position.

Ali has an equally large smile on her face. "I'm so glad you found me too."

Andrew is still looking around the orb. He tries standing up and balancing as the orb ascends. He looks like he's trying to surf. I try not to laugh but fail. He collapses, sits back, and releases his breath. We trade glances, and I feel motivated for the task at hand.

ANDREW

As we step out of the orb and back onto precious land, I feel like a superhuman. I climb onto a large boulder near the shore and breathe in deeply, absorbing every ounce of fresh air I can.

Stella and Ali share an embrace before she gets back into the orb. When it rolls back into the water, Stella turns and walks toward me. I stretch my arms toward the sky and laugh. "I have never felt so alive!" I hope Stella feels the same.

"Who knew visiting aliens on a spaceship could feel so refreshing?" she jokes, joining me on the boulder. She hugs herself in the breeze, and I rub her arms and back.

"This has been the most unbelievable experience. It's exhilarating, terrifying, and so beautiful all at the same time." I let out another howl.

She smiles big and leans in close. "I'm sort of panicking, though."

"I know!" I yell. "Wait, panicking?"

"Yes! What the hell are we going to do?"

"I see what you mean. Let's go inside and warm up." I hop off the rock, and we walk in stride, connected at the hip. We experienced something life-altering together, and it's hard to deny I feel closer to her because of it.

I slide open the glass door, and we're greeted with a joyous welcome from Chester. He's sliding around on the wood floors, wagging his tail and yelping.

Stella plops down on the couch, and I offer her coffee, tea, water, beer, and wine. She chooses wine. I pour us each a glass and meet her on the couch.

She has her hand on her forehead. "Can you imagine if we tried to tell our families what just happened?"

We roar in laughter. "My sisters would definitely not be okay. They'd be calling some psychologists."

"Yes," she says, still laughing. "My mother would stop everything to come evaluate my mental state. She would totally freak out."

When my laughing finally subsides, she says, "You know, I feel so lame saying this, but you are a really amazing person."

"Nah."

"It's true. This all happened so fast. You have helped me tremendously, and I'm basically a stranger."

"But you don't feel like one."

"I feel the same way. I find it amazing how well we get along, and how easy it is to trust you. I'm surprised at how close I feel to you without knowing much about you. It's like we're old friends who haven't seen each other in years."

"Stella, you do know me. I can tell you how I was raised, where I went to school, where I've lived, and it won't make much difference.

You know me because we are connected. We've been through a lot together in a small amount of time, and we've witnessed each other's character. When I look at you," I pause to emphasize my sincerity, "I see the most beautiful, most kind, elegant, compassionate woman I've ever met, and I'm thrilled to know you."

Her eyes tear up, and she exhales fully. "And now you make me blush." She takes a big gulp of wine and settles back into the couch cushions. "Have you ever been married?"

My heart sinks, as I'm sure she is thinking about her husband. "No, I have come close a few times, but something always kept me from pulling the trigger. I have been consumed with work and secretly loved the idea of retiring early, so I made that my priority. I finally saved up enough to live comfortably here back home."

"New York, right?"

"That's the one. I enjoyed it for the most part, but it's too crowded for me."

"I can imagine," she says and takes another sip. "So, your family is here?"

"Yep, both of my sisters and their families. They live here on the island. My parents always wanted us to stay close and spend time together. Luckily, we all like each other. I can't get enough of those kids. They crack me up. They remind me of when I was young, you know?"

She hums her agreement. "Do you miss your parents?"

"I miss them so much." I sigh, putting my feet on the coffee table. "I miss sharing good news with them. I miss how seriously they took my questions when I had any. My dad was the quiet one, but being out on the water fishing or climbing together put me in the right state of mind to tackle any problem."

"Sounds like you had a nice childhood."

"The best. And your parents? Are they around much?"

She takes a sip and lets out a breath. "My mom moved to Arizona with a boyfriend a few years ago. They have since separated, and she has a new beau, but she does really well there and has a good group of friends. She loves the weather."

"Ha! Stark difference from Maine, I'm sure."

"Totally."

"And your dad?"

"He left the picture. Single mom all the way!"

"Oh, I'm sorry. Although, I've heard single moms are superheroes."

"Absolutely."

"Are you curious about him?"

She repositions herself and pets Chester next to her on the couch. "I mean, I was curious when I was younger, but at this point, I don't care to know him. He chooses to live his own life. So, why would I waste my energy thinking about someone who doesn't care to know me?"

"Yeah, I can see that."

"It was really painful for me as a child knowing that he didn't care to be in my life, but instead of letting it hinder me, I focused on my amazing mom and how our relationship was enough for me. So, I guess I keep my guard up on this subject, but I don't like to worry about it."

She looks down, still petting Chester. I feel sad knowing anyone caused her pain. I question what kind of man could abandon his family. If he only knew the incredible woman she became.

"Your nieces and nephews? How old are they?"

"There's six of them." I chuckle. "I'm not going to guess all of their ages. I need to be a better uncle, for sure. The oldest one is in first grade, I think. Lots of little munchkins."

"They must be thrilled to have you so close by."

"You'll definitely have to meet everyone after we . . ."

"After we save the world?" she asks. "Or rather, the alien world?" We laugh.

"Yes, after we save the alien world."

"Good. I'd love to," she says and smiles.

We gaze at each other. I feel so happy in her company, and I wonder if she's thinking the same thing.

"Andrew, I might have to take you up on your offer to let me stay here."

"You're more than welcome. There're two guest rooms. Take your pick."

"Thanks. I can't imagine how I'll sleep tonight, but I should try."

"Absolutely. Let me know if you need anything."

She gets up and walks down the hall. Chester follows her to her room and watches as she closes the door. He looks at me, clearly hoping he'd get to sleep in her room.

"Sorry, bud!" I whisper. I bring our glasses to the sink, turn off the lights, and head to my room.

As I lie in bed, knowing she's in the room next to me, I feel an overwhelming sense of responsibility—for her, for Ali, for her people. Together, I know Stella and I can do anything.

—◦◦◦∿∿∿∿◦◦◦—

When morning comes, I get out of bed and wonder if she's awake yet. I'm pleased to see her in the kitchen making coffee.

"Good morning!" I say with a groggy voice.

She turns around and smiles. "I hope you like your coffee strong."

"The stronger, the better."

"Good. I also made some toast and eggs."

"Amazing. Thank you."

We sit down at the bar in the kitchen and drink coffee with our simple breakfast. I love how messy her hair is and how she doesn't seem to care about it.

"Did you sleep okay?" I ask and blow on my coffee.

Stella tilts her head from side to side. "I tossed and turned for a while. I couldn't get their faces out of my head. And then I couldn't stop coming up with ideas of how we could get things going for Ali, and then I'd get side-tracked worrying about my little earthly problems, like finding a new place to live."

"Hey, no rush in that department. I need the company."

"You're too kind. We'll see how that goes. Right now, I'm really feeling the weight of last night. Did you come up with any ideas?"

I finish the last bit of egg on my plate and lean my forehead on my hand. "It has to be something urgent. Something major."

She hums.

We remain sitting. I'm deep in thought, making plans for how things should go. It seems she's doing the same.

When we talk about our ideas, we finish each other's sentences, and every thought she has makes me appreciate her more.

On our third cup of coffee, we have our plan.

"Are you ready?" I ask, sure and unsure at the same time. I've never lied to the police before. Stella nods, encouraging me.

"You told Ali the plan?"

"Yes, she knows."

"Okay, here we go." I pick up my phone and call 9-1-1. "Hello, please send an ambulance! I just saw a plane crash into the ocean behind my house. I'm on my way out to see if there are any survivors now. Please hurry!" I give them my address and hang up.

"Wow, you sounded pretty believable. Let's get out there and keep our story straight."

We scurry outside and take out my dad's old canoe. By the time the police and ambulance arrive, we've paddled out to sea, and I wave to them. "Over here!"

One speaks into their radio, and we head back to shore.

"Officer, I can't find anyone," I say. "It was like an asteroid hitting the water. Splashes a hundred feet high. It must have been a jet because it was traveling at high speed."

"And there's no sign of life?"

"No. And I haven't found any wreckage or parachute. Something isn't right."

"And you saw the plane crash as well, ma'am?"

"Uh, yes, I did. I'm sorry. I'm—I'm in shock."

"I understand. I've called the coast guard to come do a thorough search. I'm Officer Preston, and you are?"

"I'm Andrew Witten, and this is Stella Frasier, sir."

"Thank you. And where were you when you saw the plane crash?"

"We were both on the porch drinking coffee." I point in the direction of my house.

"Okay," the officer says, scratching his chin. "There's a chance the plane crashed farther out than it appears. If you didn't find anything close to shore, I'll send the guys into the deeper waters as soon as possible."

"I could see how it might be farther than I thought."

"What size plane did you say?"

"It happened so fast, but with the splash it made, it had to have been going very fast. Faster than any Cessna you'd see around here."

"Did you hear it coming?" he asks, looking through his binoculars.

I cross my arms and act like I'm taking time to think. "Now, that you mention it, no, I don't think we did." I look over at Stella, who is holding her hand over her eyes, searching the waters. "Stella, did you hear anything?"

She shakes her head. "Just, uh, just the crash. The sound of the impact," she says, then turns back toward the water.

Officer Preston lowers his binoculars. He juts his jaw, moving his tongue over his teeth, and appears to be sucking out food.

"Did your neighbors come out? Say they saw something?" He puts his hands on his hips and looks at the houses next door.

"I'm not sure if there's anyone in them. They're vacation rentals. But I guarantee you they'd be down here if they had."

I see the Coast Guard in the distance. There's a boat about a mile off the shore and a helicopter coming from behind us.

Stella dramatically falls into my arms, and we pretend to be very worried about the imaginary plane and pilot.

The officer speaks into his radio, "Do you see anything out there?"

"Nothing yet, sir."

"Okay, let's go inside and let the Coast Guard search. If there was a crash, they'll find it. I've got to ask you some questions."

"Sure, of course," we say in unison and lead the way inside, sneaking glances at the water.

Officer Preston sits at the kitchen table, and Stella fetches some waters.

"Okay, Mr. Witten, Ms. Frasier, I have to admit, I'm not sure there was a plane crash."

"I don't understand. Where could it have gone?" Stella asks.

He reaches for his pad and pen. "You say it was traveling very fast, yet you heard no engine?"

"No engine noise at all."

"One of the problems we have is that there are no planes missing. We checked with air traffic control on the way here, and every plane flying in the area has been accounted for." He scratches his eyebrow with his pen. "Maybe you saw an optical illusion with the sunrise and the horizon. I've seen strange things before myself."

"There is no doubt in my mind we saw a plane crash," Stella says in a stern tone.

"You know," I lean over the table, "there's a sharp drop-off just on the other side of that island. Could the Coast Guard use radar or something to scan the ocean floor?"

"There is usually a lot of evidence on top of the water when a plane crashes. Lots of debris. Sometimes, there's smoke in the air from the failed engine."

"Then, what could it have been?" Stella asks. "An asteroid?" We stare at each other, pretending to be confused.

"One of our divers found something," his receiver calls out.

The officer's eyes open wide. He looks at us, then leans into his radio. "Are there any survivors?" He does that tongue thing again.

"Uh, sir . . . you better get down here."

"I'll be right down." His brow is creased when he looks up. "I apologize, guys," he says as he scoots out of his chair. He clears his throat. "You were right to call us. Now, you need to let us do our job." He holds his hands out and insists that we stay in the house. "I will let you know any news as it comes."

I watch him leave and wait until he's off the porch to put my hands on my head in disbelief.

Stella jumps. "They're about to find an alien spaceship!" she whispers.

"Act natural! Act cool." I stand straight. "Back into character."

She points her thumb over her shoulder. "We're not actually going to wait inside, are we?"

"Not a chance," I say, opening the glass door.

"We're concerned for the pilot."

"Exactly. We need to know that they are okay."

We head down to the shore. As we get closer, my sarcasm melts away and becomes genuine worry. It was fun playing our little game with the police, but the seriousness of our efforts is sinking in. These people are about to find something extraordinary.

Leaving a safe distance between us and the officer, we keep back about thirty feet from all the commotion. A few more divers drop into the ocean, and officers scatter around the shore, making phone calls and whispering to each other. One of the coast guard boats pulls up to shore. A soldier jumps out and walks up to Officer Preston.

"We're going to have to close off the area for investigation."

He tilts his head down. "Any idea what's down there?"

"Right now, it's too hard to tell. Close off the area and keep them inside." The soldier points to us, and Officer Preston looks over his shoulder.

"Hey, guys." He comes toward us, eyes squinting. "There's a lot we need to figure out. A lot of unknowns. We're blocking off this section of coastline."

"What do you know?" I ask.

He sniffs and pulls up his pants. I bet he wishes he could be searching the scene.

"Well, it could be a number of things. Illegal drug trafficking, a stolen plane, or an accident with military training programs."

"Military training program?" asks Stella.

He holds his arms out to either side as if to herd us like cows. "We aren't sure yet. Now, it's better if you two wait inside. We'll know where to find you if we have any more questions."

As we turn toward the house, I notice he stays behind.

"Oh, no." Stella takes a step toward me. "They're going to cover this up and call it a training accident."

"That's okay," I say, putting one arm around her. "They know we're watching."

We walk hip-to-hip back up to the house, quietly speculating how far they're going to take the military training story.

A helicopter flies overhead, and two police cars pull up in front of my house.

Stella leans in close. "Should I tell Ali they should move their ship? I'm worried they are about to take their presence as a bad sign."

"No, we need their ship for leverage. If we get rid of it too soon, we lose our proof. Trust me."

When we enter the house, I hear a knock on the door. Stella peers through the window and gasps. She holds her finger up and runs to the bedroom. They knock again, and she emerges, rummaging in her purse.

I open the door and am greeted by men in business clothes.

"Hello, I'm Special Agent Brian Spieth, FBI. May I come in?" he asks, very professionally. He flashes his badge. Two guys stand behind Spieth with earbuds. Their sport coats bulge near their waists.

Spieth looks to be nearing sixty with grey hair and sun-spotted skin and has an unusually tan face with aging yellow eyes.

"Yes, of course. Did you guys use your radar to find the plane? I knew it was down there somewhere."

"Why don't we have a seat, and I will ask you a few questions."

I motion for the table or couch. He chooses the couch and sets out a recorder as he sits, elbows leaning on his knees casually. His eyes scan the room. "My report states there was a woman here as well."

"Yes, Stella. She's resting. This has been quite the morning," I say. "She's in the other room." I hope this is a good opportunity to set things in the right direction before he starts recording.

"So, are you the local FBI agent? Or did you fly in from somewhere?"

Agent Spieth looks surprised and clears his throat. "Well, you might call me a local, but as you can tell by my southern drawl, I did not come from this area. I work in the northeast most often, yes."

"So, what would you say is your area of expertise?"

"I have a few different specialties. Fraud being my main focus." He stares hard at me, blankly, almost like a threat.

"Let me ask you this—"

"Excuse me, Andrew. I am here representing the United States of America, and what you saw today is classified military information. You must understand—"

"You can't honestly believe that what's underwater down there is part of the military. Have you seen it?" Is he simply following orders, or is he aware of what's going on?

"Whether I have seen it or not is beside the point. I'm here to ensure your safety, and I need your cooperation on this matter. We have some paperwork for you to sign that establishes your allegiance to the United States—"

"You mean a non-disclosure agreement?" I smirk. There's no way I'm signing anything. "Have you ever met them?"

"Who?" he asks, visually frustrated.

"The aliens."

Spieth straightens, reaching for his radio.

"Oh, look who it is . . ." Stella says.

He releases his grip on his radio and stands. "Hi, I'm Special Agent Spieth. If you don't mind, I have a few questions for the two of you." He glares at me, and I understand there's no more funny business.

"You don't remember me, do you?"

Confused, I look from him to her.

"I'm sorry, ma'am. Remind me of your name."

"Stella Frasier. Daughter of Frank and Nancy Frasier."

She walks over and sets her old drawing of Ali on the table. Agent Spieth's eyes widen, but the rest of him remains placid.

"Remember me, now?"

"As a matter of fact, I don't."

"You know very well who I am and what this drawing represents. You convinced my family there was a child predator stalking me, and my entire life, I've thought maybe I was delusional for thinking I met someone from another world. Well, how many other alien cases have you covered up since then?"

His face lightens to a jovial yet concerned expression. "There are no such things as aliens, darling. Now, hold up. I don't know what this has turned into, but it's going to stop right now," he demands, holding his arms out defensively.

"You know," Stella says, "the same little girl I met in my backyard all those years ago has come back to find me for help. Her name is Ali, and she's in that ship down there."

"What?"

"Yes. We know the aliens. They are nonviolent creatures, and they need our help," I say.

Spieth's tan face turns a more reddish hue. "I was not prepared for this charade, and I don't know who put you up to it, but please sit down."

I don't appreciate the pushback, but Stella and I sit. "Agent Spieth, you don't have to pretend anymore. We know that's an alien spacecraft down there. Getting the FBI's attention was our goal today. We need to know who to connect with to make a peaceful negotiation for the aliens."

"I have a signal that will tell the ship to move locations. I can use it at any time for proof that we're communicating," Stella says.

"Oh, really?" He sneers. "In that case, tell them to go back where they came from. Ha!"

I'm frustrated with how he's treating Stella, and I stand. "Is there any chance you could take us seriously?"

Agent Spieth gets up and matches my energy. "No, you need to take me seriously. If you don't sit down and answer my questions, I'm going to take you into custody for disorderly conduct."

"Please think about this," I say. "We want to help the military and the aliens. We can do both. Please, just listen to what we have to say. They mean us no harm."

"I'm going to give them the signal," she says hesitantly.

"Are you threatening the United States?"

"Look, Agent Spieth," I say, "we are not trying to threaten anyone. We simply want you to know that *we* know there are aliens parked in my backyard. You don't have to try to cover it up. And we have valuable information that can benefit the military, the government, science, and our future in the cosmos. This is bigger than you and me. Will you please give us a chance?"

Agent Spieth puts his hands on his hips. "And if I don't?"

"If you don't, Stella can simply tell the aliens to reveal themselves. She can tell all the ships parked on planet Earth to rise up out of the water and present themselves to humans. They are a peaceful race and would commit no act of war, but do you really want to cause mass hysteria around the world simply because you wouldn't give us a chance to be the middlemen?"

"Give us a chance," Stella says with desperation in her voice.

From the look on Spieth's face, it's obvious he knew this day would come. He looks at the floor and scratches his neck, and then picks up Stella's drawing. He stuffs the page in the back of his notebook and folds his hands.

I don't feel like this guy will break easily.

His face gets hard. His eyes lose their luster. "You think you're the first humans for the aliens to use against us?"

We both stare at him wide-eyed. "That's the point of this," I say. "We are not against you. They are not against you."

"Look," he says. "I'm not sure what you think you know about these guys. I'm gonna be real honest, and you better listen up. They have captured our people, tortured them, brainwashed them, created bio-warfare. They are not what you think. Now, are you going to side with these ultimate manipulators, or are you going to side with your fellow humans?"

"What are you talking about?" Stella yells. "Ali would never do that. Don't you dare try to flip this around. You're the manipulators!"

"Code two-four-two."

The front door bursts open.

"Tell Ali to get out of there, Stella." She looks scared but nods.

"You are under arrest for refusing to retain classified information, and for threatening the United States of America."

Stella and I stare at each other as we get shoved into separate squad cars with handcuffs.

Fuck.

STELLA

My whole body is tense, shaking, with clenched fists. I refuse to believe what Spieth said is true. I have always felt confident in my ability to read people's demeanor, and I believe Ali has been genuine and honest. To think that it was all a ploy makes me physically ill. I close my eyes and concentrate on communicating with Ali in case they take us too far away.

"Ali, they are taking us somewhere. They're trying to turn us against you, but I won't let them. We'll be okay. I don't know where we are going."

"Stella, I'm right behind you. We're in this together. This could be a good thing. It means they are taking you seriously. Keep it up! Let me know if things turn bad."

I drop my shoulders and let out a breath. Opening my eyes, a surge of anger for my captors hits me. But being defensive will do no good. I turn in my seat, looking for a car or a UFO following us, but

I see nothing. Is Ali following us, or was she using a figure of speech when she said she's behind us?

Turning to the front, I find a squad member staring me down with a mean mug. He has no sympathy for me. Part of me wants to give up. I don't see how we can get out of this. If they won't believe a word we say, what's the point in trying anymore?

We come to a stop at a group of buildings I've never seen before. They appear strangely ominous with their dark concrete exterior and tinted windows. It is rather futuristic looking with dihedral edges, resembling a mountainside. I expect to see a major road, but it's a small dirt one at the end of the driveway. I should have been paying more attention. Without notice, they open the squad car door and yank me out.

"There is no reason for excessive force, although I'm sure you find pleasure in pushing around a woman." I stand straight. "I have ears. I can follow verbal instructions just fine. What's wrong with being polite?"

"I do apologize, ma'am. Sometimes it's hard to maneuver in handcuffs."

As they lead me inside, I see Andrew step out of his squad car behind me. I hope they're not going to keep us separated. I can't do this without him. I turn to see him again, and he mouths, "Don't say anything."

I face forward, pretending not to have seen anything. When we enter the ominous-looking building, they tell me to stand on a red X and allow the machine to detect dangerous levels of radiation. They secure my handcuffs to a pole and back away.

A giant folding arm raises out of its cubby and expands its append-age cone to scan me from top to bottom. It emits a green light. I guess my levels are not dangerous.

They lead me into an interrogation room and set a stack of files at the far end of the table. Again, they attach my handcuffs to the table as if I'm some sort of criminal. Agent Spieth sits and clears his throat, outwardly unfazed. I wonder how many times he's run through this same routine in the past.

"Ms. Stella Frasier, you believe you have made contact with an alien within the last seven days?"

I open my mouth to speak and then remember Andrew telling me to keep quiet. I close my mouth and maintain eye contact. Spieth shuffles the files and bangs them on the table.

"The thing is, Ms. Stella, when things enter our atmosphere from outer space, it's highly likely they will have elevated levels of radiation. When a meteorite makes it to Earth's surface, even the dirt and gravel surrounding the impact contain high levels."

"What's your point?"

"My point is, ma'am, that our machines indicate that you have not been in contact with anything from outer space. So, I'm beginning to lose trust in you. I'm wondering if this was all a hoax." He looks at me with judgment in his eyes.

I bite my lip. "Is this a bogus intimidation tactic? And even if it isn't, does radiation linger for decades?" I ask through my teeth. Doesn't he know Ali and her people have been here for at least thirty years? Of course he does. He's trying to get me to talk.

Part of me wonders if radiation is why his skin is a strange shade of yellow with what look like scarred blisters. Maybe he's gotten too close a few times. I start to doubt and question my standing. What are the chances there is more than one alien species on Earth?

"I see that you recently lost your husband," he says.

"Don't bring him into this. He has nothing to do with what's happening." My voice seems calm, but inside I'm livid.

Agent Spieth lets out a big breath and stays silent for a moment.

"Would you say it's easy to prey on vulnerable people such as yourself? Don't you think it was convenient for your friend, *Ali*, to get back in touch with you when you were so desperate?"

I'm shocked. He's turning this around, manipulating me. I huff to dismiss his efforts, but I can't help wondering if he's right.

"Why didn't she reach out to you while your husband was still alive? Do you think Ali is a figment of your imagination to distract you from reality?"

"Stop it! Stop it now!" I yell, holding back tears. "Do *not* suggest that I have made this up. Could you be any more cliché?" My face is getting hot. "You should be ashamed. How dare you exhibit the same predatorial behavior that you are insinuating Ali used against me."

"Ms. Frasier, it says here that you've been seeing a therapist lately."

"I've been seeing a therapist for years," I snap back. "There's nothing wrong with that. It doesn't mean anything other than I take my mental health seriously."

"Would you say you need help coping with reality?"

"Don't be ridiculous! Where are you getting this information about me, anyway? Have you been keeping tabs on me? Ever since my first encounter?"

"Not me, personally, but the US government has, yes." He looks down at his papers again. "My records indicate you have been actively partaking in hallucinogenic drugs."

"What?" This could be bad. "My doctor prescribed micro-dose medication for anxiety. It is not nearly enough to hallucinate."

Agent Spieth stares intensely into my eyes, leans forward, and whispers, "Are you sure?"

I shake my head. "I see what you're doing. You're pathetic. The FBI found you, the most boring and shallow person on the planet, to keep your head down and follow orders. You're not willing to question anything? Seriously?"

Every muscle in his face goes slack. "I have great respect for our nation, and although I may not understand every rule in the book, I follow them, trusting the process to benefit the greater whole."

"Yeah, what a cop-out . . . excuse the pun."

He shuffles his papers, seeming to debate what to ask next to give me more doubts.

"Is this really your job? You come around to people's homes and convince them they are dreaming? Or lying? You find that sort of life rewarding?"

He continues reading through the files.

"Don't you have an ounce of curiosity? About the universe or life itself? Is it impossible for you to feel empathy toward other life forms?"

He grins. "Have you ever heard of the Exotics Club?"

"No."

"We all get together and hunt exotic animals for fun."

"Oh, that's nice . . ."

"My fondest memory is gettin' a polar bear with a bow and arrow." He laughs to himself. "You should have seen that thing run. He was massive."

My hands tighten into fists. My jaw clenches. My teeth grind. Tears well in my eyes, and my throat tightens. He enjoys seeing me like this.

"I've also killed an elephant, a few lions, a giraffe, some—"

"Enough!"

"So, to answer your question, no. I don't give a flying fuck about any other life forms here or anywhere else."

I nod aggressively, trying not to let my emotions take over. "I'm glad to know the clichés are true. Our country is controlled by disgusting, selfish assholes who have no souls."

ANDREW

The men sit me down in a small room with only one window, which is in the door, and they lock my cuffs onto the table. They immediately leave the room, I'm assuming to go interrogate Stella. She will be able to handle herself, but I still hate being away from her. I need to wrap my head around what's going on.

Agent Spieth admitted not only that aliens exist, but also that he's dealt with them before and that this is a recurring stunt they pull.

This guy is really good at acting like he knows everything, but I'd like to see how much he really knows about Ali and her people. Was he making all that up to manipulate us?

That guy has to be full of shit. He just tried to come up with something to say that would both shock us and make us question our place in the equation. It's a power trip. It has to be.

I bend toward my handcuffed hands and rub my face trying to come up with a plan.

Agent Spieth opens the door and sits without any eye contact. He shuffles his papers and puts on reading glasses.

"Before you say anything, Mr. Spieth, I'd like to remind you that this is an incredible opportunity for our scientists to learn more about Cosmic Slip, the way these aliens travel through space. Our technology is light years behind what these people have, and this is our chance to—"

"Oh yeah? Then why have they been hiding in the dark like scared little rabbits?"

He's got the cognitive complexities of Elmer Fudd, apparently.

"Wow, that's the most ignorant thing I've heard you say so far. They feel pity for us," I explain. "They are so far advanced they see us like wild animals. They don't want to ruin our process of evolution, but they can, and they should, in my opinion. Humans are flat-lining, and we could use their help."

"Trust me, son, they don't want to help us."

"You're wrong. They want to, and they need our help. All they want to do is *leave*, sir. Let's give them what they need for safe travel. I mean, when was the last time you actually had someone to communicate directly with the aliens? Don't waste this opportunity and treat it like some random UFO sighting. It's more than that, and you know it."

"Mr. Witten, we have an entire agency working to defend our planet from aliens and galactic interference. This is none of your business, and it's not up to you to decide what happens next."

"Oh, it's not?" I say, with a hint of rage in my voice. This guy is incapable of seeing past his defense mode. "I took you for a smarter man. Do yourself a favor and give that agency a call. Do you really think we don't have a fail-safe?"

He leans back and takes his glasses off. He starts cleaning the lenses with his shirt and asks, "And to what are you referring, Mr. Witten?"

I smile. "If you bring Stella in here so we can talk to you together, I'll try to explain things in layman's terms." And I give him a large, sarcastic smile, but my heart beats out of my chest waiting for his response.

"Ms. Frasier is in the other room signing paperwork right now."

"What?" I scoff. "She would never do that."

"She finally came to her senses . . . just like you will. Come on, Andrew. You've made your point. It's time to stop the charade."

He's lying. His lack of respect for this situation is really getting to me. It's time to use our fail-safe. I'm not going to let our government continue this pattern.

"Picture this. Imagine all of the coastal cities seeing the alien spaceships at the same time, nearly a thousand ships. News breaking, and all the smartphones capturing video footage . . . If you can't take us seriously, I'll tell the aliens we failed. They asked for our help, and we failed. They can take matters into their own hands, now."

Spieth stares at me, smirking.

"Test me. I don't care anymore. If you want to single-handedly be the one to expose alien life to the world, then go ahead and make us sign the papers."

He sets his glasses down, pushes his chair away from the table, and leaves without a word. He won't admit it, but he knows this case is different from those in years past.

Agent Spieth brings Stella in. She sits next to me. I let out a long breath and don't break eye contact. She is crying but looks relieved to see me. She doesn't deserve to be here. I try to reach out to her, but my handcuffs prohibit me. I tell her with my eyes to go along with me.

"Agent Spieth, what makes our situation special is we have a method to communicate directly with the aliens. Have you ever had that opportunity before?"

"What you saw was a military training program gone wrong, and we need your compliance," he says as if he's reciting from a textbook.

"Okay, we'll tell Ali to send every ship in the United States to China and Russia. They'll be more open to the idea of receiving advanced technological intel," I say. "Or better yet, just forget it all. I think every human on planet Earth deserves to know aliens exist and that the government has been hiding it from us for decades. Let's just take one for the team, Stella. Let's let the world figure out how to help the aliens."

He slams his hand on the table, startling Stella.

"We've been dealing with this for much longer than the two of you. We have learned lessons the hard way with these guys, and we don't want to make the same mistakes we have in the past."

I feel a warming sensation on the back of my neck, and Stella says, "She's here."

STELLA

"Who is here?" Agent Spieth asks. He appears uneasy.

"Your best bet is to pretend she is human and bring her in here with us. As far as anyone knows, you're questioning witnesses to the plane crash, right?"

"You mean Ali? The girl from your drawing? Is here? Right now?" He lifts his hand to his earpiece and looks at the door, possibly wondering if I had seen her in the window.

I peer over at Andrew, who looks calm and collected. "She will not hurt you or anyone here," he says. "Please allow her to come in so we can all figure out a solution."

He taps his earpiece. "Is there someone here to see me?" He drops his gaze, then his eyes bolt up at me, and the sweat on his forehead drips into his eyes. He wipes his face and pushes his chair back. "Send her in."

He waits at the door, then cracks it open only an inch as if to second guess his options. He looks at Ali with fear and disgust. Glancing at the agent who brought her in, he says, "Please call for Senior Officer Swanson and his colleagues. They need to fly in immediately. This is a Code Skunk. We'll need backup to surround the building and the hallways."

The other agent nods and disappears.

Andrew stands as much as he can. His fury is visible by the beet-red color of his cheeks. "You called for backup? You won't need any weapons. She's harmless!"

"It's okay, Andrew," Ali says, holding her hands up. "Let them do what they need to do to feel safe."

Andrew slowly sits back down and waits for Ali to speak.

"Agent Spieth, is it? May I introduce myself?" she asks with her hand out.

He stares at her hand, the disgust and offense clear on his face. He gestures for her to sit at the end of the table.

"These two say you're an alien," he says, pointing to me and Andrew.

"Yes."

"And I'm just supposed to believe that?"

Ali pauses, playing with her hands. "That was my ship under the ocean you found earlier."

"Prove it."

"We stayed hidden about one hundred meters down just behind the island near Andrew's shoreline. One of the divers saw us first. Our radar indicated that your satellites picked up GPS location and locked our position. When we moved into deeper waters, you lost track of us."

"If that was your ship, then how'd you get here so fast?"

"I took an orb, a small craft, and I followed the cars from the sky."

I see Andrew's eyes widen. He mouths, "They can fly, too?" to himself.

Agent Spieth's eyebrow lifts. "How come we didn't see it jump out of the water and fly around above us?"

"We are using advanced alien technology that you will not understand."

"Mmhm . . . Where is your ship now?"

"Do you want GPS location?"

"Yes."

"43.409976, −67.046398"

He writes the number down on a piece of paper and opens the door. He hands the officer outside the paper, mumbling orders.

"I'll have to get that verified," he says.

Ali nods.

"Ali is what you go by?" he sputters.

"Yes. It's nice to finally meet you."

He seems to have a dry mouth and settles for nodding his response.

"Agent Spieth, I come in peace. I know this must be uncomfortable for you, but please hear me out." She folds her hands politely on the table and tells me telepathically everything is going to be okay.

"As you know," she begins, "we have stopped here on Earth during our travels. We've stayed longer than we anticipated. You see, we were thrilled to learn of another planet with intelligent life, and we have desperately hoped to make a connection. Through our years of efforts, it has become clear our presence is not welcome, and we respect that. But spending so much time here has depleted our resources. Our planet has been thawing from its great freeze, and we know Earth could provide a jumpstart to its healing if we gather certain minerals before we leave."

Spieth seems tense still, but he's listening. He holds a finger up and touches his earpiece. He puts his head down, then crosses his arms.

"Looks like your ship is where you said it'd be . . ." he says. His eyes fall onto Ali.

"How can I convince you to trust me and my people?"

"First, tell me why we *should* trust you?" he says, exaggerating his southern drawl.

"Why shouldn't you?"

He sits back in his chair and rubs his forehead. This is going to be a long process.

"To start, you fly your crafts over no-fly zones. You've caused irreparable damage to fighter jet pilots' mental health, and you've caused an overall distrust among our citizens against the very agency that is meant to protect them. You've stuck around for so long that we assumed you've been here plotting how to take over our planet."

"We've been figuring out ways to communicate with you. We have always tried to avoid causing fear among your people and realize the importance of maintaining our covert existence."

Spieth stays silent.

"May I be blunt?" she asks.

Spieth looks around, carefree, as if to say, "Why not?"

"When we first came here, it was clear to us that your civilization was not prepared to acknowledge other life in the universe. But we've felt a shift lately. There's a lot of attention on the subject, and I'm curious what your thoughts are. Do you think humans are capable of accepting this fact, now?"

He glances around the room as though he's giving his answer some thought. "There's no doubt in my mind some people would be able to handle the realization. But we have this thing on our planet called religion. It brings great comfort to those who need it, and I believe the religious people on Earth would not take too kindly to your existence."

"I see . . ."

I'm surprised at his genuine answer. He must have been in the

FBI dealing with strange cases for so long that he can stay calm and levelheaded. I can't say if it would be the same if a newer, younger agent was assigned to our case.

"Ms. Ali." Agent Spieth clears his throat. "Would you consider yourself the leader of your people?"

"As it pertains to communicating with humans, yes."

"Do you or your people intend to cause harm to humans or planet Earth?"

"No."

"Do you intend to claim any part of our planet or atmosphere as your own?"

"No."

"Are you willing to communicate peacefully and fairly with the American government, pledging your allegiance with us?"

"Yes. Any and all information shared will stay between us."

He nods and repositions himself. "Look, there is some truth to what you've said. There has been a recent shift, which has made my job extensively more difficult. And it might be time for us to let your existence be known to a certain group of scientists and military personnel." He peers over at Andrew with defeat in his expression. Maybe Ali's presence has softened him a bit.

Andrew's face lights up, and he looks at me with a combination of hope and disbelief.

"We've been preparing for a day like this. We have a designated group of NASA scientists who remain on call for Code Skunk, which is a separate NASA division under military surveillance."

"We find it to be of great importance to keep a positive relationship with Earth, especially since we have only explored one-half of this galaxy. If we could remain in communication, it could benefit us both."

Spieth holds his hands out in front of him. "I have already reached farther than my jurisdiction allows, but we will get you in contact with Officer Swanson, who is, as you might say, someone of great importance to our secret programs. He will be able to provide you with some answers."

Agent Spieth gets up, takes his paperwork, and leaves the room. Finally, we're all alone. I'm relieved we are together again, and things are moving along.

"Ali! You did it!!"

She smiles at me, holding her cheeks.

"This meeting will go down in history. I can't believe I was here to witness it," Andrew exclaims.

We all try to hug, but since Ali is the only one without handcuffs, she stands and embraces us.

"What made you decide to follow us?" I ask.

"I couldn't just sit back and let you two get arrested without at least trying to help."

She sits in her chair and looks as if she doesn't know where to begin. "I took an orb and followed the cars, then hid it behind some trees. I wasn't sure where you'd be inside the building, but I followed Stella's voice in my head. I found the reception desk, where I informed her Agent Spieth was expecting me. My nerves did something weird, at that point."

"Oh?"

"I was trying to explain that I needed to speak with Agent Spieth about the plane crash, and when I could sense she had doubts, I couldn't control my vibrations."

"What happened?"

"They really amped up, and the windows bowed and nearly shattered."

Andrew leans forward. "Did it scare them?"

"It started to. But I reminded myself how important this was, took a deep breath, and gained control. That's when the receptionist got a call from Spieth. I guess you had told him I was here. Perfect timing," she admits.

"I wasn't getting through to him. He wasn't budging. But having you here made all the difference," he says.

"And now, it's looking like they're really going to give us a chance to get you what you need. You're one step closer to going home."

"You know," she says, slowly relaxing in her chair, "you could come with us." There is a hint of a smile on her face. I'm so shocked I can't speak. "From what I've been told, my planet is very similar to Earth and could easily support human life. I would love to be introduced to my home planet with both of you by my side."

My heart sinks a little. I smile to be polite, but Andrew looks over the moon.

"You mean we could actually go on your ships, and travel a hundred thousand light years, and survive?"

"We do not measure in light years, but yes. Depending on how long we explore the other solar systems, it could take up to an Earth year to get back to our planet."

"One year! That's all?"

"Wouldn't that be exciting? Imagine starting a new life on a new planet," Ali says, with excitement and hope in her voice.

"Hold on, guys. Let's take this one step at a time," I say—my signature motto these days. "Our first goal is to make nice with the military. We need to make plans so that you guys actually get what you need for traveling. Are you even sure your planet is ready to sustain life again?"

"Oh yes, it has been thawing nicely. Our probes show us the

temperatures are within a comfortable range, and the vegetation has rebounded well. We have many plans in order to ensure the wildlife can flourish again, including us. All of our homes and buildings are unscathed due to our preparations before we left."

"Sounds incredible," Andrew says, like he's daydreaming.

"Well, it's only because of the two of you that we're making progress to do this the right way."

—∼∿∿/\/\/\/\/\/\∿∼—

About an hour goes by, and the door opens abruptly. A man walks in, older and hopefully wiser than Agent Spieth. He introduces himself as Senior Officer Gerald Swanson.

"You'll have to excuse my messy hair." He rubs his hands through his thinning hair. "The helicopter always makes it wispier than I intend." He smooths it out a few more times and says, "Hi there," then cheerfully shakes our hands. He offers to remove our handcuffs.

This guy is not intimidating like I imagined he would be. He seems happy and nice, so far. He sits and asks us if we need anything to eat or drink, while he sets his coffee mug on the table with his laptop and files.

Why isn't he at least a little intimidated by Ali? She is an alien after all.

"I have reviewed the tape from your time here with Agent Spieth, and it brings me great joy that we have this opportunity to speak. Two superheroes and one alien. Straight from a comic book!"

His jovial attitude confuses me. I look to the others, and they seem to agree this guy isn't what they expected.

Officer Swanson clears his throat again. "Let me give you some background. I've been the head of Unidentified Aerial Phenomena management with the defense department for over thirty years, and our focus has been to gather intel before someone else does." He laughs and peers at Ali.

"A few years ago, when our fighter pilots got footage of your little tic-tac, I was assigned to prepare a special group who'd be ready for a situation like this. What was that thing? A drone?"

Andrew jumps in, "It was a small white cylinder-shaped craft spotted by some fighter jets. It made headlines."

"Oh yes, I remember seeing that on a TV somewhere," Ali says. "That sighting was unintended. You are referring to our solar batteries. We send them up to charge. A technology we'd be happy to share with humans."

Andrew and Agent Swanson share a glance. "I'm not too sure oil guys would be thrilled at that idea, but maybe we can figure something out."

It dawns on me that resource scarcity is in the US's favor. This is still a military guy, no matter his rank, so oil means control.

Andrew starts to say something but is interrupted by Officer Swanson.

"I've had my theories about what sort of creature might be flying those things," he says to Ali. "I never imagined a pretty young lady like yourself."

The tone in his voice makes me squeamish, and I feel the urge to nip it in the bud. "Ali has been slowly altering her DNA for years to appear more humanlike."

"Holy shit! That'll wake you up."

"As funny as this may seem, Officer Swanson, we are very seriously trying to help an entire species survive, as well as prevent mass chaos, while simultaneously creating a long-term relationship with an alien planet that is clear across our galaxy," Andrew says.

"You're right, you're right. All jokes aside, I'm giddy with excitement." He turns to look at Ali and sits up straight. "It is truly an honor to meet you, and I am at your service. We greatly appreciate this opportunity to speak with you, and I feel lucky to be here in my position. I hear you're interested in making some sort of treaty?"

"This is our hope, yes. But I'm worried about my ship. There's no need to feel threatened. I gave you the ship's coordinates for credibility, not for you to engage it with your nuclear weapons."

His happy-go-lucky attitude stops. "How did you know that?"

"My people and I have unique ways of communication."

"You can understand why we need to protect our planet, right?" He fiddles with the pen in his hands.

"Absolutely, which is why we have always sought permission for supplies."

"Here's the deal. We won't take your presence as a threat as long as you let us keep you under surveillance. Our missiles are locked on you, but it's only for our protection."

"Yes, but—"

"It's our duty to protect our citizens. We have to take whatever precautions we feel are necessary."

"Have we initiated any sort of violence against you?" Ali asks, and I silently cheer her on.

Swanson leans on his elbows on the table. "We take your presence as a threat."

"Doesn't that seem a bit ignorant?" Andrew says.

"You know what they say. . . . Ignorance is bliss," Officer Swanson replies with a sarcastic grin.

I put my hand on Andrew's shoulder to try to calm him down. His face is beet red.

"I thought the whole point of making a treaty was to trust each other," Ali says, sounding disappointed. "Officer Swanson, are we wasting our time here?"

"They've been here for decades without initiating war. They're not going to start now that they finally have a way to communicate with humans," I add.

He taps his fingers on the table. "If we're going to work together to get you what you need, we need to have eyes on your ship at all times."

"I'll agree to this if you disengage your weapons."

He straightens and sets his pen down. "Fine. My team of scientists will have more questions for you. They may be from NASA, but they work for me. Don't forget it. They will speak with you regarding your space travels. I will let the group know the time has come."

Ali's face brightens, and she says, "Thank you!"

"And I understand that you'll need to extract minerals from Earth in order to depart?" he asks, taking notes.

"Yes, we use certain renewable minerals as an energy source for travel, as well as for replenishing our soils on our home planet."

"And you need us to do the mineral extraction for you?"

"I think that would be best, as our methods might draw too much attention."

Swanson purses his lips. "And then you'll be set and on your way."

A grin appears on her face. "Yes."

Clasping his hands on the table, Swanson gives her a cynical smile. "We'll be in touch." He gathers his seemingly useless files and says, "I think this is a great time for us to break for the night, but I need to know you will keep this under lock and key. Feel free to go home, call your family, let them know about a quote-unquote plane crash you witnessed, but do not tell anyone what we're all really doing here. We don't need any media attention." He stops by the door. "Have you told anyone else at this point?"

"Are you kidding?" Andrew says with his brows furrowed. "This is not something to bring up as regular banter between friends. We'd be shunned if we told someone."

Swanson laughs under his breath. "Great, we will get in touch soon about our next meeting. If you need anything, please call me directly." He hands each of us his flashy FBI business card. "Let's get you back home, Ms. Ali."

After he leaves, an officer holds the door open. I guess we're free to go. In my excitement, I let out a shriek. Did this really just happen? I stop and glance at Ali. She has her hand on her ear, then covers her mouth to giggle.

"Officer Swanson just vomited in the hallway."

"What?"

"I could sense he was hiding his nerves, and from what I just heard, his nerves got the best of him. He did seem to be acting strange to me."

I laugh quietly with her, and my lips crack from smiling so big. "Ali," I squeal. "We're making progress. I'm so happy we can go home." As I utter those words, my stomach sinks. I don't even have a home. I slam my hand on my forehead.

"Stella, both you and Ali are coming to my house. Bottom line. I've got two guest rooms and plenty of food. We need to stick together from this point on. My home is your home."

"Chester! Oh, I bet he has to pee. Let's get out of here."

"I guess you'll ride in a squad car with us, Ali."

"I'll send someone to retrieve the orb."

ANDREW

When we pull up to my house the police cars are gone, and all that remains is the yellow tape surrounding my yard. I can hear Chester barking from the living room window as we jump out of the squad car.

"Thanks," I yell, waving as it leaves.

Chester is ecstatic, running all over the place and sliding to a stop on the wood floor. "Gosh, I bet you're hungry, bud!" I fill up his food and water bowl and crash on the couch.

"I'm starving," Stella moans and collapses next to me.

"I need to meet with my family and share the good news," Ali says as she heads toward the back door.

"Wait. I thought your ship had to stay put while it's being watched by surveillance."

"I gave them the coordinates to another ship," she admits. "Please, contact me if you need to talk." She smiles and steps through the door.

Ali's words from the interrogation room keep echoing in my head. Stella nudges me with her elbow. "What is it?"

"Ali made sure Swanson trusted her, so it makes me question why she would lie about which ship's coordinates she gave them." Stella nibbles on her thumbnail.

"Maybe it's just as simple as she wanted to be able to go home at night."

"Maybe. I hope you're right." She nudges her face into the couch cushion. "This is so wild."

"That's an understatement."

My stomach growls. I could cook, but I'm exhausted. "Let's order some Thai."

"Mmm, sounds good," she says, barely lucid.

I reach for my phone, and it vibrates. I look down at Stella, who is fast asleep on my shoulder. "Hey, Claire," I whisper. "I was just going to call you." I can't tell her the agents had my phone during an interrogation. I saw her missed calls and made a mental note to call back but forgot.

"Andrew. Where have you been? I've been worried sick. You didn't show up for dinner last night, and you haven't been answering your phone. I thought you were dead! Your car was home, but where were you? I came by earlier today, and there was police tape everywhere."

"Gosh, I'm so sorry. I completely forgot about family dinner night. See, we witnessed a plane crash into the ocean, so we've been dealing with that."

"What? Are you okay? What happened? Wait . . . We? Who else is with you?"

"Well, I made a new friend. We've been hanging out," I say, trying to sound nonchalant.

"Andrew, you have a girlfriend? Already?"

"Nice try. We're not there yet."

"Yet? Oh my gosh. You have to bring her over for dinner."

"I will when the time is right. We still have a lot to deal with for the police, and plus, we're still getting to know each other. I don't want to scare her away with all our family sarcasm."

She moans dramatically. "Okay, I really need to know what exactly has happened," she yells. She's more impatient than I anticipated.

"Look, we just got home, and we need to get settled. I'll call you soon, I promise." I hang up before she has a chance to argue. I open my food delivery app and order from Green Roof Thai. I order a variety of things, hoping to get at least one thing Stella might like.

She stays curled up on me until Chester's barking startles her awake. I grab the food from the front door and meet her at the kitchen table. I spread all the plastic containers across the surface.

"Thank God. I could eat a horse." She opens a container and dives in with her chopsticks, then stuffs her mouth with lo mein in true Thai fashion. Mouth full, she moans.

"I wasn't sure what you like, so I got a bit of everything," I say, and take a bite.

She nods and glugs down a beer with impressive confidence.

"I'm so sorry." She holds her hand in the air, silencing me.

"I'm in heaven right now," she says. She sets her beer down, and her smile fades. Maybe heaven was a trigger.

I knew this might all come crashing down on her. Her husband, her home, her alien friend from her childhood. She's got a lot going on.

"Good food can have that effect," I say.

She spins the bottle on the table, eyebrows creased.

"Hey, they threw in some spring rolls," I say, staring just as intensely at her as she is at her beer.

"Yeah, I'm sorry. I have the urge to write in my journal. I think that would help me process some things."

"Of course. Absolutely. You should. Take as much time as you need. The guest room has towels if you want to shower. Let me know if you need anything else." I stand and search for a pen in my kitchen junk drawer. Out of the corner of my eye, I see her watching me with her head tilted.

She smiles and takes the goods, also the lo mein. I watch her walk down the hall, then glance at Chester, who is drooling all over the floor. I toss him a chunk of spring roll and sit back in my chair.

Inhaling deeply, I lean my head back into my hands and stare at the ceiling. I close my eyes and enjoy the quiet, the peace. Having Stella here feels good. I want to be wherever she is. What we experienced together is special, and I can't deny I have grown attached.

I stand and stretch and go to my beloved piano. If I play, will it bother her? I open the top and make sure the felt is dropped so it won't be too loud. I play a quick chord to test its intensity, and it sounds like a distant dream echoing through the night.

I dabble here and there with a few pieces I know by heart, but one song is stuck in my brain. I've never heard it on the piano, but I don't have a guitar lying around, so I try my best. After about an hour of trying and failing, I'm frustrated. I totally ruined the song. I should have just listened to the record.

I stand and turn to head to bed and see Stella in the doorway.

"Led Zeppelin?" she asks. "Sorry, I didn't want to interrupt."

"Oh, that disaster?" I motion toward the piano. "Yeah, that's embarrassing. I don't know why I tried to play that. I'm sorry you had to hear me butcher it."

She smiles and giggles. "I will say the original is truly beautiful. What's the name of it again?"

"It's called 'Thank you,'" I say, scratching my jaw.

"That's right. I always loved the last few seconds. It reminds me of a ray of sunshine."

I want to tell her *she* reminds me of a ray of sunshine.

"Me too." She twirls the end of her hair, leaning against the door frame, looking majestic. "Hey, I know it's a workday tomorrow, but I'd love to do something with you after you get off."

"Gosh, you're right. I guess we can't just sit around and wait for a call from NASA. We should go on living our lives in the meantime." She laughs.

"Exactly. Might as well have a little fun."

She smiles and looks down. "I should get back around four."

"Perfect."

She turns and starts back to her room but stops at the doorway. "Andrew?"

"Yeah?"

"Thanks for dinner. Good night."

I grin and wave from the piano. "Good night, Stella."

STELLA

I wake up before the sun, tangled in a mess of blankets and sheets. I hop in the shower and realize I have to leave extra early in order to catch the ferry. It's strange going back to work, but the FBI is still working on setting up a meeting for us with NASA, and I can't abandon my students.

Most of my work clothes were saved from the flood, but I'm going casual today. I've got enough on my mind. I pull on some jeans, sneakers, and a cardigan. I glance in the mirror and decide against going barefaced. A little mascara never hurt anyone.

Andrew must still be asleep because I don't see him. I don't worry about saying goodbye and head out. I drive onto the ferry, turn off the engine, and stay in my car for the commute. Some people get out of their cars to stretch, feed the birds, or lean over and watch the water. It's only a ten-minute ride, but I can see why those few moments of quiet are important. It's a nice start to the day.

As happy as I feel right now, I can't help but want to hide. I have a secret so big. Even if I shared it with people, they wouldn't believe me. I have the most readable face in the history of human life. I'm an open book. How am I going to pretend like everything is normal?

When the ferry stops and I drive off, I look back at the island in the distance with an eerie feeling it was all a dream, and I get the urge to drive by my old apartment. I check my watch. I have time.

I pull into the parking lot and look at the mess. The construction crew has torn out all the innards of the walls and floors and tossed it to the curb awaiting trash pick-up. They weren't kidding about keeping the mold at bay. I guess they didn't want to take any chances. My stomach sinks thinking of what I would have done without Andrew and Ali that day.

I turn the key and hardly recognize the space I used to call home. Just like a murdered carcass left for dead in the forest, slowly eaten away and decomposed, only the skeleton remains.

The kitchen cabinets are gone, the built-in shelves removed, and the ceiling and floors are bare wood framing. There is nothing left of me here. I'm happy it can be saved, and the space reused for a home again. I touch the frame around the door and wish it well, hoping it will bring the next family as much joy as it did for James and me.

As I approach the door to leave, I see where our wedding photo would be hanging if the walls were still intact. I'm overwhelmed with guilt as I realize how quickly James was pushed out of my life. It's apparent to me now how much the simple act of kissing our wedding photo as I left our home weighed on me, because I'm relieved now to leave without him there watching.

I say goodbye to our home for the last time and head to my car.

The rest of the drive to school is quiet and heavy. I wonder if I'll be able to pull myself together enough to teach at my normal capacity. I park in my designated spot and find my way into the classroom.

The bell rings, and kids flow in, looking exhausted, yawning even. It's a Monday, for sure.

"Good morning, class!" I exclaim, nearly sarcastic. I walk to the whiteboard and scramble for a meaningful quote to start our day. I settle for a word: Music.

"Today we're talking about music. How has it changed over the years? How do you choose music that moves you? Does it need a sick beat? Or how about heartfelt lyrics?"

"Or the evil rhythm set forth within that of heavy metal?" Joey asks, holding the metaphorical power of metal above his head.

"Hey man, whatever floats your boat." I chuckle. "So, write about music however you want today. Do you play music? When do you first remember hearing it? Is there a song you love because your mom or dad loves it? Twenty minutes. Go!"

I sit behind my desk and admire these tiny humans scribbling down their thoughts. They're really the same size as me, or larger, but they have so much growing to do on the inside. I'm proud that I have a minor part in that, even if it is just one year in high school.

In their minds, they're on the precipice of social catastrophe, facing the end of childhood and becoming self-aware, free-thinking adults who could make one wrong move to ruin it all. Asking them to be open and honest in class gives them a safe place to address their feelings.

Of course, there's always the funny guy who thinks it's pointless to dive into emotions with a random grouping of kids at a public school English class. They crack jokes because they already take life lightly. I'm extra hard on those kids because, deep down, I think their emotions run the highest. They are expert deflectors.

As the day goes on, I am pleasantly surprised with the students' written responses. The topic of music brings out their personalities and big debates. We get to know each other a little better.

The last bell rings, and I get butterflies thinking about what Andrew has planned for us. I eagerly pack up and head to his house.

I pull into the driveway as Andrew lets Chester out of the front door. The dog runs straight to the driver's side door and jumps on the window to greet me.

"Hey, buddy!" I say, gently opening the door. Andrew is leaning over the porch railing, wearing a long sleeve crewneck shirt. His arms show their strength as they support his weight on the wooden rail.

"Hi," he says, grinning.

I smile back. "Hi."

"Are you ready for our great adventure?"

I reach the porch, and he takes my bag. "What should I wear?"

"Anything you don't mind getting sweaty in," he says, leading the way into his house.

"Are we going on a hike?" I ask and sneak into my room.

"Sort of!" he calls from the kitchen.

I settle with keeping my jeans on and swapping my sweater for a t-shirt and meet him by the table.

He looks me up and down and nods. "First stop, the shed." He waves me forward to follow him.

The shed doors are open when we reach it, making me think he'd spent the day rummaging around it, but I'm surprised to see it's nicely organized, and filled with shiny gadgets I've never seen before.

"What is all this?"

"Rock climbing gear." He takes down a rope from the wall. "My family and I keep all our gear here for easy access. What size shoe do you normally wear?"

I scratch my head, trying to find the right words to let him down softly. There's no way I'm going rock climbing. "Nine," I hear myself say. He grabs a couple pairs of shoes from a cubby and stuffs them in a bag. He proceeds to grab many other things.

"What's that?" I ask fearfully.

"This is a harness."

"What's that?" I point to some contraption in his hand.

"The belay device."

"What?"

Andrew adds it to the bag and then puts his hands on his hips. "Stella, don't worry. This will be so much fun. I promise."

"I've never rock climbed before. I really don't think—"

"You'll do great." He grins and shakes my shoulders. "Let's go set up the rope."

I follow him to the shore, and he throws the rope over his shoulder, grabs some metal gadgets, then drops the bag.

"We'll come back this way after we set up the rope."

We walk slightly uphill toward the top of the cliff.

"This was my favorite thing to do as a kid . . . and as an adult, actually."

"Kids can do this?"

"Totally. My nieces and nephews have been doing it since they were two. They climb these routes like it's nothing now."

If a kid can do it, I certainly can. "And your sisters?"

"Yep, they climb too."

He crouches near the cliff edge where a series of metal loops, probably twenty, are set into the stone.

"These are the anchors." He tugs at them, and they hold. "We drilled them onto the face of the wall as well. Typically, you attach a quick draw to anchors and clip your rope into them as you climb, but since you're new to climbing, I'll set up a top rope anchor."

"Sure, I'll pretend to know what you mean."

He laughs. "These are carabiners, and they can hold up to a thousand pounds. You can trust them. We're always picky about our ropes, and you can trust them, too." He loops the rope a few times and ties strange-looking knots at its ends. He attaches two carabiners to the rope, then hooks the carabiners to the anchors. A couple more knots in the rope and two more carabiners at the bottom. He definitely knows what he's doing.

"Now, I'll just feed this rope through the carabiners, and we can tie in at the bottom."

He stands and guides me down the hill, touching the small of my back.

"I'll be honest. Out of all the things I'd imagine we'd do together this afternoon, rock climbing was not one of them."

"If you want, you can take me to one of your ballet classes to get back at me."

"Revenge! I love it. Great idea."

"I'm filled with good ideas," he says, making me laugh.

When we get to the shore, he shows me how to step into the harness and tightens it around my waist. He gets down on one knee and helps me put on special shoes, which remind me of pointe shoes.

"Comfy?"

"Miserable."

He chuckles. "They're supposed to be tight. It gives you better grip on the rock."

I'll believe it when I see it.

He ties one end of the rope to my harness and the other to some gadgets on his harness and pauses, holding my waist. "Do you trust me?"

When I look up, my stomach flutters. I nod.

"I've got you." There is sincerity in his eyes. He slowly lets go of my waist and takes a step back. "So, you'll want to start by finding a good grip with your hands and work your feet up."

I'm shaking as I approach the wall and look up the face for the first time. "That's way too high. I can't climb that."

He smiles. "You climb as high as you want, Stella. I can lower you whenever you tell me."

I feel around the wall for anything big enough for my hand.

"Grab that jug." He points to a tiny ledge above my head.

I reach up and find it to be grippy. With both hands on it, I find one for my feet and pull myself up. It's exhilarating. I quickly look for another hold for my hands and reach it with ease.

"Amazing, Stella! Keep working your way up. Use your arms like hinges. Keep them straight until you have to pull up. That's it. Perfect."

There is something rewarding about this. It's a puzzle, and I'm solving it as I climb.

"Are there creatures living inside these cracks?"

"Probably."

I smile but keep climbing. There's a long ledge out above my head to the left. I could reach it if . . . I look around, analyzing my options, switch feet, and step into a pocket. I'm leaning pretty far to the right, and my fear of falling kicks in. I double-check my knot to make sure it's still intact.

"You're a natural. Trust your feet. They're solid. You can reach it."

My arms tire, and I realize now why he wants me to keep them straight. I lean back farther, lengthening my arms, trusting the rope. I swing my body to the left as I pull up and reach the ledge. It wasn't as far away as I thought.

"Whew," I scream, completely thrilled.

"That was incredible. Fantastic," Andrew yells from below, and I look down at him.

My grip tightens, and I shriek.

"The rope has you. I've got you. You're not going to fall."

My legs are quivering, and my arms are aching, but I see another pocket. I fear what might be lurking in that hole but reach for it. Nothing bites me. I work my feet up more and feel solid. It's like choreography. When I get it right, my body locks into place.

"This is incredible."

"I knew you'd love it."

I'm out of breath, but the anchor is only a few more moves away. Loving the challenge this brings to my muscles and my mind, I stay strong. I'm flexible, so I reach my foot up to the same ledge my hand is on. One more move to the right and I can make it to the last hold before the anchor. I stretch my leg out far, dig my toe into a crack, and make the reach.

"Yes!" Andrew yells.

I pant, sucking in all the oxygen my lungs allow, and let myself sit back into the harness. The rope stays tight.

"I'm going to lower you now. Nice and slow."

My arms and legs throb, but I feel amazing. Empowered. When my feet touch the ground, I scream, jump onto him, and wrap my legs around his torso. He catches me with ease.

"You cannot tell me you've never rock climbed before. That was amazing." He sets me down, still holding on to my waist. My arms stay on his shoulders. My breathing is deep, and I'm smiling so big my face hurts.

"Andrew, that was incredible. It was like I was dancing on the wall. It sounds silly. But I loved it so much." He grips my waist tighter.

"I saw that. Your ballerina legs knew what they were doing up there. I can't believe your arms didn't burn out. You stayed up there the whole time. Such a champ."

"Thanks."

"You ready to catch me?"

"What?"

"My turn to climb!"

"What? No, I don't know how to work these things. What if I drop you?"

"It's easy, and you won't drop me." He walks over to the wall where a chain is hanging and attaches it to my harness. He takes some gadgets from his harness and puts them on mine.

"When the rope loosens, you pull out the slack here. When it's time to lower me, you use this hand to pull this handle and slowly let the rope through. Always keep one hand on the bottom to make sure the rope doesn't slip."

"Ahh, no. I'm not doing this."

He smirks, implying that I, in fact, am doing this.

"Let's practice." He climbs a few feet off the ground and hangs with one arm pointing to the belay device, telling me where to pull.

"See, now if I fall," he drops without warning, "it catches me. But keep your hand there. Yes. Okay, now lower me."

I keep my hand on the bottom rope and use my other hand to pull the lever.

Andrew screams. I scream. I look up, and he's laughing.

"I'm kidding!" He laughs some more. "I'm sorry."

My mouth drops open. "Andrew! Don't ever do that to me again."

He's still chuckling. "I won't. Okay, you're doing good. Slowly release the rope from your hand on the bottom, and you're done."

I follow his instructions.

"See?" He holds his hands out.

I roll my eyes.

"You ready?"

"I guess."

He climbs. His movements are so fluid. He knows exactly where to place his feet and grips the wall mostly with his fingers. He pauses at a jug, and I catch up with the slack.

"There're so many routes on this one section. You can decide how intense you want your session to be." He pauses and points to the sections. "This is a good crimp. There are tons of them. See?" He walks along the wall and shows me another.

"This is a good pinch, and you already found the pockets. There's a lot you can do here."

"That's exciting," I call out, focusing on my belaying. Before I know it, he's at the top, and I have to lower him. I'm nervous but follow each step carefully. His feet touch the ground, and I let out a sigh.

He hugs me and whispers in my ear, "You did it." My neck tingles, and he tucks the hair behind my ears, making me weak in the knees.

"Ready to go again?" he asks, face just inches from mine.

"Again?"

"Yeah. You did so great. Now, you can try a different route."

My heart sinks. I don't want to disappoint him. "But my muscles."

"Okay, let's keep the ropes up, go inside, and eat. And then we'll see how your muscles feel."

"Yes." I clap and jump.

"How does leftover Thai sound?" He tucks my arm into his as we walk.

"It's better the next day, obviously."

"I haven't even gotten a chance to ask you about your day."

"Oh, it was great. I was pleasantly surprised at how normal I felt, considering our eventful weekend." He opens the door for me. "Have you heard from NASA?"

"Not yet."

"Waiting is so hard."

He takes the leftovers and pops them in the microwave. "No kidding. So, what got you into teaching?"

"Honestly, I took an American Literature class in college. It was the first time I felt seen, if that makes sense."

"You connected to the class?"

"I enjoyed my classwork. For once, I had interesting assignments. I will never forget my college English professor. She really opened my eyes to the beauty of bleeding onto paper, spilling your guts. The way she dissected each piece of literature and conveyed the message behind the words made it feel like the authors were in the room discussing their work. I longed to know some of the authors. Dead celebrities who had so many incredible things to say, and who live endlessly through those who read their books."

He's smiling at me. "Books are an underrated art form these days."

"That's so true. In my college years, I yearned for a time when people felt things so deeply and honestly, like those authors from class. People seem so shallow these days. The intricacies within human emotion are what make being human so unique and worthwhile."

"That's beautiful." He takes the leftovers out of the microwave and sets them out. "You really are something special."

"Don't embarrass me." I wave him off. "What about you? What did you do for your job?"

Andrew sighs deeply between bites. "Nothing special at all. I worked in a laboratory in the summers during college, and I wish I had pursued that instead of corporate America."

"Why didn't you?"

"My first job right out of college offered me too much money to refuse. It was a great opportunity, and it sucked me in, always offering large bonuses and raises. Before I knew it, I was too far in it to seek a different career."

"So, you just quit?"

"Pretty much. I was at a party, and a bong got passed to me. The pot was laced with LSD, and I guess I had a spiritual awakening of sorts. That's when I met Ali. She looked like a shimmering goddess in the night sky and totally blew my mind with information. She told me she needed help, and it was all I needed to hear to motivate me to leave the city."

"That is so amazing. Good for you."

"It's weird, I know."

"It's not weird. It's funny you mentioned LSD. I have a prescription for micro-dose psilocybin to treat my anxiety."

"What? You can get a prescription for that?"

"Apparently. It's nice to have them when I need it. For me, they chill me out and force me to focus on things that are real. It grounds me, if that makes sense."

"Mother Earth. Amazing."

"All natural. Nothing better."

We have both had our fill with the leftovers. Andrew leans over the kitchen counter, smiling like he knows I know what he's about to say.

"Do you—"

"Want to go climbing?"

"Yes."

"Yes," I agree.

"Yes!" Andrew cheers, jerking his fists in the air.

ANDREW

We climb until the sun sets. Our muscles ache. We smell terrible, but it is so much fun. We pack up and walk back to the house. I'm high on endorphins, and every time I sneak a glance at her, I catch her doing the same.

Stella runs ahead and gets in the shower. I'm finding it hard to hide my feelings for her. In a normal scenario, dating would be a drawn-out process. But our situation is clearly different. I need to tell her how I feel.

I take a quick shower and set out some fruit and yogurt on the coffee table for a snack. She comes out in her pajamas and sits with me.

"You need to refuel after climbing so hard. That was awesome," I say and bite into a strawberry.

"It was the most fun I've ever had. I'm not exaggerating."

"I knew you'd love it."

She crosses her legs on the couch. I want to say something, but I'm not sure where to begin.

"Can I show you something?" she asks.

"Of course."

I notice now that she's holding her journal. She flips it open and hands it to me.

"I process my thoughts better when I write things down. I had a lot on my mind, and I wasn't sure how to share my feelings. I don't want you to read my *entire* journal, but I bookmarked the entry I wrote last night." She pushes the notebook to my chest. I'm shocked. I doubt this is a good idea.

"Are you sure?"

"Yes. I don't want to butcher it by trying to summarize."

Dear James. I immediately look up at her, but she urges me to continue.

Dear James,

I always pictured us growing old together, raising a family, and playing with our grandchildren. I have refused to believe that you're actually gone, and part of me still can't believe it. Everything was so perfect. We were perfect. Why can life be so cruel? Although we spent nearly a decade together, I feel like we were only just getting started. We had so much to look forward to. Wherever you are, I hope you can feel my immense love for you, and how you will always have my heart.

When we were together you had my whole heart, which is why I felt so completely dead when you died. I had to start over, try to live without you. It was miserable. It was like I had to grow a new heart for survival purposes, just large enough to feed my body the oxygen it required to live another day. So, now that I've had time to recover and survive, I've grown to appreciate my new heart. I feel strong, determined, and inspired. I'm trying to make you proud. I know you wouldn't want me to crumble.

It would be an understatement for me to say that a lot has happened since you left. My world has been turned upside down. I blamed the doctors for a long time, and then I blamed myself for not urging you to see a doctor sooner, and then I blamed you for trying to tough it out. I'm done blaming people. Blame is for the weak.

Not long after you left me, our home was destroyed, which forced me to be strong again. Herold died. I wonder if you two are off playing Texas hold 'em in a bar somewhere in another dimension. The thought brings me comfort.

A part of my past has returned to me; a part I never shared with you, actually. Ali. She's an old childhood friend who stuck around long enough to find me again, and she needs my help. I think you may have met her somehow, somewhere. She's incredibly brave and inspiring, and I'm going to do everything I can to help her. Her company has been a welcome distraction from all that I have lost, and she has introduced me to someone else.

I'm writing to you in my temporary home, Andrew's house, where I have found solace during this chaos. Andrew is someone you would totally get along with. He's incredibly kind, intelligent, and honest. If I'm honest with myself, I can admit that I'm drawn to Andrew in more ways than one. I wasn't prepared to have feelings for someone so soon, but I don't want to feel guilty for it. It feels right, I know it.

James, you still have my heart. You took it from me, and I want you to keep it. But this new heart I have is aching to grow. I didn't feel right about starting a new relationship without writing to you, symbolically letting you go. My soul will always yearn for the day we reconnect somehow, and I will always love you, James. Until then, I hope you can feel relief knowing that I am not crumbling; not anymore. I'm endlessly grateful for the time we had together. Rest in Peace, James, and I will see you down the road.

Love,
Stella

My heart is racing, and I look up at Stella, who seems eager for me to say something. How do I put into words the aching I have? She has loved someone else. I'm grateful she feels confident enough about her feelings for me that she seeks to confess to her late husband. How can I put into words the intensity of what I feel for her without sounding like I'm merely agreeing with her, when I drew the same conclusion on my own?

"Stella, I—"

"Shh. Andrew, please don't say anything. I know it's a lot to take in. This is something really personal that I wanted to share with you."

I inch closer, placing my hand on her arm and then around to the back of her head. I tuck her hair behind her ears, look into her eyes, and whisper, "You're really something special."

I can't wait any longer. I have to kiss her. She puts her hands around my neck and plays with my hair. She pushes my face to hers, and my entire body melts.

———∿∿∿∿∿∿∿———

I roll out of bed when I hear Chester barking and whining at the back door. It isn't a territorial bark, so I know it must be Stella or Ali. Although, Stella will be at work. I pull on some pajama pants and stumble to let Ali in.

"Good morning." I yawn.

"Andrew, we must speak."

"Right, I'm glad you're here. Let me make some coffee. Would you like some?"

"No, thank you. Did you get a call from anyone yet?"

Mid-pour, my phone rings, and I pause to look up at Ali. She motions for me to quickly pick it up, and I oblige.

"This is Andrew. . . . Yes, today should be fine. We could do four p.m. Excellent, thank you." I hang up and finish pouring my coffee.

"They finally set up a meeting with NASA for us. And they want to meet as soon as possible." This is too good to be true, which is never a good sign.

Ali shifts her weight. "I have thought long about how I might begin to explain space travel to NASA, and I think that no matter how much I explain, the only way humans can comprehend everything is to evolve another five hundred years, at least. Earth's technology is nowhere near the level needed for Cosmic Slip. Humans have been stuck using the same propulsion methods for a century. I hope they don't expect too much from me." She sounds frantic and looks very worried and anxious.

"I can understand how this could be intimidating to you," I say, "but you might be surprised how capable these scientists are at grasping new ideas. I say, let them have it. Give it to them straight. Be honest and provide guidance. It's not your responsibility to teach them every step of the way, so don't stress out about the details."

"Yeah, I think they are more concerned with making sure we leave Earth. I'm excited, but nervous to hear the questions they have for me . . ."

"Speaking of questions, I have a few. Which minerals do you need exactly?"

"We need calcium, silicates, and oxides in order to create new crystals to power the ships as well as grow more food. We can manipulate atomic structure to create various crystals for different levels of energy within the ship. The minerals we need for our planet come from ocean-cooled lava."

"Okay." Maybe I'll wait until the meeting with NASA to unload all my queries about that. "And how exactly should we ask to obtain these minerals?"

"We have underwater capabilities to extract the lava rock, which could go unnoticed, but the surface minerals will require actual digging."

"And your planet doesn't have lava?"

"Oh, it certainly does. But if we wait for the volcanoes to naturally nourish the soils, it would be a long time before we could grow quality food. There's no way to predict that, and we simply want to expedite the process."

"We'll have to see how the meeting goes this afternoon. I'll have to get in touch with Stella." I grab my phone and shoot her a text. "NASA meeting today at 4! We'll meet you at your school after dismissal!"

"Andrew," she says. "Do you think this will all pan out?"

"Ali . . ." I sigh.

"Because, I mean . . ." She pushes her hair out of her face. "What if this has all been a waste of time, and I've ruined your life, and Stella's life, and humans will try to kill us, and we're all—"

"Ali." I grab her shoulders and look her in the eyes. "You're letting your human DNA overpower your alien DNA. You're having doubts, which is normal. Trust me, I've had them too. But we've done everything right. We've followed the rules. We've avoided violence. We've asked for permission. And just because things are going smoothly does not mean things can't work out how we hope. Okay?" I say, and realize I needed to hear this myself.

"You're right."

"You've been working to get to this point for so long. As much as you need proof of the good in humanity, trust me, I need it too." I rub her arms, hoping to shake off her worries.

"Thank you, Andrew," she says, patting my hand.

"You're welcome. Now, let's eat breakfast and get ready to meet Stella in the city. We've got a date with some rocket scientists."

"Breakfast is typically served in the morning, Andrew." She points to her wrist as if it wore a watch.

"I see your point, although I must have slept through breakfast, and it's my favorite meal of the day."

She laughs at me. "Okay, I'll eat breakfast for lunch as long as you make your famous breakfast sandwich with the fried egg."

"Have you been reading my mind?" I grin and reach for the English muffins on top of the fridge.

STELLA

After school, Andrew and Ali are waiting by my car, and my anxious excitement sinks in. I glance around, trying not to look suspicious, which, I'm sure, makes me look wildly suspicious. "Is it finally happening?" I whisper.

"Yes," Andrew replies and greets me, his arms wide open. We hug, and he kisses my cheek.

"You look very refreshed, Stella." Ali smiles in her quiet manner.

"That's surprising. My body has never been this sore in my life." I glance up at Andrew. "Having a good day at work helps, too. How are you guys?"

He leans over and elbows Ali. "She's a little nervous, but I reminded her that we're all in this together, and it'll work out. It has to."

"Oh, Ali, I'm nervous too, but with excitement. This is good. Things are moving along. Where are we meeting them?"

"An office downtown. Let's go."

When we arrive at the building, I can sense Ali's angst. It makes me wonder what else they talked about while I was working.

"We mostly talked about my insecurities in conveying necessary information with the scientists."

I smirk and wink at her. She grabs my hand and links arms with me as we walk inside.

Upon entering, I see a conference room where Officer Swanson is standing, arms crossed. He's speaking with a few seated men. He reaches for his earpiece and looks in our direction, then nods to the men and opens the glass door.

"Good afternoon. Thank you for coming. Ali, hello." He seems just as nervous as he was the other day. "You'll be pleased to know we have flown in our brightest team from NASA, including a very special guest, Neil Husk."

"Neil Husk?" I shriek. "Neil Husk is here?"

Officer Swanson lifts his hands up and settles me. He looks over his shoulder at the closed conference room door. "Yes, but strictly for counsel. He's been leading NASA in the latest space travel endeavors."

"Who is Neil Husk?" Ali asks.

"He's the billionaire space-guru genius who built his own line of ships to send celebrities on space adventures. He supposedly has an IQ of one-sixty and goes to every red-carpet event with his supermodel girlfriends." I sound more like a high school valley girl than I intend.

Andrew looks unfazed by the fact that we're in the same building as the richest person in the world. "So, everyone in there knows about Ali?"

"Yes, but no one else knows, and we plan to keep it that way. They have been sworn to secrecy and understand the importance of the matter. That it's an issue of national security."

We all nod at him, and he leads us into the room. I shake my arms. My nervous energy is clinging to me like house flies. I refuse to make a fool of myself in front of Neil. Play it cool, keep it together, Stella.

As soon as we walk in, the NASA crew stand, Neil being the last to do so. I nervously stay quiet. Ali snatches my hand and squeezes it hard. Her eyes bulge out of her head, and her cheeks lose their color.

"Don't freak out, Ali. He's just a celebrity." I try to loosen her grip on my hand.

"No, he isn't just *a celebrity."* She doesn't take her eyes off of him.

Officer Swanson is still introducing us to the group, and I can tell he's getting to my name. *"What do you mean?"* I lean out to shake Neil's hand.

"She means I have a particular secret I'd like to keep."

I trip over the chair in front of me and fall to the floor.

"Hi, I'm Neil Husk. It's nice to meet you, Stella." *"I trust you and Ali will keep my secret?"* He leans down to help me off the ground, as does Andrew.

"I'm sorry, Mr. Husk, Stella doesn't meet many celebrities." He laughs.

"Hi, yes, I can keep—I mean, yes, I—nice to meet you, too." I shake his hand firmly.

Officer Swanson introduces Ali to Neil. They exchange a hand-shake, and although it is silent in the room, my head may explode.

"I thought you were dead!"

"Far from it," he replies bluntly.

"Why did you leave us?"

"I wanted to."

"Don't you care about us?"

"Yes."

"Then what are you doing?"

"Many things."

"Come home," she pleads.

"Not a chance."

Their hands separate, and Ali retreats, trembling, probably with anger. I was afraid to get involved in that conversation.

Officer Swanson continues with the introductions. "Scooter Williams is the head of Exploration. Sam Devine leads the research programs for space matter, and Christopher Mandle is Director of Technologies."

"Ms. Ali, it's a dream come true to have you here," Scooter says. "We heard you were hoping to excavate minerals you need for space travel?"

Ali motions her hand toward the table, asking for permission to sit. Everyone stands and apologizes, then takes their seats.

"Yes," she replies, avoiding eye contact with Neil. "It would be our greatest accomplishment if we could collaborate amicably with humans to get our ships ready for traveling back home."

"You know," Neil says, "we have been researching different methods of propulsion in our labs."

"Is that so?" Her tone implies she isn't interested in anything he has to say.

"I have been working with this NASA team experimenting with revolutionary space travel ideas, and I'm curious if they coincide with your technologies."

"What are you doing?"

"Neil has brought up the most incredible ideas for space travel." Christopher leans his elbows on the table. "And he's been with us through the entire project. We feel we have an incredible advantage in the field having him on our team."

Neil and Ali exchange glares.

"*Are you trying to come off as some hero?*" she asks.

Neil leans back in his chair, crosses his legs, and rubs his chin.

"Let me ask you, Ali, by any chance, do you use antigravity propulsion?"

Ali blinks a few times. "Yes, but—"

The NASA team cheers, and Scooter gets out of his seat and high-fives Neil. A huge smile breaks out on Andrew's face. He is as interested in all of the science just as much as NASA.

When Ali stands, the room calms. "As much as I'd love to share the exact science of our space travels, I'm afraid it would do more harm than good. The goal here is to get me and my people home, away from Earth, without causing fear and panic among your people. We can relay back our discoveries on our return travels."

"It just so happens that Neil has encouraged us to collect minerals needed for his studies," Scooter says. "We've accumulated a ton. I'm hoping we have what you need already. But, Ms. Ali, we want to be involved with someone who could provide some answers. Is there anyone else who might be willing to speak with us?"

She looks down at the table. "Unfortunately, there were only a few of us who went through the DNA alterations so many years ago, and I am the last survivor. You would not be able to successfully communicate with my people in their natural form. But . . ." She looks up at Neil. "I think your colleague is probably giving you some great ideas."

Sam sets his glasses on the table and clears his throat. "Is there any chance we could see one of your ships?" His hope and anticipation are clear through his squinted eyes.

Ali lets out a breath and tilts her head. She seems uncomfortable. "Right now, we don't have any to spare. But I would be willing to bring one team member down to meet my family while we deliver the materials. You could ask your questions then, with me there for translation."

Neil's eyes get wide. "Yeah, maybe Sam would be the best guy for that."

"Oh, I don't know about that."

"Why not? You'd ask all the right questions," Andrew says.

"Something tells me Neil would have some good questions, too," I add. "I'm sure they have many questions as well."

"Many." Ali's voice is so low, she might be talking to herself.

"The way I see it, Neil is the one with all the revolutionary ideas. He might be the best bet for conveying important details," Christopher says. He looks down at his papers and sneaks a peak at Ali's face but seems embarrassed and thumbs through his pages.

"Okay, I'll do it," Neil says. "I'll get all the information we need, and then you and your people can be on your way."

"You should know . . ." Ali readjusts herself in the chair. "Andrew and Stella have been true heroes in helping us. It's because of their open-mindedness, their kindness, and their persistence that we have come this far. I have offered to have them return to our planet with us, if they so choose."

The NASA crew's jaws drop, and Sam stops chewing on the end of his glasses. "What an incredible opportunity. You could be our intel on the new planet."

My cheeks get hot, but I stay quiet.

Andrew can't contain his excitement. "Yes. Ali mentioned, and it's obvious to any human, Earth is nearing the end of its life cycle. As painful as it is for anyone to admit, it will become a dead planet soon." He throws his hands out in front of him. "Timing is imperative to our survival, and we can't miss this opportunity. Ali's planet could potentially sustain human life. It would be an incredible journey, and an incredible triumph to blend our two species on one planet."

"Another option," I say, "is that Ali helps us extend the life of Earth by providing her wisdom on clean, renewable energy sources."

Ali glances at me. "Or both. But having humans on our planet would require you to live by our standards, not humanity's. We would have to educate you on our lifestyle and housing situations before you decided to move humans across the galaxy."

"Wait. How many years are you thinking? You think Earth will die within a few hundred years?" Christopher asks.

"If you continue living this way, yes. If you make some changes, Earth's lifespan could be prolonged another ten generations."

"And you'd be willing to share your planet with us?" Scooter leans over the table.

"Humans will have saved our species. The least we can do is return the favor. Plus, we still have the entire other half of our galaxy to explore on our return trip home, and we will certainly be looking for habitable planets."

Scooter, Sam, and Christopher seem like they are trying to stay calm.

"How do you propose we communicate a hundred light years apart?" Scooter says.

Swanson reaches for his earpiece and leaves the room. I'm relieved he's gone. He's not really interested in what's going on.

"There will be some trial and error," Ali says. "But just like I said, you must keep an open mind on things. I can communicate with Stella telepathically, but I'm not sure how far that will go."

Everyone's jaw drops again. Christopher points to me as if to double-check that what he heard is true. Ali and I nod, but Neil lifts his shoulder, dismissing it.

"How exactly do you travel so far, so fast?" Sam asks.

"Well . . ."

"It's called Cosmic Slip," Andrew says.

Christopher's eyes narrow. "Cosmic Slip?"

"Yeah, Cosmic Slip?" Neil says with a hint of attitude.

"It's the term I coined when I learned about her travels. When Ali first communicated with me, she briefly explained how high-speed space travel is possible, and the only way it made sense to me was to think of it as slipping through time and space."

"We have evolved much more than humans in certain ways. We connect with our ships and the universe on a deep, personal level that is difficult to explain."

"They use dark energy like a slipstream."

"Unbelievable," Sam whispers.

A noticeable grin appears on Scooter's face. "Cosmic Slip. I like it."

Andrew reciprocates with an equally large smile. Neil lets out a "Pff" and rolls his eyes.

"Wait." Sam taps the table. "Can you read anyone's mind?"

"Telepathy is our standard form of communication. You must be open to the ways of the universe and its emotions. Stella and I have a special bond, and our souls are spiritually connected. I cannot say if anyone else holds the same capacity as she, but I have yet to meet any other human who does."

"You said the universe is made up of emotions?" Scooter asks.

Ali's eyes grow wide. "Of course it is." Her voice gets louder, and she pulls her hair to one side.

It must be exhausting trying to explain things that are so obvious to her species.

"What I mean is, although it may seem silly to you, yes, the universe is exploding with emotion everywhere you look."

A quiet comes over us all. We glance around at each other.

We needed this reminder. This goes much further than who can build the best rocket to the moon or what technologies we're missing.

We humans have a long way to go to have spiritual connections to the universe and its insurmountable abilities.

"I think you're overestimating the mental capacity of the humans. Even if you build an exact replica of one of our ships, they wouldn't hold the level of consciousness needed for space travel," Ali says while looking at Neil.

He stares at the floor, then stands abruptly and peers through the glass.

"Do not pretend to have a clue as to what I am doing here. And how dare you force me to deliver supplies with you. Don't you know that will do more harm than good? Sometimes I question your own mental capacity."

"Your family deserves an explanation, and you know it," Ali says, getting teary.

"It looks like we can learn a lot from you and your people," says Scooter. "All the more reason we should figure out how to stay connected to you on your journey home."

"Speaking of which, how soon can we gather the minerals?" Ali asks.

Neil turns and faces her. "We'll have them ready by tomorrow. The sooner you can get home, the better."

"So soon?" Scooter asks. "But we still have so many questions."

"Write your questions down, and I will get answers when I deliver the materials. They've waited long enough."

ANDREW

Our drive home is heavy with silence. Tomorrow, everything is over. Ali will have what she needs for her people and planet. She'll go home. Our mission will be complete. If I'm honest, I don't want this to end. Traveling with Ali would be a dream come true.

It's obvious Ali wants us to join her family and go to her planet. She wants us to stay together. Will I be able to convince Stella to travel across the galaxy with me? Will humans be capable of living on a different planet? Can we survive on their diet?

When we get home from what seems like the longest car ride of my life, we all collapse on the couch.

"So, what food do you eat?"

Ali sits up straight and runs her hands through her hair. "We eat plants and animals. We farm and hunt. Our diet is very simi-lar to that of humans. We have studied the chemical makeup of our marine life compared to yours, as well as what toxins differ between our two species. We have considered the risk for foodborne illnesses and treating any ailments you might develop. While we might have a simpler approach to living, we are a thousand years ahead of you in technologies, and that includes the medical field. We would be able to care for you."

I looked over at Stella enthusiastically. She keeps looking at her phone and staring out of the window.

"You think we could be there in a year of space travel?"

"Actually, we have been discussing this, and we feel it might be better to cut down on that time. While we do have much exploring to do, half of us could go straight home, while the other continues to map out the galaxy."

I rub my hands through my hair and consider the weight of the moment. What can I say to Stella to convince her of the magnitude of this opportunity?

"If Stella and I go, how will we communicate with Earth? I thought Stella was the key feature in your plan."

"That's a good point. We could work on your satellite technologies. Once we map out the galaxy, slipping through the cosmos will take one-tenth of the time."

Stella looks at me, and not with a pleasant expression.

"Are you serious?" she asks. She checks her phone again, stands, and gets her purse. I jump up and grab her hands.

"Stella, we should talk about our options. This is scary, I know, but it could be our adventure. You know how much I care about you, right?"

She squeezes my hands and then pulls away.

"I need some space," she says and leaves. I turn to Ali. She looks tired and discouraged.

"What was going on in her head just then? Could you tell if she was okay?"

"Honestly, I was so caught up in my own thoughts with plans for tomorrow, I wasn't paying attention," Ali says. "I'm sure she'll be okay. She just needs to think things through."

I walk back to the couch. "You're probably right. Gosh, my sisters would kill me if I left. And Stella would really miss her mom."

"We can come back to visit, and when you consider the impact you will have on saving future generations, it seems like a small price to pay."

"The answer is simple for me. I want to go. But Stella needs me. I need her. You have gifted my life with so much meaning, and I feel like it's too soon to say goodbye. I owe you at least—"

"Andrew, you do not owe me anything." She sits back and puts her face in her hands. "You and Stella have been so brave for my family. I owe you everything. I have selfishly wanted you to join us because, in my mind, it's a win-win. But I'm realizing how difficult it would be to leave your home and your family and start over with strangers in a new place. It would be a sacrifice for you at first, but I truly believe you would be happy with us. If you and Stella decide to stay home, do not worry about saying goodbye to me. We will see each other again. I promise."

Chester puts his paw on my knee. He's done it a million times, asking for a belly scratch, but his timing seems too coincidental.

I scratch his chin and pull him onto my lap. I lean my head back and catch a glimpse of the stars through the window. My lifelong dreams have been to reach the stars, find a greater purpose. As much as the science guy in me wants to explore deep space and be the hero who saves humanity, my heart belongs to a beautiful star already. I belong wherever she is, and she wants to stay.

"I have a proposition."

"Let's hear it."

"I agree with you, with NASA, that it would be extremely beneficial to have humans join your trip home."

"Okay . . ."

"And you trust me, right?"

"Of course."

"Do you remember me telling you about my science buddies?"

"Yes."

"Zain would be the perfect guy to go with you. Come with me now. We have to talk to him."

"Don't you think it's a little late? We're leaving tomorrow."

I grab my phone and text Stella, "Don't worry, everything will be okay. Ali and I are running an errand. We'll see you back at home!" I snatch Ali's hand and lead her straight to the car.

On the drive into the city, I tell Ali all about Zain. "He's kind, generous, inquisitive, and an incredible scientist. He and I used to challenge each other with barbaric math problems and calculate ridiculous hypotheticals of quantum mechanics just for fun. As brilliant as he is, he's very humble and inclusive with his work. He's genuinely a good guy. He's devoted his life to his lab and supporting fellow scientists and mathematicians. He isn't married and might just be up for this. The problem is getting him to believe me."

"If he's your friend, he should trust you."

"I hope it's that simple." I will need to be very careful with my words. If I come off too eager, I could push him away.

When we arrive at his apartment, he is shocked to see me and quickly invites us in. Ali stays behind me.

"Zain, meet my friend Ali." I coax her forward. "You're going to love her."

"Pleased to meet you, Ali," he says and shakes her hand.

She looks around the place. "I like your apartment."

"Thank you. I don't spend a lot of time here, but it serves its purpose." He waves us in, and we follow him through a small entryway, past a small dining room table that could be the same one he had in college. The living room features a whiteboard on the wall instead of typical décor.

We sit on the couch, and Zain sits in a recliner and rests one ankle on his knee.

"What brings you to my place tonight?"

"You're not going to believe why I'm here, but you have to try." I pause, gathering myself. "Remember when I visited the lab? We both discussed dark energy in relation to space travel?"

He nods, sneaking a glance at Ali.

"And I'm not sure if I told you how that idea was brought to my attention, but it came from Ali, and it's actually how she got to be here."

Zain snaps out of his trance and looks at me. "Here? As in my apartment?"

"Here, as in Earth," Ali replies.

The color leaves Zain's face, and he somehow chokes on his own saliva. I rush to the kitchen and get him a glass of water. As much as we joke around together, he knows I'm being serious right now.

"I'm just going to tell it to you straight because I know you can handle it." I tell him calmly and slowly about everything I know—Ali, Stella, and what has happened, right up to our meeting with NASA. "The FBI has known they exist, and basically ignored their existence."

"I knew it," Zain exclaims, but he's looking off into the distance. I appreciate his enthusiasm. "That's not all. Ali invited Stella and me to join her on their trip home to see about potentially making their planet the next one for humans whenever Earth is no longer livable."

"Oh my God," says Zain.

"But . . ." I move my hands outward. "I thought you'd be a better candidate . . ."

"Oh my God." His eyes are still wide, and he sets his glass down on the coffee table between us. He slaps himself across the face.

Ali looks at me with one eyebrow raised, and I gesture to give him a moment to process this. I stand and go to the whiteboard. I draw a general sketch of our galaxy and mark where Earth is compared to Ali's planet. He slowly walks up with his hands on his head.

"No way . . ."

"You want your mind totally blown?"

Zain doesn't move but holds his breath.

"Less than a year of space travel. Then, one-tenth of that on the way back to Earth."

"Whhhaaaatttttt?" he says and paces around the room.

"Basically, the world needs you to be a secret agent on a mission to another planet where you can gather all the information you want and find out if humans could live there."

"Why isn't NASA using one of their astronauts? Why me?"

"We aren't in contact with the entirety of NASA. This is a small group formed through the FBI to work on classified missions. Plus, Ali invited me and Stella, not just anyone. I convinced her to let me ask you, and she trusts me."

Zain turns to Ali and, very hesitantly, asks to see her hand. She agrees, and he holds it and turns it over, rubs his fingers on her palm, and then looks at her in amazement.

"I always pictured myself as one of those people standing on top of a skyscraper holding a sign that said 'Take Me with You' if aliens ever came to Earth. I don't care if this is a dream, or if I'm having a brain aneurysm, which is probably the case. There's no chance I'm missing this."

Ali smiles, cheeks blushing. I jump up, and Zain and I fake punch each other.

He suddenly stills and starts a checklist of everything he wants to bring from his lab. He's in full geek mode, talking to himself, pacing, thinking out loud.

"Your cat seems to really like me," says Ali. The cat is sitting and purring on her shoulder.

"That's very surprising. My cat is usually very shy. Oh! My cat!"

"Chester has always wanted a playmate. I'll take her." I lay my hand on his shoulder. "There's one more thing . . . and you might want to sit down for this." I guide him to the chair. "You're leaving tomorrow."

"Cool, cool. This is fine." His face goes blank. "Tomorrow? That's impossible!"

"Well, NASA is delivering our minerals tomorrow, and we will leave shortly after. So, it depends on when we get what we need."

"NASA is okay with me going? I'll be in contact with them?"

"Yes," I say, keeping things simple. I know they will be relieved to have someone else to send with Ali. I may go to jail for telling Zain top secret information, but I never signed the papers. Hopefully, NASA will back me up.

"I won't sleep tonight in order to gather everything I will need. What kind of plug should I bring for my computers? US? European?"

Ali giggles. They most definitely do not have plugs inside their spaceship.

"And who will I put in charge of the lab while I'm gone? Emily. It has to be Emily. And my apartment—"

I hold up my hands. "You're freaking out a little, but I don't blame you. How about I take care of your apartment while you're gone. No problem."

With her attention never leaving the cat pawing at her face, Ali says, "Don't worry, Zain. Your plugs will not be useful on the ship, but we will still be able to accommodate your technology."

"How? Don't answer that. If I start asking questions now, then I'll never be able to pack in time." He rubs his hands on his pant legs a few times, staring at the floor. There's a calmness about him now, as if he's really letting this sink in. He sits down in his chair and slowly turns to face me. "If I didn't trust you so much, Andrew, I'd be kicking you out. But this is actually happening . . . isn't it . . . you wouldn't lie about something like this."

I kneel on one knee next to his chair. "She introduced me to her family, man. I saw their faces. These are real people who need our help. I would go with you if I could, but Stella isn't ready for it. For Stella, it's *enough* to save them and send them home, but it's not enough for me. I need to know more, you know? I know you know. But the choice is yours. You're the only person I trust enough to send with them. If you don't want to go, I completely understand. If you do want to go, I understand, and I'll back you up no matter what. I trust Ali with my life. You can trust her, too."

He wipes his teary eyes on his sleeve and sighs deeply. "Well, I'm going to ignore all my fears. I won't let them keep me from seeing the universe. Ali, if you'll have me, I'd love to join you in your travels."

She smiles and hugs the cat. "It will be exciting and challenging. My only request is that you remain honest with me. You have to communicate your fears and tell me anything you will need. We'll have to trust each other. Can you do that?"

Zain nods. "Of course, absolutely."

"Good!" I say, clapping my hands. I grab his shoulder and shake it. "You'll do great, man. We need to go find Stella and fill her in. We'll come back to get you in the morning."

"Yes, get out of here. I have too much to do. You're in my way! Sheesh!" he says. We all smile, and Ali peels herself away from the cat.

"See you soon, Zain."

He may have blushed, but I can't say for sure.

As we step out into the hall, Ali grabs my hand and squeezes it tight. Her eyes flicker and she gasps.

"Stella! Stella is in trouble. Let's go!"

STELLA

I have a bad taste in my mouth. I hate leaving Andrew this way, but I said I needed some space. Neil is obviously nothing like Ali, but he's an alien. Why would he betray his own kind? How could his family give up looking for him? Is this a secret I need to keep from Andrew?

My phone vibrates in my purse. It's another text from an unknown number. I was getting texts earlier but ignored them. I was too distracted.

"It's Neil," it reads, and my heart skips a beat. "If we're going to trust each other with my little secret, I need to share my side of the story. Can you find a way to meet with me alone?"

"I trust Ali, not you. But I will keep your secret for now," I type and hit send.

"Stella, there's more to Ali that you need to know. Meet me for coffee at Main Street Café in an hour. It's important. Please."

I stuff my phone back in my purse and get back in my car to think. This is getting more complicated by the minute. My stomach sinks. The look on Andrew's face when Ali told NASA she invited us to go with her was like a little boy on Santa's lap.

I don't want to break his heart or keep him from his dreams, but I'm staying home. I'm not ready to leave. If he really wants to go, I won't stop him. Saying goodbye tomorrow will be the hardest thing I'll ever do. Either I beg him to stay with me and he resents me for it, or I let him go and regret it for the rest of my life.

When I begin driving, I'm going nowhere in particular. I'm at a loss for words, torn. I'm curious about what Neil has to say, but I know it would be wrong to meet with him in secret, right? I don't want to believe any of these aliens are evil.

Why did Neil choose to rebel against his family? What if there are more rebels?

If Neil wants me to keep his secret, he will answer some of my questions. I head for the coffee shop.

As I pull into the parking lot, my heart is beating out of my chest. I force myself to remember that although Neil is one of the most famous celebrities in the world, he's a fraud. He's been lying to everyone. And for all I know, he's lying about Ali.

My ego might have something to do with my decision. He's a celebrity. But another part of me wants an opportunity to hear both sides of the story. I'm skeptical. Yet the way Ali cowered behind me in the meeting makes me want to defend her, stand up for her, and get some answers.

Neil is inside wearing a baseball cap and staring at his phone. It's not a popular time of day for coffee, so the shop isn't crowded. There are no paparazzi or bodyguards. Who would ever expect a billionaire to come to this tiny coffee shop in Maine?

I walk inside and wait by the door, taking my last deep breath of reassurance to play it cool. He glances my way, stands, and pulls out a chair for me to sit down with him.

"I'm so relieved that you decided to come."

"Relieved?" I ask as I sling my purse over the back of my chair.

"Coffee?"

"Sure, I take it black, thank you."

He waves his fingers, and a man standing nearby approaches the table.

"She would like a coffee, black, please," Neil says without looking at him.

The man's wearing a suit and looks completely out of place, so he isn't a barista, but rather some sort of assistant for Neil. He delivers my coffee, and Neil completely disregards his presence.

"Stella, I feel like we should clear some things up. You see, when my . . . family and I made the decision to alter my DNA in hopes of connecting to humans, I never dreamed I'd end up where I am today."

"And where did you think you'd end up?"

"I had no idea. I knew the main goal was to ease our way into society to form relationships and gain access to Earth's resources amicably. Sound familiar?"

My stomach sinks, and I feel my face flush. Is he implying Ali is simply following orders?

"What's wrong with handling things amicably?" I ask.

"Do you honestly believe they needed our help? Since you've seen first-hand how advanced they are."

"*Our* help?"

He clasps his hands on the table and looks down. "Stella, it's easy to see that you are a good person."

"I'm not sure I can say the same for you."

"But you need to understand I want to help the humans. My family just wants to help themselves. They want to take what they need and leave. I, on the other hand, intend to lead the humans into space travel and aid in their discoveries. To quicken their advancements."

"Why don't you just tell them the truth? You'd be able to show them a lot more."

He sits back and scratches his chin.

"In all my years on Earth, I have learned a lot about humans. Humans are vain, selfish creatures who take pride in slow progress. If I reveal too much too soon, there would be confusion and panic. It's important to take things at a slower pace."

"What about Einstein and Newton? I'm sure some people thought they were bizarre, but they never let up on their discoveries. If you really wanted to help us, you'd go all in."

A smile stretches across his face. I search for signs of his alien DNA but can't see any. His eyes are tired and strained.

He looks around the coffee shop and clicks his tongue. "I'm surprised Ali came through. I never thought she'd be tough enough to make a difference. In my old society, I was treated like an average Joe. Nothing special. Ironically, I found the alien society was nothing special either. My parents sent me off onto a foreign planet, hoping I'd make them proud. They underestimated my level of intelligence. Instead of following my parents' orders, I realized I didn't want to manipulate the human race into providing for my family. I was at the forefront of an amazing opportunity to help the humans instead."

"You're twisting their words."

"Am I?"

"Yes! You claim you're helping the humans, and you might be, but what's in it for you? Sure, you're helping us technologically, but look at you. You're worth billions. You're a celebrity who dates supermodels.

You have NASA kissing your feet. You're not so average, are you?" I fall back against my chair. "I think you're helping yourself."

Neil spins his coffee cup between his hands and leans in toward me. "And you can't see yourself enjoying a little fun along the way? When I abandoned my family and their plan, I felt so much relief and freedom. The truth is I can't wait for my family to flee the planet. We don't need them."

I squint and tilt my head. "We?"

"As wrong as Ali is about everything she's doing for her people, she's right about one thing. You're special. You must have an old soul . . ."

". . . *since your level of consciousness allows you to communicate telepathically.*" He grins. "You could play a key role in the development of space travel and training programs. You and I could live this lavish life together and be remembered forever as the power couple who saved the human race."

I suddenly remember Ali mentioning to Neil how a certain level of consciousness is required for space travel.

"A power couple? No, no, no," I say. "I will not let you manipulate me. You are a pathological liar who wants to be worshiped, and I will not submit to you."

"Any other woman would kill to be with me." He sneers.

"I'm sorry I wasted your time," I whisper as I scoot my chair back.

He grabs my hand, and when I start to pull away, he grips it tighter.

"I had high hopes for you. I was wrong."

Something is wrapped around his finger, and I try to push his hand off. I feel a prick near my wrist, and a warming sensation travels up my arm. My brain is on fire.

—∿∿∿∿∿∿—

"Wake up, Stella."

I try to open my eyes, but my head hurts too much.

"I'm sorry I had to do that to you. But you pose a threat to my plans."

I muster up the strength to open my eyes and see Neil standing over me. I go to gasp, but my mouth is taped shut. My hands are bound. My legs are strapped to a chair. I meet Neil's gaze, and my eyes fill with tears, but I don't take my eyes off of him. My heart may explode out of my chest. I want to yell at him, but I can't.

"I can see why you'd be upset with me," he says, turning his back to me, and peers out of the window.

It dawns on me I've seen that image before. We're in the conference room where we met with NASA earlier. The entire first floor is one big open space, and this glass room sits in the middle. The lights are off, but the blinds on the street windows cast eerie shadows on the floor, and passing cars light up the room with their headlights.

"Before you came into the picture, I had everything laid out perfectly. First," he says, holding out one finger. "First, make a bunch of money. Second, display my scientific abilities. Third, get NASA to trust me. Fourth, become the hero who helps save humanity." He steps around the table and looks deep into my eyes. His darkness is truly visible for the first time. "You were right. I was going to be worshiped. Shit, I already am. Then, you and Ali had to barge in and disrupt my process."

He pulls a chair in front of me, sits down, and scratches his chin again. "I tried to tell you she's dangerous, or ignorant, really, and you refused to believe me. I offered you a position in my plan, and you refused." He looks up at the ceiling. "It was a one-time shot. I couldn't let you go and risk you ruining my reputation. What am I going to do with you?"

"*You're going to—*" There's a horrendous pain inside my head. I scream and find it hard to catch my breath with my mouth taped.

"Oh, I'm sorry. I forgot to tell you the concoction I created for you is a neuro-path inhibitor, which makes it very uncomfortable to speak telepathically."

Sweat drips down my neck. It's difficult to keep my head up. I need to find a way to tell Ali. The pain is too much. Andrew might not come looking for me. I literally told him I needed some space. I didn't mean this much. I sob. I have ruined everything. Curiosity killed the cat. Why do I have to be the stupid cat?

"You know what should be embarrassing for humans?" Neil asks himself. "Just how easy it was for me to become a rich celebrity. I knew I'd have to dumb myself down to seem believable and trustworthy, but this was too easy. You humans have such a narrow view of surviving. No wonder only a few people are acknowledged for their intelligence. School, career, family. Talk about dull. How can you possibly expect to make any difference in the world, the universe, if you keep going down the same limited path? Honestly, your race needs me. I am the necessary component humans need to survive in this universe."

Even Neil is losing interest in his conversation. He looks over at me as though he is expecting me to reply, as if he forgot I can't speak. He walks toward me and slowly removes the tape.

"Neil," I whisper, "I need my medicine. I need water. Get me my purse. My pills are in my purse." I start coughing.

"You humans. That's another problem. If you just let the sick ones die off, you'd have much less of a population problem, and all the sickly genes would be eradicated. You'd be a far superior race than you are now." He reluctantly goes to the other side of the room to get my purse.

"Sure, I'll give you your medicine. But you'll have to do something for me in return."

"And what's that?" I ask nervously.

He leans against the table with my purse in his hands, sifting through the contents.

"You need to convince Andrew to go with Ali when they leave. I can't have him here disrupting my plans. And you . . . you can go with them and live a happy alien life with your boyfriend, or you could still change your mind about being my partner."

"I can't tell. Are you a good guy or a bad guy?"

"Well, it depends, my dear, on the narrowness of your mindset. But seeing as how it's pretty black and white with you, I doubt you could understand."

"Maybe if you opened up my neuropathways again, I'd be more likely to understand," I reply with sass and cough some more.

He puts my purse down and chuckles. The contents of that purse are important, and I cool down a bit.

"I'm willing to figure something out with you. I know I seem special, but I'm only human. Which means, I can't deny that I yearn for a lavish life. If you could provide for me and keep me safe, I might be able to make it work," I plead. I stare into his eyes. "But, before I can do that, I really need my medicine. Please. My frail human body depends on it."

He looks down with a pitiful expression and once again sifts through my purse. He pulls out the pill bottle my counselor prescribed me.

I have at least ten pills left. If I take them all, maybe I'll be able to communicate with Ali like Andrew did.

He takes a bottle of water from the fridge under the table and pours the pills into his hands.

"All of them," I say. He puts them in my mouth, and I swallow almost the entire bottle of water. God, I hope this works.

"Better?" he asks, looking a little uncomfortable with the situation.

"You really need me, don't you?" I eye him.

"Oh, don't flatter yourself. I don't *need* you. It would be very helpful if you did what I asked, but there are other avenues. There always are."

"You know," I say, panting, "you think you have everything figured out about humans. But you're lacking some of the most important characteristics. Authenticity, empathy, and kindness." My stomach is warming up with a tingling sensation.

"Humans don't have any empathy toward planet Earth." He leans against the table again. "Earth is dying a slow death, and humans will die with it if I don't help them now."

"Ali wants to help us. You want to be worshiped," I say, losing my focus as my mind wanders into a dreamlike state. The room is brighter than before, and Neil is radiating a beautiful aura of red and orange light. I'm displaying white and purple. I close my eyes and focus on seeing Ali. I know if I try to speak to her, it will be too obvious to Neil. I focus on Ali, hoping she'll hear my message.

"Neil, if you want me to do you any favors, the least you could do is untie me," I say, struggling to keep my mind focused. "And if you want to impress me, set me up at the conference table and treat me with respect. Talk with me, so we can work something out." I focus on the room and imagine Ali being here with me. My mind wanders, and my muscles relax.

"If I untie you, you'll try to escape. And then I'd have to shoot you." He walks to the side of the room behind my chair and returns holding a glamorous revolver, made with what appears to be very high-quality materials. Intricate details along the stock expose its sophistication. He holds it on his lap, then opens the chamber and displays the bullets, locked and loaded.

His face reads indifference, and he lifts one shoulder. "Come to think of it, I honestly don't care if I kill you. It makes perfect sense. If I kill you, then I can deliver the materials to Ali and send them on their way. I'd still be able to play dumb with NASA and answer their little questions they have for her. And then, my team and I will have nothing standing in our way," he says, and then he points the barrel at my face.

His tone is threatening, and his sneer is evil, but I'm not afraid. I have a different point of view. I have a certain peace about dying.

I think of my mom, and my eyes tear up. I think of my James, and my heart aches. I'm so thankful to know Ali and hope so badly she can get home. I think of my sweet students. And then Andrew . . . My heart, my love. I picture him, and how he held my face when we kissed. It was easy to fall for him, and he so eagerly wants to take care of me. I cry. I'll never get the chance to tell him I love him. I do have a reason to live, to fight. I could never leave him.

"Wait!" I hear a blast, and my world goes black.

ANDREW

The thought of Stella being in trouble makes me physically ill, and I suppress the urge to hurl out of the window while I'm driving. Ali is next to me with her hands on her head, trying desperately to connect with Stella again. She has only gathered bits and pieces of a message Stella sent. She's in the conference room where we had our meeting earlier.

"She's with Neil!" Ali cries.

"What? Why?" Did he take her? Did she go willingly? She was swooning over him. Either way, I'm going to kill him. "Is she okay? Did he hurt her?" I step on the accelerator.

"I can't reach her, Andrew. I don't trust Neil for a second. I think he may be doing this to her. Keeping her from being able to communicate with me. Drive faster."

"How could he do that?" I ask, pushing my Bronco to its limits.

"Neil is not human!"

"He's an alien?"

"He's like me with altered DNA. We thought he was dead all this time, but he has been busy becoming a celebrity."

"And this was something you decided to keep a secret?" I ask and swerve around a slow car.

"Well, I was still thinking everything through. I only just found out today. Apologies later, let's go get Stella."

I run the next two red lights and barely make the green. I jump the curb and stop half on the sidewalk and half off, facing the wrong way on a one-way street. We hop out and run to the entrance. It's locked.

I bang my elbow at the corner of the glass so I can reach in to turn the lock from the inside, but this glass is surprisingly thick. I nearly break a bone trying again and again.

I can barely see through the blinds. Neil has a gun.

"ST—"

Ali covers my mouth. "Shh . . ."

I desperately look for something I can throw at the window. A trashcan. I run over and yank it, but it's bolted to the ground. I settle for the metal lid. My heart is beating harder than it ever has before. I'm going to kill this guy.

"Stand back," I demand.

Ali doesn't move.

"Neil has a strange look on his face and—" She gasps.

I peer through, and Neil is pointing the gun at Stella. My life flashes before my eyes as if the gun is aimed at me.

I cock my arm with the trashcan lid.

Ali screams at the top of her lungs, and I get knocked to the ground. I roll over and see Ali releasing a blast of vibrations. I can't get up. The glass surrounding the first floor of the building shatters, and the conference room crumbles.

When my ears stop ringing, I look up. Stella is strapped to her chair, lying sideways on the floor. I bear crawl until I can stand and run to her. Trembling, I reach for her head. I might see her brain spewed on the floor, but thankfully her head is intact.

"Stella, I'm here!" I say. Tears obstruct my vision.

"Am I dead?" she asks.

"No, I've got you. You're okay. Don't worry." I push her chair up and start to untie her when I remember there's still Neil to worry about.

He and Ali are staring at each other. Neil slowly gets up off the ground from behind the conference table, and Ali is near the reception desk. It could be a scene from a Western. I speed up the task at hand and whisper to Stella, "Let's get out of here. Can you walk?"

"Get the gun." She squints in Neil's direction. "He can't see his own evil. He has to be stopped."

I let out a deep breath, finish untying her, and steal toward the gun. Neil and Ali haven't moved a muscle and haven't broken eye contact.

I try not to break their concentration and creep very slowly. A shard of glass shatters under my shoe, and Neil jerks his head in my direction. We both leap for the gun.

Neil gets a better grasp, and I grab a handful of glass shards and throw them at his face. He screams and recoils. Sitting on the floor, he appears distraught, probably over the prospect his good looks might be tarnished. He draws out a large piece of glass from his cheekbone. I take the gun, pushing past my throbbing hand and dripping blood, and aim it at him. I didn't know I was capable of murder until now.

"Why shouldn't I kill you right here, right now?" I'll kill him in a heartbeat. "Do you have any idea what it's like to love someone with all your heart, with every ounce of your existence?" My throat tightens up. "And then watch some alien asshole try to take that away? Because, Neil, it's a very terrifying feeling." I hear sirens in the distance.

Neil looks down. "I was wrong to think humans could adjust quickly enough. I mean, look at you. All you can think about is your little love story with your little human. How pathetic." His mocking tone makes my finger tighten on the trigger.

"That's the difference between you and me," I say, mimicking his tone. "There's nothing little about falling in love. It's monumental, earth-shattering, and it's something I'd die for. You think you can help our world? Our world is lacking passion, honesty, depth, and needs more love stories. Our world does not need another selfish, power-hungry billionaire. Go back where you came from. Humans are better off without you, I promise."

"You think I could just drop everything and return to the family I abandoned?" He shakes his head and shrugs.

"Yes," Ali calls out from behind me. "Come home with us, Neil. We can work through this. Please!"

"I'd be a failure all over again. I'd be better off dead."

The sirens are loud now.

"You're a failure here, too, now," I say. "The police are about to arrest you for kidnapping and attempted murder."

His expression darkens. "How do you think they'll treat me in prison?"

"Awfully, I hope."

"Hands up! Put the gun down!" an officer yells from behind the broken glass. "Nobody move except the man with the gun. Put it down, now!"

I don't take my eyes off Neil, and I slowly place the gun on the table, put my hands behind my head, and back up toward the women.

"This man kidnapped Stella and held her hostage in this room." I jerk my head in her direction but don't break eye contact with Neil. He's still watching me with a dark grin on his face.

The officers keep their weapons raised and run toward us. Neil jumps up from the floor and reaches for the gun. The officers fire. Neil falls to the floor.

I stare at him in shock.

The officers continue forward, calling an ambulance on their radio, and check for a pulse. I watch as Neil's eyes go blank, and a single tear falls with his last breath. A sense of relief washes over me, knowing he can never hurt Stella again. I hold her against my chest and kiss her head.

"Was there an explosion? Is anyone else hurt?" asks an officer. I turn to Ali, hoping she can come up with an explanation, but she's too shaken.

"No, officer, we're not sure how that happened. Ali and I found out Stella was in trouble, and when we saw he had a gun, we jumped into action. Can I make a phone call?"

"You have somewhere to be?"

"No." I reach for my wallet, pull out Swanson's card, and turn it for him to see. "I was instructed to call Officer Swanson if anything should change during his investigation."

"The FBI?"

"Yes."

"Sure, call him. But do not leave the vicinity." He points at the mess and turns toward the paramedics. "By the way, is that who I think it is?" he asks, jerking his thumb over his shoulder.

"Yes, it's Neil Husk."

His eyes get big. "Uh oh."

"Neil knew what he was doing. He knew you'd do your job. This was no accident. He was trying to kill Stella. You saved us." He'll probably still be judged ruthlessly for killing a celebrity.

The officer shuffles his feet and readjusts his belt. "Let me get that paramedic," he says and leans into his radio.

I quickly dial Swanson's number.

"Hi, Officer Swanson." I look down, not sure where to begin. "We got into some trouble downtown."

"I'm not too far from there. Are the local police involved?"

"Yes, they're here. We're at the conference room."

"Don't say a word until I get there. I'll let them know I'm headed your way."

"Thanks. And you might want to prepare yourself. Neil is dead."

"Dead? Good grief. Save it for when I get there." He hangs up.

I look down at Stella, whose face is streaked with tears.

"Andrew, I am so sorry. This was incredibly selfish of me."

"What happened?"

She begins to cry again, and my stomach drops. "He convinced me to meet with him to hear his side of the story and what his plans were. He gave me an ultimatum to join him in his plan or die."

"You met him here? Alone?"

"No, we met at the coffee shop. Then when I wouldn't agree with him, he drugged me. I woke up here. I tried to call for Ali, but the drug he gave me blocked my abilities somehow."

"I heard you, Stella." She pulls Stella into an embrace. "It was different this time. I couldn't hear you exactly, but I felt what was happening and saw sporadic images."

"I convinced him to give me my psilocybin. I was hoping it would open up my mind enough to get word to you, and—"

"It worked. Gosh, I'm so sorry, Stella. You must have been so scared."

"I was." Stella looks at me and grabs my waist. "But I'm not anymore. Andrew, I need to confess something. I cannot bear the thought of you leaving—"

I kiss her hard. "Stella, I am not going anywhere. You have my whole heart. I love you. Those three words seem inadequate, but it's true, I love you." I push her hair behind her ears and kiss her again.

"The shrooms are still swimming around my bloodstream, but don't let that take away from what I'm about to say."

"Okay . . ."

"When Neil pointed his gun at me, all I could think about was you, and how I wasn't ready to say goodbye. I feared you'd never know how deep my feelings are for you. That I'm in love with you."

I hold her face with my hand. "I could never leave you."

"I don't want you to resent me for keeping you from traveling with Ali and fulfilling your childhood dreams."

"Andrew already took care of that. We've got someone else ready to go."

"Someone better. The perfect person to go," I say and grin.

"Who?"

"My best buddy, Zain. He's a better scientist than I am, anyway. Plus, he and Ali will get along great." I look over and see Ali blushing. I wrap my arms around Stella and hold her tight.

"What the hell happened here?" Officer Swanson yells across the room. He steps lightly through the broken glass.

I hesitate to break my gaze from Stella to speak to him, but when I do it's just in time to see Neil being carted off in a body bag.

"Hi, Officer Swanson. So, this is a difficult matter to discuss. Um, well, you know our special friend Ali here? It turns out that Neil was . . . see, he was actually like Ali." I glance around to make sure no one else can hear us. "I'm not sure I'd let anyone do an autopsy on Neil, just in case he's a little different than a full human."

He goes pale and coughs as if choking on his own saliva. He calls to the paramedics, "This body is to be transferred to the FBI immediately for autopsy." He stops the stretcher, whistles for his team, and waits until Neil is in the right hands to let go. He turns around and crosses his arms, looking down at the floor.

"You're lucky we were downtown. This could have been a shit show for the rural police. Neil Husk? Really?"

"If you're wondering if there are any more out there like me, Mr.

Swanson, you don't have to worry. The others have died in previous years. Neil was missing for so long, we thought he died, but he changed his identity and decided to live a human life. I didn't know until I saw him today. I am the last one alive."

"Why didn't you say something to us?"

"I should have, and I'm sorry. I was shocked and confused and hurt. I didn't know what to do." Tears stream down her face, and Stella holds on to her shoulders.

"I'm sorry, Ms. Ali. " He rubs his forehead. "I can't wrap my head around how someone like him can get so rich and famous, while no one notices something is a little off."

"Correction, I think everyone thought he was a little weird, but couldn't put their finger on it. I know I did," I say. I hope Ali doesn't take offense.

"He *was* always a little odd, wasn't he?"

Stella and I nod as the paramedics wave us over to inspect our injuries.

"At least now it makes sense why he had so many radical ideas and insights for science and technology," I add.

"NASA will lose it. They will totally lose it," he says under his breath. "Okay, I'm going to have one of my colleagues come take down your statement on what happened here." He looks around the room and sighs. "And Andrew, you'll be hearing from NASA on our plans for tomorrow. Obviously, there will be some changes."

"Yes, if you talk to them first, tell them we have some good news." I hope there will be no issues with the new plan. I'd rather break the news to NASA first and allow them to approve before I tell Swanson.

STELLA

Today is the day. Today we say goodbye to our friend who we have worked so hard to save and somehow managed to. Thankfully, I took a couple sick days at work to witness the departure.

When Andrew told NASA about Zain last night, they were familiar with his lab and were supportive of Ali inviting him on her return trip home. They understand the importance of Ali choosing the traveler. Zain is thrilled NASA thinks he is well-suited for researching and collecting data. One scientist on board is much better than no scientists on board.

I head down to the pop-up tents scattered on the shore. Even Andrew's backyard is filled with the NASA crew, who are preparing for Zain's travels. NASA went ahead and rented the neighboring vacation homes to ensure there wouldn't be any onlookers.

In order to remain covert, the military delivered the minerals via helicopter to the twenty GPS locations Ali gave them. The helicopters carried out massive pallets and dropped them in the ocean early this morning. Thankfully, the amount of minerals provided will ensure a large area of land on their planet will be thoroughly nourished, and the rest will be used as needed to power the ships.

Ali and the others agreed to let Zain join them, collect data for up to one year, and then return to Earth to share information. He will be gone a maximum of three years, including travel time.

When Andrew brings back Zain, I am quickly introduced to him. In an obvious rush, Zain hands me his cat, who now purrs in my arms. I watch him shyly offer his arm to Ali and walk with her to the NASA team members. They poke and prod him, jotting down temperatures and measurements.

NASA adds new high-tech software and gadgets to his bags. We have about thirty minutes until the scheduled departure, although, with the frenzy, I doubt we'll be on time.

Andrew finishes his private conversation with Zain and comes back to stand with me.

"What'd you ask him?"

"I wanted to make sure he was really okay with all of this. Give him a chance to back out if he wanted."

"I see. And what did he say?"

"He said he's never been more sure of anything in his life. He's all in. I knew he would be."

Andrew and I stay on the outskirts, trying not to interfere or get in the way. Andrew crosses his arms and scans the area. "This is a monumental moment in history that will probably stay hidden for years. Will the world ever be ready to acknowledge extraterrestrial life?"

"Right?" I add. "We've all been sworn to secrecy and have to go on living the rest of our lives knowing we aren't alone in this massive universe. Makes you wonder what other secrets the government is keeping. I heard they have like eight UFOs in Area 51."

"I've heard there's always some truth to rumors. It only takes one drunken night to spill intel."

"And then word spreads?"

"Word spreads, but no one really knows for sure."

"Oh my gosh," I gasp, "do you think we'll see a cheesy UFO documentary about this event in ten years? With fake animation and horrible narration?"

"Those are sort of my guilty pleasure."

"Mine too!"

I stroke the kitty in my arms. Andrew's got the look of a man watching his kid graduate from college: pure pride and joy. He may not be going up into space, but he knows he'll be a part of this project forever. His best friend is going into space. He will not take this lightly.

"Do you think they'll be able to do this? Travel through space and time? With a mere human?" I sound like Neil deGrasse Tyson.

Andrew laughs and rubs his hands through his hair, then grabs me by the waist and looks up at the clouds. "It seems completely unbelievable, doesn't it?"

"Completely."

"With human space missions, everyone is so nervous, hoping nothing explodes. But I don't know, this seems safer in a way."

"I know what you mean."

"When I asked Ali how they'd get around the fact that Zain doesn't have their level of consciousness, she said they'll have to sedate him. Put him in a dream state."

"That's so interesting. I wonder if I'd have to do that."

"You want to find out?" He nudges me with his hip.

I smile, and he grips me tighter and kisses my head.

"Soon, they'll be on their way into space utilizing a higher consciousness to access dark energy, using it like a current in the sky. Cosmic Slip," he says.

"Will sedation be hard on his body?"

"He'll only be sedated while they're slipping. There will be breaks when Zain is awake and can truly experience their way of life in space. But any astronaut will suffer some physical discomforts."

"This is so intense. It's so thought-provoking. I'm overwhelmed trying to absorb it all. And Zain is actually going to experience it. Today. Cosmic Slip," I repeat, loving the sound of it. "Do you think you'll get credit for coining that term? It's so catchy. You should be in the textbooks for—"

"You're chatty when you're nervous, aren't you?" He peers down at me with that big handsome grin.

"It's just a lot to take in." I set the cat on the ground, and she rubs against my legs.

"I know. I'm sleep deprived, but I've never felt so awake and alive. This is really happening."

Ali leaves Zain with the scientists and walks over to us with her head hung low. I'm so relieved we get to help her, but sad to see her go.

"Well, you did it, Ali!" I say, trying to stop my voice from cracking. I hold her face in my hands as tears fall down our cheeks. "Thank you for trusting me after all these years. Thank you for saving me when I needed saving. Thank you for lifting my spirits during my grief. And for providing me with this unbelievable adventure. I will miss you so much." I hug her again.

After wiping her tears, she clasps my hands and looks at us. "You two have given us another chance at life. You could have run away, but you chose to be brave and fight. You could have given up and sent me away, but you looked for answers, for help. I can't thank you enough." She doesn't bother wiping away her tears again and hugs us both.

"This isn't goodbye," Andrew says. "We will find a way to communicate more effectively. For now, we're thankful for the satellites. We will see you when you get back."

"Absolutely." Ali slowly steps away and meets Zain in a different tent for photographs. They head toward the water, and she beckons an orb. When it rolls onto the sand, they step inside and wave before the door shuts.

Everyone is staring, speechless. There is not a noise to be heard as they descend into the ocean.

A few moments pass, and vessels emerge from on the horizon, like stars glinting on the waves. They rise ever so slightly off the water, and then, within the blink of an eye, they're gone. No smoke trails or slow ascension—just gone.

For decades, alien spaceships have been hiding in Earth's oceans, and now, they're gone in an instant. The world will go on, not knowing the magical encounter we've all shared.

I stare up, hoping to get one last glimpse of our friends. We all look at each other, silently acknowledging we are part of something special. There are no FBI agents or NASA scientists. We're just humans working together and with the universe. We take turns hugging each other.

Scooter's hands are in his pockets as he walks, head down. He starts to talk but takes a breath before he starts again. "Stella, Andrew, I want you to know how much we care about Zain out there. We'll be monitoring our satellite communications constantly, and we'll fill you in as much as we can. We want to invite you to come see our temporary comp site in a couple days. We'll be able to track their travels, to a certain extent. All of us here," he points to the crew packing up, "we're family now, including you two."

Andrew shakes his hand firmly. "Thank you, Scooter. We would be thrilled to be included every step of the way, if you'll have us."

"Zain's part of the family, too. We want you guys in the loop. We'll see you soon."

"Perfect!" I say.

Saying our goodbyes and helping pack up the last of the equipment, I feel so much gratitude. Andrew and I head back inside and sink into the couch.

I notice Chester in the kitchen staring up at the cat, who has found her way to the top of the refrigerator.

"What's the cat's name?" I ask, watching Chester's tail sweep the tile floor.

"Wow, I'm embarrassed. I don't know. In the heat of the moment, I never thought to ask. This all happened so fast."

I take a deep, cleansing breath. "We're going to have a lot of free time together." I lean my head on the couch and smile in his direction. He scoots closer and puts his arm around me.

"The world is our oyster, it seems."

"We should start with naming the cat."

He smirks. "How about we check her collar."

"Wow, I must need some coffee." I walk over to the fridge and lift the cat. Chester jumps, sniffing intensely. I sneak a peek at the cat's pink collar. "Her name is Galileo."

"Oh, that's clever!"

"So clever! We can call her Gal, for short." I look down at Chester. "You be nice to Galileo," I say with my hand on my hip. I put her down, giving her a head start away from Chester.

"Yeah, you better listen to your mom!" Andrew shouts as they scurry off into another room.

I tap my foot on the floor. "Have I reached Mom status with Chester already?"

"If you're okay with that."

I express my joy at this news by reaching my arms out, and I chassé into a pique turn. I extend into arabesque and hold. Andrew is gawking at me. I release down and laugh in embarrassment.

"What? You don't have a happy dance?"

He laughs quietly.

"I never gawk at you when you spew out your science jargon."

"That's because science jargon is very unsexy. You dancing through my house is very sexy. Get over here, you ballerina."

I walk with my most elegant ballet technique and fall onto his lap. "I am a delirious ballerina who desperately needs a nap."

"No time for naps," Andrew says and kisses my neck.

"You haven't slept for two days. You must be tired." I chuckle, knowing quite well where this is going. He picks me up and carries me into his room.

"I want you so bad," Andrew mumbles through our kisses.

"I need you."

"Are you sure?" he whispers, giving me chills.

"So sure."

He takes my shirt off and kisses my neck down to my breasts, tugging my bra to the side. I unclip it and throw it. My body is quivering, waiting for him to kiss me again as he lays me on the bed.

I take his pants off, and he removes his shirt. He's built like a god. With ease, he lifts me up and slides my pants off. I feel no sense of insecurity or shyness. I hold on to his neck, arching my back with every breath, as he lay on top of me. He flips me on top of him and brushes my hair behind my shoulders. I throw my head back in ecstasy.

We melt into each other . . . completely and thoroughly.

———〰〰〰〰〰———

What seems like hours later, after the comforter and sheets have been kicked off the bed, we lie entangled in our moment of bliss.

"Move in with me."

"Well, I kind of already have."

"That's true, but you know what I mean. Don't leave," he says, tugging on my shoulders. "Let's meet each other's families. Let's do this."

"I'm definitely eager to meet your sisters. Let's do it." I watch his eyes grow heavier with every breath. "Get some rest."

"I wonder where they are now," he whispers right before he falls asleep.

"Me too."

I am exhausted as well, but something is nagging at me. I can't pretend to understand alien technology and their advanced forms of space travel, but what is so interesting to me is the level of consciousness needed.

How many years would have to go by for humans to have that natural ability? Are the aliens going to help Zain reach capacity?

Humans are getting less and less conscious as time goes on with so many apps and social platforms as distractions. I am able to speak telepathically with Ali, so does that mean my consciousness is farther along than most? Maybe I have a bigger purpose in all of this.

I roll over in bed, imagining Ali and Zain traveling through the galaxy, brainstorming together, planning together. I hope Zain is adjusting well. I can't imagine being the only human on a space mission. He didn't have a single doubt, which says a lot about him.

I wonder if I'll change my mind about traveling to their planet in three years when they return. Will I really be able to deny Andrew the chance again to travel the galaxy? What about my mom and Andrew's family? I put my hand on my head and admire Andrew's broad chest as it rises and falls with each breath. We are exactly where we need to be, for now.

Finally able to relax, I relish the opportunity to catch up on sleep. I ignore our growling abdomens and close my eyes.

ANDREW

I t's bright outside when I wake, and I check my phone. It's past four. I haven't slept this late since college.

I roll out of bed and go to the kitchen to make some coffee. While it's brewing, I head to the porch.

Stella brings me a cup, and we sit, soaking in the sun's last stretch of heat as it inches its way closer to setting. I'm thankful to call this star ours. Our sun that sits the perfect distance of 93,000,000 miles away to give us the perfect amount of energy and warmth to survive.

"I can understand why some ancient civilizations worshiped the sun," Stella says with eyes closed, letting the sun soak in.

"I know. It's a great star."

"How many stars are in our galaxy? I know I've heard the number before."

I stare into the distance. "Somewhere around a hundred billion."

"BILLION? A hundred BILLION? The number I had in the back of my mind was way off." She looks shocked, and I laugh. She's so animated.

"How are they going to sort through fifty billion stars and their surrounding planets?"

"There's only a small area around the galaxy that is habitable. I never got into specifics with Ali, but she made it seem like they're spreading out, going in different directions to scan as much as they can in the least amount of time. If they scan something that has potential, they'll check it out in depth."

"Ah, yes. My feeble human brain cannot compute."

"It will be interesting to see how the communications work with the new satellites."

"NASA launched a rocket into space with new satellites just for this occasion?"

"There are thousands of satellites orbiting Earth. New satellites are constantly being built to replace older models, and it takes about an hour for a rocket to send a satellite into orbit. And technically, Neil Husk's company made the launch, which is painfully ironic. They have announced his death and that the company will be run by their chief operations officer until they vote someone in to be CEO."

"So, then their COO must know what is going on."

I sigh and stretch my arms up. "Not sure about that. I guarantee NASA will control all communications through the satellite. Neil's company was just willing to set it up for us."

"Neil was working so closely with NASA. I wonder what they're going to do now."

"I'm not sure about his business, but NASA isn't too bent out of shape about the loss. They potentially have direct communication with an alien species who is willing to share their knowledge of space travel."

"That's true."

"Which reminds me." I turn to her. "I want you to meet my family. Let's go to my sister's house for dinner. I've never brought a girl home, so I'm sure they'll be thrilled."

"Never?"

I laugh, a little embarrassed. "No, really. I mean, I've had my fair share of girlfriends, but none that I knew I wanted to marry."

"Oh," she says, leaning closer with a grin the size of Texas. "Is that the stipulation? They have to be marriage worthy? I see . . . wow. You must really love me." She chuckles, cheeks blushing.

I lean in to kiss her. "Stella, I would marry you right here, right now. We are destined to be together. Soulmates, if you will. I know it deep down in my gut. I want to spend the rest of my life with you."

Her eyes are wide as if she's surprised by my seriousness. Her tears fall, and I wipe them away. I kiss her again, and again.

She pulls away and takes a breath. "So, let's talk about tonight. Everyone will be there for dinner?"

"Yes, but don't worry. Everyone will love you. And, if they don't, then they're blind."

"I will be fine to wear these casual clothes?"

"Of course. I'm sure everyone will be in hiking clothes. We're outdoorsy people. But the food will be delicious, and the wine will be expensive. My sister went to culinary school."

"Oh, which sister?"

"Claire. She does real estate but could totally have her own restaurant if she had the time. Sydney is an architect. She designs restaurants and small businesses."

"They need to team up."

"They've talked about it, but Claire doesn't want to miss nights and weekends with her kids, which are the busiest times for restaurants."

"I can understand that." She sighs. "I'm so nervous. Forgive me ahead of time if I don't seem like myself. I get introverted and awkward when I'm nervous."

"Everything is going to be fine. My family is easy to get along with. Don't stress. Let's go."

We jump in the Bronco, and Stella keeps quiet, staring out the window. As I surf the radio stations, she flips the mirror down and inspects her hair. It's messy, as usual. She moans and flips the mirror up with force. I laugh and start singing loudly. I'm trying to make her laugh, but I'm failing. A smile is all she musters.

She turns the radio down without warning, forcing me to stop singing. "I'm just letting you know I'm not ready to answer questions about my past. This will be an uncomfortable night if I have to drudge up my sappy past and risk everyone feeling sorry for me. Do they really want to know that I'm a widow who lost her home because a guy died upstairs while filling up the tub, who then joined forces with their brother to save an alien race that had been hiding on Earth for over thirty years?"

"Stella, you're rambling."

"Stop the car." She braces herself on the dash in front of her. "Please, right now!"

"Okay, okay. Pulling over."

"It has dawned on me that I have no idea what to say to your family. I do not like pity. It's the worst feeling in the world when someone feels sorry for you. What if they ask how we met?"

"We met through a mutual friend."

"Who?"

"Ali."

"Ugh, well I know that, but what if they ask who Ali is?"

"Look, we don't want to lie to people. Be as honest as you can. Obviously, you'll leave out the fact that she's an alien. For example, I technically met Ali at a house party."

"You mean when you were hallucinating?"

"Yes, but do they need to know that? No. Okay, let's practice. And how did you meet Ali?"

"We were . . . childhood friends, I guess."

"See? Easy."

"Okay, I do feel a little better. But I'm not ready to tell people about James or my house. I'll get emotional and embarrass myself."

"If you do, my sisters would cry with you. Don't hide your feelings. But you don't have to divulge your entire past tonight."

She pushes her hair to one side. "Okay, you're making me feel a little better."

"My sisters are genuine people. You'll be fine."

She nods and smiles.

"You ready?"

"Ready."

I squeeze her knee, and we take off.

STELLA

As he opens the door to Claire's house, Andrew is tackled by a swarm of giggling children. A tall, beautiful woman with sandy blond hair like Andrew's walks down the hall and introduces herself.

"Please excuse these wild animals. Hi, I'm Claire. Come on in." She gestures for me to walk around the rambunctious kids and into the kitchen.

"Your kids are beautiful! And so is your house, wow, I love this." I stop at the water lily–esque painting. Claire keeps walking, and I hurry to catch up.

"Oh, thanks. I found that at an art fair. Do you know how to use a chef's knife?"

"I think so, but now I'm nervous."

"If you could help me chop the herbs, I would be so thankful. My sous-chef got distracted," she says, waving her hand toward the back-yard where it appears the husbands and Sydney are playing cornhole.

"What are you cooking?" I ask, overwhelmed by all the dirty bowls and utensils on the counter.

Claire digs in the bottom drawer of the fridge and pops back up, holding chives.

"Seared scallops with lemony brown butter and capers for us. Fried fish for the kids, and lemon pudding cake with fresh fruit for dessert."

"Wow, this is an impressive menu."

Claire looks relieved and proud. She clearly likes to be a good host. I take the chives and search for a cutting board.

"I will admit that I have reason to celebrate." She winks at me.

To my relief, Andrew walks in with only one kid hanging from his arm instead of five, and I smile at his disheveled hair.

"Hey, Sis. Have you met my girlfriend?"

I cringe slightly at the term. I haven't been referred to as a girl-friend in ten years. Looking at Andrew out of the corner of my eye, I say, "I would prefer to use a different term, but I can't think of one that suits us."

"My Lady? My Girl? My Boo? My—"

"Partner?" Claire says.

"I like that one." I'm relieved she stopped him before he said something like *my princess*.

"Yes," she replies, tossing him a bottle of wine to open. "We have met, and she complimented my menu for the night. She has good taste. I can tell."

"And I'm excited to meet Sydney and the rest of the family."

"Andrew, go grab everyone. Dinner is ready."

He opens the back door and yells, "Dinner!" Claire's shoulders jerk up. She scowls in his direction and rolls her eyes.

"Who are you calling for? All the neighbors?" He smiles as if proud to have already annoyed his older sister.

The husbands walk in, and we exchange pleasantries. Sydney is the last to enter, exuding a natural radiance and welcoming smile. She's tall, like Claire, but with dark hair. Both could be in a magazine.

"All of you are so beautiful. I'm Stella." I stick my hand out to greet her, and she hugs me instead.

"Look who's talking." She laughs.

"Everyone, bring your plate," Claire yells, as she stands by the stove, holding her spatula.

Andrew hands me a plate and smiles, as though telling me I can relax now. We all find a spot at the table and say cheers to good food and family.

I am surprised and pleased to see how easy-going everyone is, how they have essentially accepted me as part of the family and treat me as such. This night is a lot less terrifying than I imagined.

While Sydney tells an embarrassing story about their high school days, I glance over at Andrew and nudge his foot. He looks at me with contentment, leans over, and massages my neck. I rest my cheek in his hand and feel a sense of normalcy for the first time in a long time. I'm so thankful to be with this incredible person—my boyfriend, my lover, my partner.

—⁓⁓⁓〰〰〰⁓⁓⁓—

When the night ends and we finally make it home, Andrew falls asleep fast. I'm still reeling from how successful the evening was, and how relieved I am no one cornered me with questions. Tonight was lighthearted and fun.

I roll over in bed, restless, trying to will myself to sleep, when I hear an owl hooting in the backyard. It gives me chills. I lift my head off the pillow, quiet my breathing, and hear it again.

Is this a sign? It was an owl that brought me to Ali. There's an old saying that your spirit is awakened when an owl makes its presence known. I leap out of bed and peer through the blinds into the backyard. It's completely dark. The moon must be hidden tonight. I pace the room. There's no chance of falling asleep while that owl is hooting. Something tells me I need to pay attention, need to listen.

I grab Andrew's sweater and a lantern from the hall closet, slowly open the glass door, and wait on the porch until I hear the owl again. It's coming from the left. I creep down the steps, trying not to scare him away. I dim the lantern and search the trees for his silhouette. The wind is calm, the ocean shore barely audible in the distance. He hoots again, and I spot him, then sit on the ground and stare, remembering this feeling from so long ago.

He turns his head, and his eyes reflect the light of my lantern. He hoots one more time and takes off.

His wingspan is smaller than I anticipated, judging from his bulky body. He soars through the night sky until he vanishes near the end of the low-lying branch. I expect to see him perched on a nearby branch, but when I stand, he's nowhere to be seen. I would have seen him fly to another tree. He was too close, too visible to simply disappear. I wander around, waiting to hear him. Even as a kid, I remember following them from tree to tree as they tried to escape my stares.

It dawns on me that Ali did the same thing the first time I saw her. She jumped through some tree trunks and disappeared. It was as if she stepped through a portal or invisible force of some kind.

I return to the tree where the owl disappeared and debate if this is me becoming unhinged, or if I'm onto something. But I'm curious. I'm drawn to this place as if magnetically pulled. I set my lantern down, grip two branches above my head, and walk my feet up the trunk until I can kick one leg over the branch where the owl was. With my arms and legs wrapped around, I crawl along the branch and scoot up as far as I can before it gets too thin to hold my weight. I still have a few feet to go to where I last saw the owl. The branch sways when I reach my hand as far as I can, but not far enough. I look down and judge the distance. It's not more than eight feet. I might break a bone, but I surely wouldn't die.

The branch cracks, and I use all my strength to jump forward. I might land on my feet. I reach my arms out to grasp another branch, and suddenly, I'm ripped apart in every direction.

There's a thunderous humming sound that reverberates through my body. I scream, but my breath escapes me. I try to open my eyes, but I can't feel any part of my body. The darkness is overwhelming, heavy and thick. I feel like I'm drowning, and just as I begin to submit, the darkness fades and a figure approaches. I'm frozen and helpless, but once I can focus, a calm comes over me. The figure is a dancing flame of light, an everchanging vivid hue. It changes into a silhouette shape of a human and my heart sinks.

I can't speak or move, but I recognize this being as if it's a soul . . . one that is very familiar to me. James.

He's how I always imagined he would look in death—not dead at all but living on and spreading his love into the universe.

Guilt and painful resentment wash over me. My heart aches, and I try to bellow out how sorry I am.

His light turns blue and indigo. The ohms get louder, which brings my focus back and quiets my heart. The sound envelopes my body, becoming visuals and feelings. He has a message for me.

He's meditating with a cloud of an aura surrounding his head and bends down and picks a mushroom from the ground beneath him. His eyes glow, and a three-dimensional grid is displayed in front of him; one that displays the galaxy continually shrinking into a group of galaxies, and the ever-expanding universe.

As his eyes dim, he grows larger, until I have to look up high. His light seems never-ending. He returns to his original form and comes within inches, it seems. He wraps himself around me, and I feel an undeniable sense of love and understanding, positivity and hopeful-ness. I wish I could display my feelings back to him, but something tells me he knows how I feel. He backs away, slowly dimming until I'm left alone in the darkness.

I'm moving faster and faster until I slam into something hard.

Lying in the grass, my head is killing me, and my shoulder sears. I roll over, and in doing so my shoulder pops. I instantly feel better.

The dark of the night seems bright and beautiful compared to where I came from. I lie on my back, catching my breath. My heavy breathing fogs in the cool air. I stare up through the trees into the sky, processing what happened.

Hoot Hoot. I jerk my head up in the direction of the sound. He's perched on a branch farther away. He spreads his wings, and this time, he flies far into the night. I feel at peace and put my head down.

"Stella?" I hear Andrew calling.

"I'm here!"

Andrew and Chester come running.

"What the hell are you doing out here?" he yells, but in a whisper. He tries to help me up, but pain shoots through my shoulder. I slowly inch my way to sitting.

I'm not ready to explain. "Just let me sit here for a minute." He looks confused, but resorts to sitting next to me in silence.

After a few deep, calming breaths, I say, "Promise you won't think I'm making this up."

"I would never."

"I've always been this way, even when I was a kid. I've been searching for signs. Signs that would reveal life's biggest secrets or something. Sounds stupid."

"Not stupid."

"I was trying to fall asleep and got distracted when I heard an owl."

"Okay, totally normal."

"But I over-think moments like that. Owls and I go way back."

He chuckles. "That's the cutest thing you've ever said."

I whack him on the leg with my good arm. "This is serious, Andrew!"

"Okay, okay. I'm listening. You heard an owl."

"Yes!" I say defensively. "So, I came outside. I found him in the trees and watched him disappear in mid-air. I, for some reason, thought I should investigate. I climbed the tree and fell. What happened in the moments before I hit the ground is the wild part."

He wraps his arm around my waist, avoiding my shoulder.

"It felt like I accessed some other dimension. I could have fallen and hit my head so hard I hallucinated, or had a near-death experience . . . I don't know. I somehow entered a heavy darkness at first, but it revealed itself to be bright and beautiful. I saw, I think, James. He was trying to send a message. I'm just not sure what he was trying to tell me."

"It reminds me a little of when I first saw Ali."

"Oh?"

"Yeah," he says. "I mean, I knew I was tripping, so I didn't let it scare me. But it felt like I left planet Earth, for sure, and there was definitely a message for me."

"Hmm."

"Stella, you are part of something major right now. The universe is obviously calling to you. It might call to all of us, but you're the one willing to listen."

He always knows exactly what to say. His sweet words make me melt, and I lean my head on his arm.

ANDREW

Stella is unusually quiet this morning. I can understand why, considering the night she had. She's sitting on the couch drinking her coffee, staring out the back windows. I love seeing her face light up with the sunlight shining through the glass.

"We're supposed to meet with NASA today. Do you think you're going to be okay to go? Or do you need time by yourself?"

She jerks her head in my direction, eyebrows raised. "No! I will have to come with you. I'll stay out of the way, but I'm not ready to be alone."

I can see her eyes welling. "Of course, absolutely." I sigh. "I'm glad you're coming. I need you there."

She goes back to looking out the windows. "Do we have time to eat first?" She sounds exhausted.

"Let's grab something on the way. I know a great bagel shop."

—∿∿∿∿⋁⋁⋁⋁⋁∿∿∿—

I wipe away the sweat on my hands as we approach the designated office building the top-secret NASA team rented for this project. I'm worried about having enough input, being insightful, but most importantly, I'm eager to see what they've discovered.

Stella rubs my arm as we enter the building and see the incredible setup. It looks like a miniature flight control room with about twelve computers in front of a big screen that displays their projected distance. There's a glass-enclosed room that was probably used as an executive office by its previous tenants. It now holds spare furniture. Engineers are at glowing tables where it looks like they are sketching prototypes of the orb that took Zain and Ali.

"Andrew! Nice to see you again. And the lovely Ms. Stella, welcome," Scooter says.

"Thank you. Glad to be here. What are we working on?" I ask. He guides us to some chairs around a small coffee table.

"You'll be excited to hear that Zain has already reached out, and he's adapting well. They have been sending messages to us each time they stop to explore. We don't believe they can communicate while 'slipping,' as you call it."

"So they're using regular radio wave technology? They must not be far." I turn to observe the big screen.

"Yes, you can see their path there. We're only following Zain's ship."

"What are your plans for when they get too far for radio waves? We shouldn't have to wait years to receive a message."

"Unfortunately, that's our only option for now."

"I have a question," Stella says. "Neil mentioned something about how humans didn't have the level of consciousness needed for space travel. Did they say sedation worked?"

He looks impressed that she remembered this detail. "Yes, it's remarkable. They claim his body will adjust, eventually, and he won't need to be sedated. But, as far as we know he's only awake when they stop to explore." Scooter leans in a little closer and whispers, "Can you imagine what was going through his head the first time the aliens sedated him?" He slaps his knee and laughs to himself. "He's got to be the bravest son of a bitch I've ever met."

"No doubt!" I wipe my hands on my pants again. My buddy is out there, and I'm scared for him. I hope he's not getting worn thin. "They must be doing a lot of exploring in that case."

"We could send more humans using sedatives if they return, and we're hoping they will. But who knows how far in the future that will be." He leans in again. "It really makes you wonder about those cave paintings with UFOs and strange figures. Maybe they came to Earth long ago, but their current generation doesn't have record of it."

"It does make you wonder," Stella agrees.

"In terms of communication, my passion in quantum mechanics has me curious if we could get creative and somehow work with quantum entanglement. I know it's been studied and witnessed even between satellites, and I wonder if we could somehow incorporate it." I know I am reaching a bit.

"Quantum entanglement. That would be a new one for us. That's the one that Einstein called spooky action at a distance, right? I remember something about that from college." Scooter leans back in his chair, and I think, judging by his age, that could have been forty years ago.

"Yes, but if we can entangle two satellites around Earth, hypothetically, we could sync up one that's here and one that's a hundred thousand light years away. They might have the tools and ability to link somehow. It's worth considering."

"Andrew." Stella stands and puts her hand on my shoulder. "Explain quantum entanglement again?"

I look up at her, confused. "Sure. Einstein describes it as when two particles are strongly correlated, they lose their individual quantum states and share a single, unified state. It's the ability of separated objects to share a condition or state."

Her face goes white. "This is it." She jerks her head in Scooter's direction. "This will seem improbable to you, but I believe the aliens communicate with each other using quantum entanglement. We just call it telepathy because we don't understand it. And I received a message from . . ." She looks at me. "A dream. And I think I'm making sense of it now."

"If that's true, if they actually use quantum entanglement, then it wouldn't matter where they are in the universe. Theoretically, they could communicate with each other instantaneously."

"Ms. Stella, you were able to speak to Ali telepathically while she was here on Earth, right?"

"Yes, but I never thought it could stretch across the galaxy. The aliens kept referring to our level of consciousness, and if I'm interpreting my message correctly, hallucinogens could be the answer." She turns to me and grips my shoulders. "Remember when Neil drugged me, and I couldn't connect with Ali? It was neuro-path disruptors or something like that."

"Right . . ."

"I had to take my psilocybin to break through. It wasn't a large dose, but enough for me to send her a message. Maybe hallucinogens enable us to find that connection or expand our consciousness far enough to be able to communicate, or even slip through dark energy." She stares at me as if hoping I'll say something.

Scooter clears his throat and puts his hand under his chin. "That's not our normal line of thinking when we're talking about space. We usually use math." He sounds unconvinced.

"Have you ever heard of an old soul?" I ask.

"Of course."

"Stella is an old soul. She's very in tune with everything that's going on. Without her, none of this would have happened. We need to look into this."

"How? Quantum entanglement communication involves extensive planning and experiments, as well as two identical mechanisms for sending and receiving information. If we go this route, we'd have to provide the aliens with a—"

"Brain?" Stella says. She's right. The soul has deeper connections than we give it credit for. "Bear with me," she pleads. "Is there a quiet room in here? A place where I could focus?"

"I'll show you." Scooter stands and leads us to the back hall, where six offices are clustered together.

I'm racking my brain trying to grasp Stella's idea. Einstein also had doubts, and he predicted there would have to be some sort of agreement between particles or secret information shared between the two that was undetectable.

Scooter opens the door with his nameplate and motions for us to go in first. Stella sits on the edge of one of his guest chairs, and I follow. Scooter takes a seat behind his makeshift desk, which appears to be a folding table.

"I know this might be frustrating as a scientist, but she might be onto something. We're dealing with quantum mechanics, which on the most basic level is very complex. I would call our situation complex, wouldn't you? I don't know the extent to which we could test this, but if Stella has a conditioned connection with Ali, they could be entangled and capable of communicating.

"And, if I'm right, humans could form a connection with an alien and gain access to communications through a soul-searching, consciousness-expanding hallucination, it seems." Stella is smiling, eyes wide with excitement, but Scooter's brows are furrowed.

"Have you ever experimented with drugs?" she asks.

He readjusts himself in his squeaky chair. "Yes, I did mushrooms in college." It appears his admission is painful.

"And how did you feel after?" she asks, sounding like a lawyer in court.

"Well." He looks off to the side, then leans back and grins. "I felt an overwhelming sense of peace. I remember wanting to play music and to be surrounded by my friends, to be outside in nature more. All good things."

"Exactly," she says. "They have amazing benefits. My therapist even prescribed me micro-dose psilocybin for my anxiety. I believe it holds incredible powers for connecting us to each other, nature, Earth, and potentially bigger things like the universe."

"Let me get this straight." Scooter holds his hands out in front of him. "You believe we can use hallucinogens to enable quantum entanglement for communicating with aliens who inhabit a planet that is one hundred light years away?"

"Shrooms or LSD may enable the connection for quantum entanglement to work. Expand our consciousness." She smiles. "I'll be the first to try it. Maybe if I could get connected with Ali, I could see if she has any friends who would be willing to connect with another human . . . cosmically speaking."

Scooter rubs his fingers together and looks back and forth between us.

I'll be the first to admit this will be nothing short of a miracle if it works. We'll be at the forefront of being able to travel faster than the speed of light. Potentially, a deeper level of consciousness is what we're lacking in order to slip.

Scooter settles back in his chair, looks at Stella, and sighs. "I'm going to let you have this one. You clearly have a special part in this, and I am in no place to sit here and judge. I have doubts, but if you're willing to be the guinea pig, feel free."

She leaps up and hugs me.

"I'll try to connect with Ali. We need a designated room for these experiments, and a qualified nurse onsite. I want to do this today. Can you make it happen, Scooter?"

"I'll make some phone calls."

"You're the best!" She runs over and kisses him on the cheek, then turns to face me, radiating from within, and sits on my lap. "You are a genius," she whispers. "What made you think of quantum entanglement?"

I wrap my arms around her and look proudly into her eyes. "When you spend your entire college career learning about this stuff, it's hard to unlearn it. I'm always thinking about it in the back of my mind."

She hugs me a little tighter. "Sounds like destiny."

———~www/\/\/\/\wwww~———

The NASA crew is surprisingly enthusiastic about putting together a makeshift "cosmic consciousness" room (which ends up looking more like a yoga studio). They remove the furniture from the glass-enclosed room and set up a projection screen displaying an endless loop of stars. There's a soft mat on the floor, fake plants for ambiance, and lots of water bottles.

Scooter negotiated a higher dose of psilocybin pills for testing. I would think Stella would be slightly nervous, but she is eager to get started.

She has a heart monitor strapped under her shirt and a vitals monitor on her arm. She enters the room with her pills and sits in the typical meditation position. We turn the lights off and wait for the drugs to kick in. We all stand on the outside of the glass, quietly watching.

After thirty minutes, she starts moving her head and looking around. Her eyes lock on the screen and get wide. She begins to hum and lies down on her back.

—∿∿∿∿∿∿∿—

Her vitals are good. Her heart rate is elevated, but still okay. I rub the back of my neck, hoping to release some tension. I don't like seeing her like this, but I know she needs to figure this all out on her own. How long is this going to take?

She starts to move her arms and leans on her elbows. I race into the room to try to help her. "Take it easy. Don't get up too fast."

"Andrew . . ."

"Yes," I say, scared something might be wrong. "I'm right here. You were out for five hours. Are you okay?"

"Five hours?" she asks, rubbing her bloodshot eyes.

"Yes, everyone has been on their toes waiting for you to wake up."

"I know what to do," she says very seriously. "I know where to go. Ali explained everything. She told me everything."

My heart might explode from excitement. "This is incredible. I can't wait to hear about it. You need to eat something first," I say, helping her up. The entire crew claps and cheers, and she smiles, keeping her head low. I lead her to the couch and bring her a muffin and coffee.

"I'd like to thank you all for your support in this bizarre idea I had, and thank you for staying with me, monitoring me," she says. "You'll be relieved to know that I got in touch with Ali." Cheers erupt again, and she holds her hand up. "And she believes in my theory. She believes any of you could make a connection. You must expand your consciousness. Does anyone else want to try?"

In a crew of about twenty people, no one is quick to volunteer.

Stella smiles. "The good news is, trying this won't kill you. I'm your example. This is safe. We'll all be here with you. She has designated a universal time slot every day at noon for one of her crew to meet in the spirit world with one of ours to attempt to match their brain sequences. I will give you specific instructions and guide your trip, so I'll be right there with you. As long as Scooter is okay with it, we can have someone try tomorrow. At noon. So you have time to think about it."

As she takes a bite of her muffin, a small man steps through the crowd. He's short, but his hair is styled to stand up tall as if to cunningly add to his height. He pulls off his glasses and fiddles with them in front of his chest.

"Hi, I'm Brent. I'm one of the control room specialists. I will . . . ," he gulps, "I will volunteer."

"Everybody give it up for Brent," I yell, and the crew applauds.

Going first is very intimidating, knowing you'll be trying to communicate with an alien somewhere in your mind. I will admit, it sounds terrifying. I will do it for Stella, eventually. And for Zain. He's the bravest of us all. This is the least I can do to show support for him. I'm proud of how brave Zain and Stella have been. It's my turn.

"Brent, you're already a hero for volunteering. If you want, I can go first. Stella and I are close, so it might be easier for her to show me the ropes. But it's up to you."

A wave of relief sweeps over Brent's face, and he exhales a deep breath as if he had been holding it ever since he stood up. He shakes my hand. "It's a deal."

"All right, you heard the woman," Scooter yells. "Everyone go home, rest, and be back by eight a.m. Good night." The crowd disperses, and people whisper to each other on the way out. The excitement is tangible. I sit next to Stella and inhale deeply.

"You did it. You really did it."

"Well . . ." she says, looking around. My heart sinks.

"What is it?"

She takes another bite of her muffin and a sip of water, then looks down and puts her hands over her eyes.

The more time that passes, the more curious I get. "You're scaring me."

"I *know* what I saw and what I experienced. *But.*"

"But . . ."

"*But* I don't know if it was just my brain making shit up. There's only one way to find out."

"To find out what?"

"To find out if I actually met with Ali and communicated with her, or if it was just some fake hallucination. I mean, that shit is intense. Ali took me to these strange places that she claims are inside us all, deep within our soul. It's a long journey through yourself, ultimately leading to this great hall of endless pillars with ancient-looking faces on every side, almost Egyptian-esque." She looks up at the ceiling. "At first, it was so scary to me. I thought I was lost. I was running as fast as I could, but there was no end in sight. The humming was overbearing at times, and the more I ran, the louder it got. Finally, I gave up and stopped running. I stopped being afraid. I realized then, in my calm state, I was in the soul itself. It's woven together, linking us all for eternity. So, I stayed there, waiting for her. Ali found me, and we embraced. She said, 'Here we can make the connection,' and I woke up."

"So, tomorrow, we'll find out if it's real. Tomorrow, if I can connect with someone in the hall of souls, then it works."

"It's worth it if it forges instant communication, right?"

"Of course," I say, grabbing her hands. "That means you should be able to connect with Ali right now. No matter how far away she is."

"Yes. I'm so nervous, and I'm so exhausted, but I have to try, or I won't sleep tonight." She holds her finger up. "I probably won't be able to sleep either way. But I need to know."

"Go for it. You've got this."

She closes her eyes and bites her lip. Then she's screaming and laughing and crying and hugging me. We jump up and down together and kiss. This got so real. We stop jumping and try to catch our breath.

"What'd you ask her?"

"I said, 'Ali, was that real? Did you really meet me in that hall?' and she said, 'Yes!'"

"Ask her how Zain is doing."

She smiles even bigger. "She already told me! As I was thinking of asking her, she answered. Zain is doing great. He's still eating the dehydrated food but has introduced some of their vegetables into his diet. He's doing great!"

"This is incredible. You are incredible." I pick her up, swing her around, and kiss her again.

"You're next, buddy." She cackles. "Get ready to have an alien hardwired into your brain!"

"When you put it that way, I'm glad I get one more day with my brain all to myself."

I notice Scooter is standing off to the side, patiently waiting for our private moment to be over. Stella pulls away from me and waves him in.

He asks all sorts of questions about Ali: their location, Zain's health status, how the slipping went under sedation. His face is bright red from asking so many questions so quickly.

Finally, Stella puts her hand on her head and turns to me.

"I'm starving."

"I know a place. Let's go."

—~~~wwwwww~~—

Stella and I stay up most of the night talking. She seems so different after her trip; so sure of herself. She was able to speak to Ali before any of this cosmic consciousness was in the cards and had that initial agreement with her counterpart. I wonder if my hallucination will be what she hopes. I don't want to let her down. What if it doesn't work for me? The whole NASA crew is counting on me.

I rummage around my messy room to find my books on quantum entanglement to ease my nerves. Maybe if I read up on it, I will be more confident. I'm enthralled in my reading but hear Stella wake up to make breakfast. She doesn't disturb me and sets my coffee and breakfast on my desk next to me.

"I'm essentially going to need to use my brain as a receiver and pretend I'm using entanglement-based quantum-key distribution the way China experimented with their satellites and—"

"Andrew, as much as you need to work this all out in your head, everything will change when you take the shrooms. Your perception of things will no longer be linear or even science-based. It happens on a much deeper level. You'll see." She walks back to the kitchen and calls out, "I didn't read any of those books."

"You're right. I'm over-analyzing it." I shut the books and rub my face. I try to eat a few bites of breakfast, but my nerves fill up my stomach.

"I will be with you the whole time, guiding you. Try not to worry."

"I'm not worried about the drugs. I'm worried about letting you down. What if my brain can't get linked? If it doesn't work for me, no one else will feel confident in your plan. What if you're the only—"

"Andrew." She steps in front of me and wraps her arms around my neck. "I am fulfilled in life knowing we saved Ali and her people and continuing to live here with you. I honestly believe this is your dream being revealed through me. This is your project. You're the NASA correspondent who thought of quantum entanglement. This is your destiny. Go in today knowing that things are moving in the right direction. This might be the next step you need to figure something else out. Keep an open mind."

She knows what to say to show me the big picture. I reach my face down to hers and lift her up. She feels weightless in my arms, and I feel her fingers run through my hair, melting my stress away with her kiss. She's wrong about one thing. She thinks it's my dream to travel in space, but that was before she entered the equation. My stars have aligned already. Whatever the future holds, she will be by my side.

When we get back to the lab, the room is buzzing. I'm greeted with high fives and chants. I feel more like a star quarterback than a science nerd about to take shrooms.

The preparations are minimal, and we enter the room together with the pills. Stella sits next to me.

"How much am I taking?"

"Do you really want to know?" she asks.

I turn to look at her and know the answer doesn't matter. I take the pills and stare at scenes from outer space—a place that has always been my biggest intrigue. Closing my eyes, I accept the darkness and fear nothing. I hear what sounds like angels singing in the distance. Then they get louder and louder.

"Follow the humming," a voice says. I know it's Stella, but it sounds too far away. I feel the world around me vanish. When I open my eyes, I'm sitting in the same spot, but I can't feel my body. The screen ahead is outlined in a ring of moving, flickering neon lights. The ring becomes three-dimensional, forming a tunnel. The ring expands until it fills my field of vision, and I enter, like Alice tumbling down the rabbit hole.

I feel myself slipping farther away from the reality I know, and I clutch my chest. Maybe I took too much. Maybe I'll never leave this place. Maybe I'm dying.

"Focus on your breathing," says the voice.

My body feels like it's being thrown and thrashed about. I picture myself trapped in the ocean during a hurricane; waves crush me before I can gasp for air.

"This is the body high. Push through."

I sink, heavy as lead. My body reaches the ocean floor, and I'm no longer afraid. I imagine myself as a boulder, heavy, having found its final resting place with the sea creatures. With no responsibilities, I observe the passing fish. An octopus peers at me with curiosity. He knows very well I am not a rock.

The sun pierces the water, and the darkness dissipates. I feel more fluid now, like I can swim. I push myself toward the light, toward the singing.

"What do you see?"

"A way out."

I surface brand new, reborn. A tingling sensation engulfs me, and I hear my name.

"Look inside yourself."

Another darkness descends, and I search for my body. I feel myself existing, but only once my vision opens do I see my actual self. I'm glowing. A grid of lights around me moves and stretches with me. The grid continues forever in every direction. I feel connected to the cosmos, in a three-dimensional net of consciousness. Every movement produces vibrations in the net that travel as far as I can see.

"Find the hall of souls."

I struggle to grip the grid, hoping to move through it somehow. An ocean of closed eyes stretches along the grid. I stare, and the eyes open to reveal themselves to me. If I stare long enough, they glow, but if I lose focus or turn my head, they dim again.

With all my willpower, I keep my gaze steady. It seems like an eternity, but I don't break away. The eyes glow brighter and brighter until they combine into one solid light. I readjust my vision and find myself in a great hall of never-ending pillars, right where Stella wants me to be.

I lean in closer to observe a pillar and see the most beautiful fractals slowly rotating and morphing into new colors and patterns, like the Mandelbrot set.

"Find them."

I break my gaze and peer around but only see pillars in every direction. Slowly, they bend and split in half, rotating until there is a reflection below each. A maze of optical illusions, endless pillars above and below, and as far as I can see.

Overwhelmed by my surroundings, I peer at the invisible floor, and that's when I see him. He's looking down at me from the other side of the universe. We're within feet of each other. He's glowing in vivid hues. I know he can tell I'm nervous, and he greets me with a smile.

He bends and touches his floor, and his hand appears to be touching the glowing grid beneath me. "*Ali sends her best. Call me Roman.*"

I can hear him speak without words! Nervous and insecure, I bend on one knee as if looking into a pond. "*I'm Andrew. Thank you for meeting with me.*" He nods, and I place my hand on the floor over his. The grid glows between our hands, spreading light in all directions.

I feel a pull from behind me. "Come back!"

Roman stands and looks down at me, giving off the sense that I will see him again. With my hand still stretched out, I see myself retracing my steps through the cosmic voyage; up and away from the pillars, through the ocean of eyes, through a starry universe, and when I open my eyes, I'm back in the glass room with my head resting on Stella's lap.

"Andrew?" she asks.

My heart is racing, nearly beating out of my chest. I suck in a few deep breaths. "Yes?" I whisper.

"How are you?"

"Water."

Stella helps me up to a sitting position and hands me a bottle of water. She's staring at me with such intensity, probably too afraid to ask if I formed the connection.

I play it cool, but I'm feeling the same as Stella did yesterday, wondering if it was all a hallucination. I don't want to keep her waiting.

"Roman? Can you hear me?"

"I hear you, brother. I'm here."

My eyes well up, and I can't hold back the relief. I'm not ashamed, and I let my tears fall. I can see Stella's shock and disappointment as she holds her hands to her mouth.

"It's okay. We can try again. I was asking too much of you. Maybe I am the only one who—"

"Stella," I say, trying to catch my breath.

"Are you in pain? Are you okay?"

I gather myself and take her hands in mine. I muster up the words and say, "I met Roman. We made the connection."

"What?" she asks, voice cracking.

"It worked! I can hear him now. I already tried talking to him.

We're communicating." We stand and embrace. I hear a roar of applause behind us, cheering and whistling. Stella and I stare at each other, crying.

"You led me there. I couldn't have done it without you."

"I'm so impressed. I'm blown away. This is incredible."

"I know," I say, holding her close. "How long was I out?"

"I have no idea." She points to someone behind the glass.

He looks at his watch and mouths, "Five hours."

"Are you famished?"

"Yes, I'm starving!"

"Let's go sit down and eat and talk it through." She grabs my hand and leads me to the couch in the common area. She hands me a muffin that I devour in five bites, and the aching in my head dissipates.

"Roman, it's an honor to know you. What role do you play in your travels?"

"Thank you for finding me. I am in charge of mapping the clear pathways for the ships. Space is filled with debris."

"I look forward to our communications. If you are with him, tell Zain what happened, and tell him we're thinking about him."

"I will, of course."

"This is exciting."

"Truly!"

I meet Stella's anxious gaze. "His name is Roman, and he works in space surveillance."

Stella squeals, and the crew surrounding us takes notes.

"Do you think you could ask him to make tomorrow's match be someone from engineering?" Scooter calls out.

"That's actually a great idea. I will. Does that mean we should let Brent wait another turn? Maybe we should match an engineer with an engineer."

The rumble of the crew grows louder and louder as more ideas spread. Stella stares at me with her hands over her mouth, eyes full of tears. I understand exactly how she feels.

This is truly monumental. The relief, the excitement, the hope. It's overwhelming. I pull her close and hold her. Our future together just got a lot more interesting.

ANDREW

The past few months have been a blur of chaos. NASA came up with a plan to match people in an order that catapulted our technologies. We now have five engineers, four space surveillance specialists, and five geophysicists connected with aliens. Stella led them all through their journeys.

Our crew has doubled in size, and we have an official documenter who takes photographs and observes our meetings and plans. As far as *we* all have come in realizing and accepting our goals, I still wonder if the general public would be able to grasp the fact that there are aliens, we communicate with them, and that humans will soon have the ability to be a multi-planetary species.

In due time, we'll be using our communications to build copycat versions of their ships. The big ones they use for space travel, and smaller ones that could replace our need for cars and small aircraft. We'll experiment with the spaceship in our oceans and atmosphere. Then, a few brave souls will venture into space. After that, dark energy.

There are special skills needed to travel at such high speed, and we're lucky enough to be able to address these issues with our matches. As great as it is to have this information, experience seems to be the most important aspect, and we are lacking it entirely.

Our history with space travel has been layered with math and engineering, predictions and precautions, and human limitations. We've been using the wrong type of materials, wrong energy sources, and our goals have been minuscule. The aliens have taught us things we couldn't have even dreamed up. We have learned how to manipulate minerals into precious stones that provide energy to the ships. We can now create rebound detectors for small particles that damage the ship. We've studied their methods of slipping through dark energy, but we won't fully understand it until we try it ourselves.

Today we are hoping to speak with Zain using my connection with Roman. Ali has been too busy translating for Zain to ever really talk with Stella. Knowing Zain, when he gets excited about something, he goes all in. I'm sure he's running Ali dry with all his questions and data collections. He's slowly learning their written language to help with his dependency on her, and he's eager to learn their math. I thought he'd jump at the opportunity to speak with us, but he clearly feels comfortable out there, and his goals are important to him.

What started as a mission to save an alien species turned into a mission to save humanity. They are returning the favor, tenfold. Our unconventional methods have won over the skeptics within our team as our quantum entanglement matches are proving to be most useful. Stella and I have been working nonstop for months. Knowing her job here is imperative to our success, she took a leave of absence from teaching.

As I stand, admiring the hustle and bustle of our crew working tirelessly to help our endeavors, I feel an overwhelming sense of pride. These are good people, who stepped up, even when it meant facing the unknown and confronting fears of uncertainty. I meet Stella's eyes through the room. She's walking toward me, nearly jumping with joy.

"Are you excited to talk with Zain today?"

"I am beyond excited. Roman said he will have some exciting news. My mind has been all over the place trying to imagine what it could be."

"I know!" She claps, getting more excited. "Do you think he's figured out all the spooky mysteries of space yet?"

"Probably not all of them." I laugh. "Although, I'm sure he's at least discovered the importance of keeping an open mind."

"Yes, he had no idea *just* how open it needed to be."

"Andrew, I've got Zain here."

"Fantastic!"

"He's with Zain now," I whisper to Stella, hoping not to lose focus. She shushes the room and points to me with dramatic emphasis.

I hear random questions being asked from the crew, which I promptly ask Roman and relay his replies. Zain answers more sarcastically than seriously, which is a great relief to us to get a laugh in.

I feel the anticipation weighing in, and it's time to ask about the big news.

"They believe," I tell the waiting crew, "that we might be capable of slipping through dark energy . . . the ones who have matched . . . and they are returning one ship to Earth to take us along under their guidance."

The room is still silent, but jaws are dropped, and arms are stretched high in the air.

"And it's Ali's ship. Zain is coming home."

The crew cannot contain their excitement, and the usual clamor commences. I continue speaking with Roman.

"Is Zain disappointed he won't get to see your planet?"

"He is more concerned with humans experimenting with slipping. He wants to go home, get matched, and properly prepare for a new mission. He wants to be able to slip. He's very jealous of those who have matches."

"Tell him we're all jealous that he's with you guys."

"You're too kind. Are you going to join the first trial runs?"

"You mean slipping?"

"Yes."

"That's a good question, and I'm not sure what the answer is yet. Will keep you updated."

"Of course. We'll keep in touch."

"How far away are you?"

"One month, max."

"See you soon."

The room is still buzzing with excitement as I snap back into the moment. Scooter whistles, and the room quiets.

"When will they be here?" he yells from across the room.

"Within the month."

"Frank." Scooter points to his left. "Let the FBI and military know what's going on. Lowell, make sure we have enough crew to evaluate Zain upon arrival. Samantha, figure out who is willing to travel back with the ship. I only want half of those who are matched to go. We need some to stay here for communications. Andrew—"

"Yes!" I blurt out in attention.

"Figure out what they expect from us and how we can prepare."

"Absolutely."

Everyone breaks off into their sectors and starts planning for the occasion. I hug Stella with my arm around her shoulders and kiss her forehead. She's awfully quiet, and I wish we were alone.

"What's on your mind?"

"I need a break," she says as she presses her temples. "Let's go home for a while."

"Sure thing." I grab our coats and lead her out of the office building. She seems distracted on the way home.

"What's going on?" I ask, hoping she's not too tired to talk.

"I've been talking with Ali, and—"

"And what?"

"I knew about her return home. In fact, it was my idea."

"Is that so?" I mumble. Where is she going with this?

"Yeah, Ali and I were talking about how exciting the whole quantum entanglement communications are and how it could open up a lot of opportunities for humans, and she agreed with me that it could be possible for us to slip through dark energy with our new level of consciousness, and—"

"And?"

"And, at the time, we decided we couldn't miss the opportunity to try it out with their guidance. They chose to turn around and head back to Earth. I told her it wouldn't feel right to send anyone out there without us since this was all my idea. We would have to be the first." She looks intently into my eyes.

My heart seems to be malfunctioning, and I pull over to the side of the road to catch my breath. I put my hands over my mouth to try to slow my breathing. She has reconsidered. She actually wants to do this with me.

"I wanted it to be a surprise. I finally opened my heart to the idea and knew that I needed to do this for the team, for you."

"Stella, this—"

"But," she says, grabbing my hands. I feel my stomach churn. She closes her eyes and opens them, spilling tears on her lap. "That was before I found out I'm pregnant."

"What?" I freeze.

"I'm pregnant. I've been too scared to say it out loud, but I'm three months in. Andrew," she cries, "I've been pregnant before. Twice. But I miscarried. So, this time, at first, I thought my cycle was off because we were so busy and stressed, but I'm pregnant. I was mentally preparing myself all this time for space travel, but I guess the universe had other plans."

"Do you realize what this means?"

Her eyes grow wide and she wipes her hair out of her face as she looks around nervously. "It means we can't be the first, after all."

I shake my head. She's only worried about my feelings about space travel. She thinks I'm going to resent her.

"It means," I say, holding her face, "that you have made me the happiest man on Earth." She cries and leans into my hands.

"Stella, as amazing as all of this is, as much as I love everything we've done together, you and our baby are the most important things in the universe to me." I lift her face and kiss her. "You are the bravest, most incredible woman I have ever known, and of all the adventures we've had, this is by far my favorite one."

She moans. "The timing is unbelievable."

"It's perfect," I whisper. "Are you happy?"

She tugs at her fingers and hands. "In this moment in time, it's hard to deny the possibility everything happens for a reason. Even horrible, painful things. I've been so worried about these aliens that I nearly forgot how special it is to be human, and I'm so thankful to be on this journey with you. Raising a baby with you seems right. It's perfect. It's as if it was always meant to be."

"I know." I rub my hands over my face. "I love learning about our new friends and their way of life. It makes me appreciate my human existence on a new level. Life is precious. We just created a new one together. How amazing is that?"

"Will you come with me to my doctor's appointment today?" she asks.

"How could I miss that? Have you told your mom yet?"

"No, I want to wait until we see the baby and make sure everything is okay." She crosses her arms tight. "My previous two pregnancies never made it to the three-month mark. Hopefully, it's a good sign that I have this time."

"Stella, everything will be okay. I know it. Do we have time to run home to tell Chester?"

Stella laughs. "Yes, I think Chester can keep it a secret."

STELLA

On our way to the doctor's appointment, anxiety sweeps into my gut, flipping and twisting with dread. It will be strange to see my old OBGYN. I will have to fill her in on the painful past of losing James. My biggest nerves come from finding out about the well-being of my baby. I'm not letting myself get my hopes up. I can't.

My first miscarriage shocked me. I was sad, confused, in a daze. But the second was traumatizing. I didn't get out of bed for days. My doctor swears miscarriages are extremely common, and that most women don't talk about them. I can understand not wanting to talk, but it makes me worry that something is wrong with my body. Something is keeping me from being able to carry a child. If I have a third miscarriage, I don't think I'll ever want to risk getting pregnant again. It's too painful.

I can't help but think of James. Not too long ago, I was pregnant with his babies. I close my eyes and imagine them all together, shining their light.

When I finally asked Ali about my last meeting with James, she said our spirits can reveal themselves in all manner of ways. James's message was so urgent he had to pull me into the spirit world. It was his way of watching over me. His message played a key role in all of our success with matches and expanding our consciousness, which makes me so happy. He knew I'd figure it out. I hope he feels my love and gratitude.

We pull into the parking garage, and Andrew comes around to open my door. "Let's go see our baby!"

I can't move. I can't hold back the tears, and Andrew scoops me up, setting me on my feet. "What's wrong?"

"I'm just so scared," I say through sobs. "I want this baby to be okay. I can't bear the thought of our baby not being okay." He pulls me in and lets me cry on his shoulder.

"You're the strongest person I know. We're going to march up there and hear our baby's heartbeat and see a blurry black-and-white photo of his or her head, and we're going to celebrate. I know it." He brushes the hair out of my face, and I nod in agreement. He grabs my hand, and we go into the elevator together.

I enter the waiting room and sign in on the clipboard next to the sliding glass window. This is a small office filled with women who have worked here for twenty to thirty years. The same office manager, the same nurses, the same doctor. Dr. Roberts is reaching retirement age.

We sit down together among the other pregnant women, who appear restless.

"She had to do an emergency C-section about an hour ago," the lady on our right says. "She shouldn't be much longer, though.

I remember mine only took about an hour. The sutures take the longest."

"Oh," I say. "So, is this your second baby?"

She leans back in the chair, resting her hands on top of her belly. She looks to be about eight months pregnant. "This will be my fourth. My first two came so fast, I had to cross my legs until Dr. Roberts could make it. But my third was breech."

"I see. I can understand why you'd want to play it safe with a C-section," I reply, feeling relieved to have a bit of a distraction.

"Those C-sections sure are a blessing, but Lord, I hope I can get away without one this last time. Recovery was much longer after the C-section."

"I see." I'm not sure what else to say, as I am not familiar with the healing process after birth. Her southern accent is comforting, and I'm surprised she had the energy to curl her hair and do her makeup. I'm a bit shabby compared to her.

She attempts to lean over and dig in her bag that's on the floor, and I resist the urge to help her. She pulls out a worn-out book and hands it to me.

"I just finished this if you need something to read. A flight attendant gave it to me when she finished it, so I might as well pass it along too."

I take the book and read the title. "*The Long Goodbye* by Suzanne Gail. Wow," I say, "she's a cult classic."

"And there's good reason for it."

"Thank you. I'll read it and pass it along. It only seems right if you put your name in it now that you've finished it. Maybe we'll see it again someday with the whole inside cover filled."

She laughs, and her pregnant belly bounces with every sound. "That's such a lovely thought. How could I say no to that?" She bends again for her purse, nearly busting open at the belly button, and retrieves a pen. She sets the book on her tummy and writes her name.

"Emily Windsor?" a nurse beckons from the doorway.

"Enjoy the book!" She smiles and follows the nurse through the door.

"I will, thank you!" I open the book and see she wrote "Flight Attendant" before her name.

Andrew jabs my arm. "I love you," he says.

I put my head on his shoulder and close my eyes. I begin to read, and time passes quickly. The other women's names are called about every twenty minutes, but I continue reading to distract myself, and the story easily sweeps my anxieties away. After about sixty pages, I hear my name. I dog-ear the page and gather my things.

Andrew puts his hand on the small of my back and follows me into the room. I sit down on the patient chair and get my blood pressure taken by the same nurse that's done it before. I wonder if she remembers me.

She jots down the results and gives me a paper robe to put on. She tells me I'm next in line and that Dr. Roberts should be in shortly and then backs out of the room with her little cart.

I look at Andrew in the corner of the room. He's sitting with a smirk on his face.

"This is why they put that curtain in the room," I whisper, pointing above his shoulder. He grabs it and pulls the curtain around him. I have nothing I'm hiding from him, but these fluorescent lights are harsh, and I deserve to change in peace. I put the paper robe on.

When the rustling of the paper subsides, Andrew peaks his head out. "Am I good?"

"Yes," I huff.

He pushes the curtain to the side and sighs, then walks over and holds my hands. In my bout of worry, I'm distracted. He turns my face so I'm looking at him.

"Everything will be okay," he says, answering my restless thoughts. I love how positive he's being, but I can't allow myself to believe it yet.

The door opens, and Dr. Roberts wheels in her laptop. "Hi, Stellaaa. Hi, Ja—" She stops rolling her table. "Hi, I'm Dr. Roberts," she says, sticking her hand out.

"I'm Andrew. Nice to meet you."

She greets me with a smile and such relief on her face that I begin to feel at ease. "I'm glad you're here. I am so excited to hear you're pregnant. Let's get some information, and then we'll take a look at that baby."

I nod, but my mouth goes dry. I answer a few questions about my cycle and what vitamins I've been taking. She is thrilled to see I should be close to fifteen weeks pregnant and then scolds me for not coming in sooner. I'm sure she understands why.

She pushes the computer aside and helps me lie back in the chair. Andrew comes to my side and holds my hand. Dr. Roberts opens my robe, lays a towel over my pelvic area, and lubricates the ultrasound probe.

"Let's see here," she says, pressing the probe onto my lower belly. My heart sinks, but I crane my neck to see the monitor.

Desperate, I ask, "Is there a heartbeat?"

"It would help if I turned on the volume. Sorry." She continues searching and readjusting the volume.

She's too quiet. This isn't good. I lie my head back on the chair and stare at the ceiling, then at Andrew. His eyes are glued to the monitor.

The most beautiful sound in the world reaches my ears.

"There it is!" she exclaims.

Andrew's hand tightens on mine as I see the outline of our baby on the screen. I look at Dr. Roberts for reassurance, and her eyes are squinted.

"That's good, right? It sounds good?" I ask, still waiting to breathe.

"Do you hear that?" She smirks.

Andrew gives a chuckle and covers his mouth. I'm too scared to ask what the smirking is about, so I just stare.

"Is it twins?" Andrew asks through his hands.

"It's twins! That's two heartbeats, Stella. Let me try to . . . oh, here they are!"

I crane my head and see both babies, side by side, perfectly healthy and beautiful. I can't stop watching them, and I feel my nerves melt away. The butterflies in my stomach change from dread to joy. My heart is rushing, gushing. My mouth is agape as I let it sink in. Andrew kisses my cheek as I stare in disbelief.

Dr. Roberts takes some measurements and confirms they are fifteen weeks old. "You are all coming along great. Congratulations, honey. I am going to take great care of you and your babies. You need to come see me in three weeks. Until then, take it easy. Enjoy this."

I nod and thank her as she leaves.

Andrew is ecstatic. He grabs my shoulders and yells, "Twins!"

I laugh and hush him. "I can't believe it," I say, wiping away my tears. "Two babies. I'm so happy." I begin to sob. He holds me close, and I hear his heart beating wildly.

"This is the best day of my life, Stella. This is the best feeling in the world." He takes my clothes and helps me dress. When I'm ready to leave, he wraps his arm around me, and we go down the hall.

I remember this hall. I remember sitting in that chair by that office door, scheduling my D&C after my second miscarriage. I felt so much guilt and sadness carrying my losses down these halls. But here I am, finally feeling joy and relief, so much relief. Those dark memories seem far away, and I squeeze Andrew's hand.

On our way back to the car, Andrew is talking a thousand miles an hour. "My sisters are going to lose it. Which room will they stay in? Or do they need separate rooms? Do you think it's a boy and a girl? Or two boys or two girls? It doesn't matter to me. I wonder how the schools on the island are doing—"

"Andrew," I say delicately, "slow down. You're panicking."

"Right. I'm just so excited." He smiles big at me, making me melt.

"I know. Me too. This is wild."

"Invite your mom up. I need to meet her. We can tell her in person."

"Wow. I don't know if I can wait that long to tell her. But it would be best. I'll call her now."

"Good! And then can I tell my sisters?"

"Yes. Now, hush."

"Mom?" I say with my throat tightening. "No, everything is great. I'm fine. I, um, need you to come meet someone. Will you come visit?" I look at Andrew and smile. "Great. The sooner the better. Come this weekend if you can. Perfect. Let me know, and we'll come pick you up at the airport. Okay, love you." I hang up, and Andrew's phone is already on a video call with his sisters. They seem impatient.

"Okay, guys, we have some news." Andrew pulls me closer so we're both in the frame. "You ready?" he asks with a big smile. They squeal and shriek, clearly irritated by the question. "Stella's pregnant!" he says and kisses me. They look at me as if to verify through me that he's telling the truth. When I cry, they cry. I enjoy the sincerity of their reaction, before I add, "With twins." His sisters are ecstatic and demand we come celebrate and have a family dinner night this weekend. We agree, hang up, and revel in this joyous moment.

ANDREW

For the past few days, I was exceedingly distracted. My mind is still torn, dreaming about humanity's potential for space travel and the magnitude of that, as well as the idea of being a father and making a family with the love of my life.

My trip on psilocybin left a lasting impact on my view of life. It was overwhelmingly beautiful and vivid and provided me with peace. Peace about life and death, peace about being connected to the cosmos, and peace about our goals. My deep connection to the universe has enabled me to understand the beauty of its endlessness. I'm eternally grateful for everything I learned before and after my trip.

Roman and I are making plans with NASA, and things are going smoothly on their return trip to Earth. Since Zain has to be sedated to slip, they are trying to work around his sleep schedule to keep him awake and active at the levels he's used to. It's taking them a little longer this way, but it's worth it to keep Zain healthy.

When we send some of our matched crew back with Ali, we will prove humans have the ability to travel faster than the speed of light. We will advance the limits of humanity and travel across the galaxy, with hopes to make the human race a multi-planetary species. Half of our matched crew is preparing for the flight. The other half is busy learning advanced technology from their alien counterparts.

As I'm walking through the lab, peeking in on everyone's work, I don't hold back my questions. Luckily, the scientists here love taking the time to explain what they're working on.

"Chang, any progress?" I ask, leaning over her worktable. She's matched with an alien named Sealia. "Hi, Andrew!" she says, greeting me with a big smile. She's holding a strange-looking material. "Sealia has been explaining to me that our composite materials used for fighter jets and space shuttles need major improvements. Our team has been working on creating metamaterials that have unusual electromagnetic properties, some even affect visibility at certain wavelengths." She tilts the material and places a pen on the other side of it. It's as if the translucent material makes the pen disappear, and I can see only the table beneath.

"That's freaking unbelievable." She hands me the metamaterial and the pen and lets me try it out.

Chang laughs. "I also can't believe how amazing it is. Imagine an entire vehicle made from this." She then puts her hands to her head and mimes her head exploding. "You wouldn't have any blind spots or engine blocking your view. Complete visibility."

"No kidding. So impressive!" I thank her for sharing and move along.

We're getting alien technology without having to reverse engineer anything, so our crew is making major progress in a very short amount of time. We are still a long way away from building a usable ship, especially since it will be powered by an anti-gravity propulsion system, a technology completely foreign to humans.

As I reach the hall, I notice Scooter leaving his office. His face is stark white, and he's absently staring straight ahead, seemingly in shock. With growing concern, I walk toward him.

"Good morning, Scooter. You feeling okay?"

He continues as if he didn't hear me. I speak a little louder this time. "Scooter?"

I startle him out of his trance, and he jerks his head toward me with a grim look on his face.

"What's wrong?" I ask.

He looks over my shoulder, then left and right, grabs my arm, and pulls me into his office.

"Swanson called," he says, and closes the door behind him.

"Yeah, he calls every few days to check in, right?"

"Andrew." He walks to his desk chair. "We're doing things in this lab that humans have only dreamed of for centuries."

"Isn't it incredible?"

"Yes, but . . ." He leans on his forearms. "Ever since we started taking engineering lessons from the aliens, Swanson has been pushing back. He says we're taking it too far."

"How could we possibly be taking it too far?" I ask, shuffling my feet. "We have to take these leaps if we want to keep up with evolution. By the time humans would figure this out, if ever, it would be too late to save everyone."

"We're talking about creating a mode of transportation that uses free energy. Ridding the world of a resource scarcity will shatter the world economy and government structures."

"Resource scarcity is what propagates war. Think about how

many other things we could focus on as a species if we didn't have to fight over oil. This can only be good, Scooter. We have to press on."

"America started as a nation that takes what it wants. That isn't going to change. Swanson said if we succeed with this brand-new technology, it will leak. Eventually, we won't be the only ones flying UFOs." He leans back in his chair and pulls his leg over his knee. "The ship the aliens are showing us can fly without making a sound. It has the potential to be invisible to the human eye. Can you imagine what other nations would do with this technology? If we're going to start flying UFOs, we have to be prepared for the rest of the world to fly them. And, as it turns out, the US military doesn't want to even the playing field."

Sweat drips down my temple. "So, you're saying humans can't be trusted? That it's better to live in a perpetual state of war than to evolve? You don't think this could unite humanity?" I ask, feeling more frantic as time goes on.

"Swanson is following orders. This comes from over his head. We have to do the same."

I stand up in defense mode. "Wait, wait. You're not going to pull the plug, are you? We could take the project somewhere else. We could sign non-disclosure agreements. Make this top secret with NASA only without involving the military. We can stop building the ship and focus on the technology instead. We could figure out how to slowly introduce this to humanity."

Suddenly, I feel sick. I'm in the same position as Neil. This was his plan all along. He was gradually revealing these technologies. The difference is his motive was personal gain and glory. He wanted to be worshiped.

Did we completely derail evolution by meeting with him? He had succumbed to the frailties of human existence. He got selfish and felt threatened when we came into the picture.

"What if Neil were the one here creating all of these new technologies?"

"First, it would be treason to take this project somewhere else. Second, Neil was nowhere near creating free energy. Not even he could explain this one to the government."

Should I inform Scooter of Neil's secret identity?

"What about our crew? They are literally dialed in telepathically to aliens. Do you really think we can keep them from connecting with their counterparts? They're scientists. It will be torture for them to hold on to this information."

Scooter takes a pen from his pocket and fiddles with it while I continue.

"What about Zain? He's on his way home."

"There's no doubt that we're bringing Zain home." He looks around on his desk and takes out a piece of paper. He scribbles a few words on it and passes it to me.

They're listening. Place is bugged.

My eyes jolt wide and meet his. I throw my hands up. I can't believe this.

"All right," I say, "can we at least eat lunch before we figure this out? I'm starving." I flick my head toward the door, signaling we should leave.

"Sounds good. Let's go." He takes his hat and jacket and leads the way. He looks at me intently and pulls his phone out of his pocket, puts it in the mail cubby by the door, and puts his finger over his mouth while he motions for me to do the same.

As we step outside, he says, "Let's just walk. I'm not sure if our cars are tapped."

"This is not okay. There's no way we can stop now. We've gone too far down the rabbit hole to turn back, and you know it."

Scooter shushes me, and his eyes dart around. "I've been working with NASA for my entire career, and I've only dreamed of this kind of potential for humans. This project has revealed so much and given me real hope for the future. There's no fucking way I'm going to let some ex-military FBI idiot tell me what to do with my team."

I jump with joy and act out my best Tiger Woods air punch. "I knew you felt the same way. I knew it!"

"Now, wait a minute." He hushes my excitement. "We've got to go about this the right way. We cannot argue with Swanson. We absolutely have to do what he says."

"What do you mean?"

"What mama don't know won't hurt her."

"But the surveillance. How could we get away with continuing if they're watching and listening?"

"We'll plan it out with the crew, but we have at least one method of communication that they can't track," he says with one eyebrow lifted.

"Genius. What will we do when we finish making a prototype?"

"We'll send the blueprints anonymously to every nation across the globe and force the US to join the revolution."

"Fuck those war-obsessed assholes."

"Fuck 'em."

"Let's do this. Tell Roman what's going on. The FBI will make us abandon the project after Zain returns, and we'll have to give up all the information we've gathered. Roman needs to pass on the message that it's up to the crew if they want to adhere to that or not. We will figure out a way to continue privately, without any suspicion from the government. The safety of our crew is the top priority."

"Got it."

"After the crew understands the cruciality of secrecy, we can proceed. We'll never be able to all meet in one place again, but there are ways around that. I've got an idea. Roman needs to relay the information to his people, who will, in turn, tell our crew at one thirty p.m. today what's going on. We need to be in the room when it happens."

"Perfect. I'll tell Roman. Listen, Scooter, thank you."

He grabs my shoulder. "For the future of humanity."

"For the future of humanity."

As we walk to the lab, I try to explain to Roman the complexities of war and government control. I elaborately apologize for the extra steps that need to be taken but plead with him to keep helping us. We decide the crew will provide me with a hand signal during the conference to give me their answer. A tug on the ear if they're in, and a chin-scratch if they want to follow the government's orders and abandon all knowledge of the project.

I pace the aisles, waiting for 1:30 to arrive. When it finally comes, there's a hush around the room. I walk to a central location where I can see everyone.

They each stare off, then their jaws drop, and a few hands cover mouths. There's a general sense of disbelief and disappointment.

As each of their gazes meets mine, I take note of their decision. Ear pull—ear pull—ear pull—ear pull. Soon, I realize everyone is tugging on their ear with enthusiasm. Not a chin scratch in the room. I begin my part of the scheme.

"Can we have everyone's attention, please?" I cough and clear my throat. "Scooter is letting me break this to you. I'm sad to say we're going to have to stop working together."

The room uproars with gasps and grumbles, enough to satisfy the surveillance.

Scooter chimes in. "We have to consider national security, and until we are given further notice, the project is a threat."

The room rattles with fictitious banter, and I'm relieved that they're playing along so well. "So, after Zain gets home, we'll collect data and provide physical therapy for anything he may need as a response to being in space, and then we'll part ways until we get further clearance."

I put my hands in the prayer position, signifying my gratitude for all their hard work. "Expect Zain in three days."

I turn and give Scooter a thumbs up. "I'm going home to check on Stella. Let me know if anything comes up."

"Will do." He grins. "And again, I'm so sorry for the way things turned out."

"It's not your fault. Hopefully, the FBI and CIA will someday see the value of being the first to revolutionize air and space travel." I wink. I'm enjoying this little game.

When I arrive home, Stella, Chester, and Gal are all sitting on the porch enjoying the weather. I try not to be paranoid about any surveillance at my house, but I need to be cautious here.

"Hi, family!" I say, giddy, and pet each of the animals and kiss my girl.

"How did everything go today?" she asks.

"Horrible." I shake my head. "Let's go for a walk."

On the shore, I tell Stella everything. I'm glad Ali didn't spill the beans and allowed me to tell her. She seems shocked and nervous but on board with the plans.

"I'm so relieved everyone wants to keep working together," she whispers.

"Are you kidding? Every scientist on the planet would kill to do something like this. There's no way they'd be able to give up so quickly."

She stops and stares out to sea. "So, what does Scooter have planned?"

I throw the ball for Chester, who whines tirelessly while he waits.

"I'm not sure yet, but he's a good guy. I trust him. If we're going to be successful, then the whole crew will have to trust one another completely."

"I agree."

"We will find out soon enough."

"Listen." She pauses to fiddle with her sweater. "My mom is bringing Moshe today."

"That's great!" I say, mid-throw.

"It is. I guess."

"What's the issue? You've been wanting to meet him, right?"

"Yes, but this is such a personal time for him to come. It would be more special without a stranger present."

"It's all going to be fine. Your mom loves him, so he must be a decent guy."

"You're right." She moans. "I'm overthinking it. My specialty."

I wrap my arms around her.

"You're not worried that lying to the FBI and CIA will be a danger to your family?" she asks with her face against my chest.

I push her out to arm's length. "Stella, if you want me to stop, I'll stop."

"No, no, no."

"I'm serious. This will be dangerous, but we have to be in it together, because we know deep down in our souls this is the right thing to do."

She nods, wiping away tears.

"We all know the severity of the situation. We will not take it lightly. You and our babies will be safe. I promise. Don't worry."

"I didn't plan on crying like this. Baby hormones, I guess."

"Eh, you've always been a crier. Don't blame it on the babies," I say, poking fun. She hits my arm and admits I'm right.

"Should we both drive to the airport, or should I pick them up and introduce everyone at your house?"

"That's up to you. Do you want time alone with your mom before I meet her?"

"I'd probably say yes if Moshe wasn't in the picture. Let's go and get this over with. Come on," she says, waving her hand.

STELLA

My mom and Moshe are waiting by the curb under the Arrivals sign.

"Was their plane early?"

"Must have been," I say as I hop out to hug my mom.

"Hi, baby girl! You look so beautiful. Here," she says, handing me her bag, and turns toward Moshe. "This is my daughter, Stella. Stella, meet Moshe."

I stick my free hand out to shake his. "Nice to finally meet you," I say, matching his face to the photos my mom sent.

"Likewise," he says, pushing my hand aside and hugging me. His cologne is strong but pleasant. He is shorter than I anticipated, but everyone looks short standing next to Andrew.

"And who is this?" asks my mom, who is staring deeply into Andrew's eyes.

"Mom, this is Andrew. We've been seeing each other for quite some time now."

"I can see now why you've been so hard to get ahold of!" she says, daintily shaking his hand. She is so dramatic.

"Hi, Ms. Frasier, I've heard so much about you."

"Oh, it's Nancy Nichols, honey."

Andrew looks at me with an embarrassed expression.

"Sorry, I never mentioned she goes by her maiden name."

"That's okay, honey. You can call me whatever you want," she says to Andrew in a deep, sensual voice.

"MOTHER!"

Andrew laughs and smiles. My mom just winks at me.

"Sorry, Moshe, my mother has apparently lost her social filters," I say, feeling my face flush.

"She had two glasses of red wine on the plane."

"That'll do it."

I attempt to put her bag in the trunk, and Andrew races over to take it from me. It is heavier than I anticipated, so I withhold my sarcastic bitchery about not needing a man's help.

The car ride goes quickly. We listen to my mother endlessly crack jokes about Moshe and their adventures. They have amazing chemistry. My mom is so excited to ride the ferry and compliments Andrew constantly. She loves that he lives off the beaten path.

"My family lives on the island, as well," he explains. "We grew up here, so we're partial to it. It can be inconvenient at times, but the lots are bigger, it's quieter, and you can't beat the views."

"I love that you're close with your family."

"We were hoping to all get together tomorrow night for dinner. Would you be okay with that?"

"Meet the boyfriend, meet the family. You two must be serious."

"We would love to meet your family," Moshe adds. "Your home is spectacular," he says as he enters and is greeted by the animals.

"His property goes to the shoreline, and the view of the stars at night is unbelievable. You should listen to him play the piano." I watch Andrew's reaction as he finishes moving the suitcases. He smiles big, almost too big, and his face turns a few shades pinker.

"I haven't practiced in a while," he says, looking at me with raised eyebrows.

He can't fool me. I know he loves the attention. "Just play part of the Rachmaninoff piece," I plead, cozying up with my mom on the couch in anticipation.

"*Just* play it." He rolls his eyes. "Okay, okay. The entire piece is about forty-five minutes, but I've only learned the first ten."

He sits at the piano, adjusts his posture, and begins. Moshe jolts his head at my mom, and she looks at me with eyes wide and jaw dropped.

It's easy to be impressed by Andrew. He doesn't slack off in any aspect of his life. He does everything with intent, purpose, and patience. He taught himself this piece simply because he wanted to play it. Sure, I want to be a prima ballerina, but I have limits. He, apparently, does not. He's a real-life superhero.

"*You know he thinks you're the superhero.*"

"*You always know how to make me blush, Ali! I'm so excited to see you! When will you arrive?*"

"*Late in the night, tonight. Zain is doing great and has already made a list of things he wants tested.*"

"*I'm sure he has. Tonight? That's early. We'll get the crew together. My mom is in town. I wish I could tell her what we've been doing together. Someday, I will. Someday the whole world will know.*"

"*I think you have more personal news to share with her.*"

"You're definitely right about that. I better get back to it."

"See you soon!"

Andrew finishes and bows his head, more out of embarrassment than for the applause, it seems.

"That was very impressive," Moshe says.

"Thank you, I think the same thing all the time. Not about myself," he says and holds his hands out, "but about the composer. He is the impressive one."

"You know how your mom and I found each other, but how did you two get introduced?" Moshe asks me. "You seem so connected."

Overdramatically, I bat my eyes at Andrew. "Well, it's not quite as whimsical and romantic as your story, but I feel we were always meant to be."

"I think it was whimsical and romantic," Andrew says.

"Well, the first time we met, I literally fell into his arms sobbing. He was there when my apartment flooded. We were strangers, but he held on to me like he knew me." I smile at him from across the room. "Our mutual friend was there and had planned on introducing us, just not in that way. Andrew helped me through the whole process and even offered me a place to live. It was like the universe had kept us apart for long enough, and when it was time for us to be together, it all happened at once."

"Speaking of 'all at once,'" Andrew says and waves me over. I get up off the couch and wrap my arms around his waist.

"Mom, we want to spend the rest of our lives together. And we're pregnant with twins!"

"WHAT?" she squeals then runs up and hugs us. "Oh, honey," she says through her tears, "I am so happy for you."

"Thanks, Mom." I can't help but cry with her.

"Are you going to stay here? Raise the kids here?"

I look up at Andrew, and we both say, "Yes."

My mom turns to Moshe. "I'm moving to Maine!" He smiles and congratulates us. He lives mostly in Israel and visits my mom when he can, so it makes no difference to him.

Andrew raises his eyebrows at me.

"Don't worry, Andrew. I won't be a nuisance. But I want to be nearby to help when you need it. I'm going to be a grandma."

"Family is the most important thing. You are all blessed," Moshe says.

I take his hand. "Tell me about this new project you're working on." I lead him to the porch to sit outside as the sun is setting.

"Wow, look at that view." He stares into the distance. "That's proof right there that God exists," he says, sitting down in a chair. "Are you a religious person?"

I find my way to the chair next to him. "Not in the typical sense, no."

"In what sense, then?"

I rub my arms, admiring the view. "I look at this same scenery in awe just like you, and I think to myself how beautiful it is, and how thankful I am for this moment, and then I admit I have no idea what God is. I feel God within me in this very moment. Although I cannot comprehend the complexity of the universe and everything in it, I am humbled to be witnessing its magnificence."

Moshe turns to me. "That's beautiful."

"I know you are a religious man, and I have no quarrel with anyone who is religious."

"No offense taken. I love to hear everyone's outlook. We all have our own path. I would never assume one is right and one is wrong. You said it perfectly."

"So, you find ancient artifacts for museums?"

"I don't find them. That would be very exciting. Unfortunately, there are still people out there who want to destroy things from history that do not align with their current views. People come to me with things that need a safe place. A letter that was hidden in a wall during World War II, ancient propagandist paintings, religious relics."

"That's really special."

"Your mom is special. She is my muse. She stole my heart from the moment we met. She looks at me like I'm some sort of saint, which is very entertaining. I love what I do, but sharing it all with your mom is what keeps me going."

"She looks up to you. She tells me about you all the time."

"I'm so happy to meet you. She speaks so highly of you. You are her pride and joy," he says, tapping my knee.

"That's so kind, thank you. I'm happy to meet you as well." I turn around to peer through the glass and see my mom gushing over Andrew, probably complimenting him some more.

"He seems like a great guy," says Moshe, gesturing inside.

"He is. I never thought I'd connect with someone after James died. But we're in a great place. I know James would be happy for me."

"Absolutely."

My mom opens the back door and announces dinner has been delivered. We all find a seat at the kitchen table.

"You know, having a baby, or um, babies in your case, will change everything."

"Mom," I say, embarrassed, "aren't we a little old for this?"

"Absolutely not! Babies are such a blessing, but they'll drive you over the edge at the same time. You won't believe how tired you'll both feel. You'll forget what it's like to have a clean house. You'll get so fat—"

"Mom!"

"It's true. You're going to look like a whale. You know, I gained sixty pounds when I was pregnant with you. Just think about twins!"

I consider throwing the pitcher of water I'm holding at her from across the table, but Andrew stands and takes it out of my hands.

"It's natural. Things will be so hard. You'll think you made a terrible mistake creating these monsters."

My mouth goes agape.

"But then, maybe when they're about three, you'll begin to see the light at the end of the tunnel. Things will get easier. The key is to stay a team. Don't let any resentment build up. Share the load. Take care of yourselves and each other. Be honest. Enjoy the chaos so you can look back together and feel happy and proud."

"Thanks, Mom," I utter through my teeth.

"I'll be here to help." She grins.

"Nancy, if my mom were still around, the two of you would really hit it off. Which leads me to my next subject." He looks at me calmly and gently. "Stella, I don't ever want you to feel worried about our relationship and what our future holds. We're going to make an amazing team, and I promise to always take care of you and our babies."

He scoots his chair back and gets down on one knee. "Our time together has shown me true love does exist. You're my soulmate. The universe brought us together. I want to be with you through it all. The sixty-plus pounds, the chaos, the highs and lows, the quiet bliss. Our future together is my greatest adventure, and I want to do it all as husband and wife. Will you marry me, Stella?" He takes a ring from his pocket and offers it to me.

I let out a quiet sob and kiss him hard, nearly knocking him over. "Of course I will," I say through my tears. He takes my hand, and I realize I'm still wearing my wedding band. I begin to take it off, but

Andrew stops me. He slides his ring right up against James's. The two rings look perfect together.

Andrew picked out a round opal surrounded by diamonds in a rose gold setting. My wedding band from James is a slightly different color of rose gold, but it adds warmth to the setting.

He rubs the two rings between his fingers, and we embrace.

My mom and Moshe stand and congratulate us. I hug my mom and take another look at the ring. It changes colors at every facet.

"How did you find this ring? It reminds me of—"

"The stars?"

"Yes. There's something so beautiful and mysterious about it."

"My thoughts exactly. That's how I see you, too."

"Great, now I'm going to cry again. You're right. I'm just a crier." I hug him and whisper in his ear, "I am so lucky. I love you."

It dawns on me that tomorrow will be a busy day for the crew. I'm going to have to take my mom and Moshe away to keep them from the shore while Ali, Roman, and Zain arrive.

"Did Ali know about this?"

Andrew glances around suspiciously. I cover my mouth and see my mom and Moshe are swept up in getting the camera on her phone to open.

"Yes, of course," he whispers. "Word travels fast when you're quantumly entangled across the universe."

"Roman told me the good news earlier—" he starts.

"They get in tonight, so we'll see them tomorrow!"

"Yes. So, Swanson will come to clean out the coms site after their arrival."

"I'll take my parents into town for shopping."

"Perfect," he adds, turning to my mom and Moshe.

"Say cheese!"

ANDREW

The sun is rising, and my brain buzzes with questions from Roman, who is waiting in the depths of the sea until we give them the all-clear to bring an orb up. Stella hurries her mom and Moshe out the door. I know how badly Stella wants to be with the crew, but she's doing her part to help.

As I walk down to the shore, I see the team has already set up tents with supplies needed for blood work and other tests. The energy is palpable, and as excited as everyone is to see Zain, we're all giddy to meet our counterparts. Opening up to anyone is an emotional feat, but opening yourself so wide as to allow someone to be inside your mind is very personal. These matches are our family. We'll be seeing them in their true form, and the crew doesn't seem intimidated.

In the distance, military boats are keeping the area clear of fishermen. The neighboring houses are filled with agents who will remain inside until the orb retreats. Having them arrive in the morning seems so public, so vulnerable. We have to trust the FBI is doing their part in ensuring the area is clear.

A glowing light emerges from the water, and the ship rolls onto shore, shining with all its glory. I stare in silence with awe and anticipation. Even after all we've seen, I'm still struck with amazement as I witness the beauty, the simplicity—the future.

The orb door opens, and Zain is the first to come out. An applause erupts, cheering for our buddy. A designated team of scientists approaches the orb and helps him get his Earth feet back. They escort him to a tent and begin their poking and prodding.

Ali is holding hands with Roman as she exits. He peers out cautiously, and I step to the orb and encourage him. He shields his eyes from the sun, but his neck glows.

"Welcome, Roman."

"Andrew!" He meets me at the base of the orb. *"Are you sure we're okay to come on land?"*

"You are safe. I promise."

He places his hand on my shoulder, closes his eyes, and breathes in a deep breath of Earth's air.

I take note of his features. He is used to seeing humans from afar, and Ali when she's on the ship, so he doesn't appear too enthralled with how I look. I, on the other hand, need a moment to soak it all in. I can't hide my curiosity. I have only seen them in their true form once before.

"May I?" I ask, reaching for his hand. He holds his hands out, and I feel his pale skin's smooth texture, turn his hands over and notice the blue veins running up his arms. It's amazing how similar we are built.

"Evolution found something that works, apparently," he jokes.

"There are definite similarities."

"Don't worry," he says. *"Zain has been examining us nearly every day on his journey. You will be excited to see his discoveries."*

"No doubt. It's probably fun for you to learn about us as well. I keep forgetting we're aliens to you."

"If I could, I'd spend the rest of my life exploring your world."

I place my hand on his shoulder. *"Maybe someday, brother."*

"I cannot stay but wanted to personally say thank you for everything."

"I should be thanking you. You're providing us invaluable information. I hope it will lead to us seeing each other again."

"I like that goal."

"We will keep in touch." I laugh.

"Absolutely." His neck glows, and he returns to his vessel.

Each matched partner exits the orb and has a few words with their counterpart. Ali stays ashore with us, and the orb slowly descends into the ocean. I welcome her back on my way to Zain's tent.

"It's so good to see you," I say as we shake hands through the people checking his vitals. He tries to speak but can't hold back his tears. He covers his face, and I get down on one knee and let him rest his head on my shoulder.

"I honestly never thought I'd see Earth again. I was ready to spend the rest of my life with them. I was going to do it. I was ready." He lifts his head. "But, damn, I'm so happy to be home."

"You're the bravest of us all," I remind him, shaking his shoulders. "I'm excited to hear about everything. Unfortunately, we don't have much time. We're about to hand over everything to Swanson and cease work until the military agrees to let us continue."

"Which will probably be never."

As far as I know, Roman communicated the plan to everyone and their counterparts. I assume he told Zain, but I can't show any hint of hope until we're away from any sort of possible surveillance.

"The most important thing is that you're home safe." I stand just as Scooter jabs my arm with his elbow.

"Swanson, two o'clock."

"Dude." Zain dips his face, shying away. "I don't want to see that guy. I might punch someone for the first time in my life."

"Ah, don't get mad at Swanson," Scooter says. "He's probably not the one making decisions. He's just the messenger."

I could tell Zain wasn't convinced, so I leave the tent to greet Swanson before he can upset anyone.

I motion toward his briefcase, which I assume is full of paperwork for us. "All ready for business, I see."

"You can thank your friends for bringing Zain home, but please encourage them to depart at nightfall. In fact, if they're still here by midnight, we will take action to remove them."

"Uh, okay. Sure thing." There's no point in arguing about their presence being harmless, and the sooner we get this bullshit over with, the sooner we can make our plans.

You'll need to park your ship in deep water until we figure out the next steps. The military will be expecting you to leave, so find a good hiding spot.

"You know, we have you to thank for a lot of things."

"Is that so?" I ask. "We could help out with a lot more if you let us continue our work."

"I wish things could be different. I really do."

"That's a really beautiful, heartfelt story. Thank you for that, Officer Swanson."

"Oh, come on. It's a win-win. You save your friends. We get them off our land."

"You think this is funny?"

"Don't get me wrong. There was potential. We were fine with

sending someone with them to gather information, but you overstepped by trying to build a prototype. That's an issue of national security."

I know what the real issue is, but I dare not go there. "Could I convince you to let us keep working under military surveillance?"

"Why? So we could be the ones to shatter our entire economic structure? Look, I know you are all hoping to win the Nobel Prize for this stuff, but you don't get it. We don't want their intel. We've got human technologies that work just fine here on Earth."

My head is about to explode. "You're missing the point, Swanson. Humans can't live on Earth forever. This is our yellow brick road to traveling in space like we've only ever dreamed of. Sending humans to find a healthier, livable planet. We're talking about free energy, erasing our carbon footprint, and expanding our time on this planet. Do you really think you're making the right call?"

"Scooter mentioned all of this to me. We have considered many angles that you'll never understand. Right now, you need to trust the system."

Fuck the system, is what I wanted to say. But it will do no good. I'm getting nowhere with this guy. This so-called senior officer with the FBI is incapable of thinking for himself. "You're right," I say through my gritted teeth. "We're very thankful for the result."

Does he honestly believe we could open Pandora's box and close it without yearning to see what happens?

I walk back over to Zain's tent, where he's chowing down on some doughnuts.

"Thank you for remembering to bring these, Scooter," he says with his mouth full. He takes another bite and closes his eyes.

"My pleasure. Looks like you're in pure bliss. What'd they feed you?"

"So many vegetables. Just vegetables." He takes another donut and dips it in his coffee.

"Sounds miserable." Scooter smacks my arm, clearly getting a kick out of this. Zain nods as he indulges in his treat.

"Your apartment is waiting for you. It might be a bit dusty, but it's still there. Are you going to be okay by yourself tonight?"

"Oh, no," Scooter says. "We're going to have to monitor him for a few days to make sure everything is working properly before we can let him go home."

"He can stay with us if you—"

Scooter waves his hands. "We've got to run too many tests. He'll be safest in the hospital for a while."

He writes *8pm tonight—Maggie's Café* in his notebook and tears the page out. I nod and place the note in my pocket, out of sight.

STELLA

I take my mom and Moshe to breakfast. We explore some cute shops and visit a nice park. I enjoy visiting with them, but I'm a nervous wreck wondering how everything is going back home.

"Honey," my mom says, grabbing my arm. "You've checked your phone for the hundredth time since we've left the shops. Is everything okay?"

I feel horrible that she's seen. I thought I was being discreet. "Gosh, I'm sorry. Andrew was having a conference call at the house, so I'm wondering when he'll be done."

She rubs her temples. "We don't need to keep circling the block. We promise to be quiet if he's still on the phone."

"Do you have a headache?" Moshe asks my mom.

"Yes, maybe too much caffeine."

"Are we in the clear to head home?"

"I'm helping them finish packing up now. You're in the clear."

"Did everything go okay?"

"Perfectly."

I take a deep breath and allow myself to calm down. "Let's go home." The trees will block their view of the commotion from the house, and they'll be too exhausted to venture out. I quickly lead them inside and bring them to the couch to relax.

"Andrew asked me to help him with something. I'll be right back." I turn the TV on for them as if they're little kids and slowly back out of the room.

When I reach the porch, Andrew is leading Scooter up the stairs. They are saying their goodbyes, and I wave and signal that my parents are inside. Scooter waves back and turns to leave. I embrace Andrew, relieved to be done with the FBI. No more bosses looking over our shoulders. It's time to focus on the new mission.

Andrew whispers, "Change of plans."

------∿∿∿∿∿∿∿------

We arrange dinner so we can introduce our families in a public setting. We arrive at Maggie's Café at six-thirty. Thankfully, we are able to reserve the back two tables, one for the adults and one for the kids.

We share the news of our engagement, and I love getting to know his nieces and nephews a little better. We let the wine flow freely and take turns sitting at the kids' table. Eventually, the adults get used to one of us being absent from the conversation, and Andrew slips out unnoticed.

I see him get into a car with Scooter and sit back in my chair, wishing I could partake in the wine. My nerves are through the roof.

Moshe looks comfortable and content sitting with my family,

listening and laughing. He isn't leaving a glass unfilled, which helps our situation. Everyone seems to be getting along well, and I haven't seen my mom laugh so hard before.

After about thirty minutes, Andrew slides into the chair next to me, wraps his arm around me, and kisses my cheek. Sydney is in the middle of telling a story about learning how to drive a stick shift, and Andrew pops back into the conversation easily.

"Is it okay to talk here?" I whisper.

"I think there's enough background noise. You didn't bring your phone, right?"

"Right."

"Scooter and I had a meeting with the whole crew. We would make plans, then I'd pass them on to Roman, who'd pass them on to his team, who then each told their counterpart."

"That's a big game of telephone right there."

"It sounds more complicated than it felt. We didn't bother you with the details while you were here. I knew I could fill you in."

"Of course."

"We're each going to focus on one aspect of the prototype, and all create foolproof detailed instructions and blueprints to bring the whole thing together. We've set a one-month deadline."

"Will the FBI be suspicious?"

"They'll probably monitor us for a while to make sure we're sticking to our word. We'll have to be incredibly careful working independently. No phones, no internet, no traces."

"What's your main focus?" I ask.

"Scooter and I are the managers. We'll be checking in with everyone throughout the month. My main focus is taking care of my future wife and our babies." He leans in and kisses my forehead.

"Yeah, right. There's no way you'll be able to keep it together over the next month without a project of your own."

"Zain and I will be in charge of deciding which cutting-edge scientists receive the information."

"You'll be good at that."

"I hope so."

"Remember that, Andrew?" calls his sister from the other side of the table.

"That was really embarrassing for you!" he says, igniting a roar of laughter.

—∿∿∿W\\\∿∿∿—

I'm exhausted after we get home from dinner, but we have major plans. Andrew informed me half of the crew still intends on leaving with Ali and Roman, no matter the cost. We're to get things squared away as soon as possible.

My mom and Moshe are toasted and will be out like a light for the rest of the night. Andrew and I aren't sure if the area is being watched, so we put Chester on a leash and take him for a harmless late-night walk.

We walk six blocks to meet Scooter, who takes the three of us to the other side of the island. There's a path through the woods to a small opening near the water. Only the moon and stars light our way. The crew is waiting, gathered on the beach. They stand when we arrive, and I suddenly feel like a royal. Ali is in the back, and my throat tightens, realizing how far she has come.

"Thank you for meeting here, everyone," I say loudly, knowing there isn't another soul for miles. "I know we don't have a lot of time, but I'll be quick. A few of you are about to embark on the greatest adventure. An adventure that will lead to astonishing changes in human space travel." I pull my shoulders back, feeling strong, confident. "You've already gone the distance spiritually and mentally when you became matched. Now comes the fun part. If you can do it, others will too. No matter how far you travel in space, and no matter how much time passes, we will make sure you're not forgotten. It will take time for our superpower to be accepted, but with our capabilities, we will find a way. I also want to thank you immensely for getting us this far. You are all so incredible, so kind, and undeniably awesome. I love you all." I walk down and begin hugging every person.

"Working with all of you has provided me with so much joy and fulfillment," Andrew says. "We aren't going to let a piece of paper keep us from working together. We aren't going to let the government or military put a stop to this mission. We can't deny this feeling in our souls to keep going." Some clap and cheer at this. "Tonight, you put your skills to the test. Tonight, some of you will be traveling to a new planet, cosmically slipping one hundred light years away. We'll be with you every step of the way. You're not alone. Trust yourself and your abilities. Prove that humans can be cosmically conscious beings and that we can begin a multi-planetary existence."

Andrew shakes hands with the six members who will follow Ali into the orb. They seem nervous but determined.

"Ali," I say, failing to find any words to explain my feelings.

She wraps her arms around me. "This is not goodbye!"

"No, of course not. I just can't thank you enough."

"Without you, none of this would have happened. We are so thankful to you. We'll take good care of everyone."

"I know," I say, wiping my face.

"We'll keep in touch!" she yells, leading the way to the orb.

It's close to midnight, and they need to leave before the military takes notice. Everyone says their goodbyes, and we watch the orb descend and disappear.

"All right." Andrew claps. "We all have a lot of work to do. Let's get started."

ANDREW

Rock climbing has been helping me take my mind off things that are outside my control. It's a great distraction. It's hard to think of anything else while you're looking for your next move. Stella is determined to keep climbing until her belly gets too big. She knows it's safe and loves sharing this passion with me.

When I'm not climbing, I'm pacing the house, playing fetch with Chester, and I've also taken up running. Zain and I came up with our list of scientists within three days. We couldn't contain our excitement. So now, it's a waiting game.

"I'm taking Chester for a run!" I call out to Stella, who's organizing the nursery.

"Okay!"

I take my earbuds and listen to some bands I enjoyed in high school. I run so fast my lungs burn.

"Andrew, we're signing off. The crew is ready to slip. We've gone over everything thoroughly with them."

I skid to a stop, surprising Chester. I try to catch my breath.

"Okay, I'm so nervous for you all."

"We are excited! It's like entering into a lucid dream state, so it might take a little practice."

"How long is the first run?"

"If they can do it, we'll slip for short spurts until they get used to the sensation."

"Best of luck. Please check back when you can."

"Absolutely."

I sit down on the curb a few blocks from my house. I rest my elbows on my knees, huffing and puffing. Chester sniffs a nearby dandelion, and I scratch his ears. I wonder about the matched crew that stayed behind. Did they just get the message, too?

I'm not going to tell Zain or Scooter until I know they succeeded. I'm hoping to find out by tonight. I get up, send my positive vibes to the sky, and head home.

Stella is waiting for me on the front porch and meets me at the street.

"Andrew! Oh my goodness." She hugs me.

I guess she got the message.

"Don't get too excited."

"What?" She puts me at arm's length.

"There's a very high probability that this won't work."

"But there's a chance."

"Slight." I head into the house. She slowly follows.

"Well, look who turned up all nervous."

"I'm simply stating the facts." I grab the OJ and pour some.

Stella has her hands on her hips, eyeballing me. "I haven't seen this side of you. You are a nervous wreck."

I set my glass down. "I'm going to be outside." I can't sit still. I go into the shed, pull everything out, and reorganize it.

I water the dry spots in the yard, spraying Chester as he gallops by. For the first time in my life, I pick weeds. I find an old tin of paint and touch up the shutters.

It's dusk, and my body is aching. I'm tired. My head is pounding. I walk to the shore. I admire the tiny rocks under my feet and the gentle sounds of the ocean. I sit on a boulder and feel grounded. My face toward the sky, I wonder what else I could do to pass the time.

"We did it."

I freeze . . . did I hear that right? *"You did it?"*

"The crew did everything right, and we slipped a thousand light years."

I crumble to my knees. I wanted this to work more than anything. I'm glad I don't have to use my real voice to communicate with Roman because I can't speak even if I wanted to. *"Roman, I'm blown away. This is amazing. Thank you."*

"It's my pleasure, brother."

"How's the crew?"

"They're ecstatic."

"I'm sure. Thanks for the update. Such a relief."

"We'll stay in touch."

I rest my elbows on the boulder and put my face in my hands. I look up to see Stella waiting near the wall with her hands over her mouth.

"I didn't want to disturb you."

I wave her over. She helps me up, and we cry in each other's arms.

ONE MONTH LATER, AT A FRENCH LABORATORY

"**D**r. Laurent. You've received a rather large package from Gregory Galileo."

"Oh, really?" He chuckles. "I haven't heard that name in quite some time. Thank you." His protégé shuts the door behind him.

"Why are you using your code name from graduate school, Zain?" Dr. Laurent says, shuffling his paperwork at his desk. He stands to go to the package, and his phone rings.

"*Allo, oui?*" His eyes widen, and he moves toward his office door. "I have just received a package as well. I'll call you back as soon as I open it."

He rushes out of his office, grabs the package, and cautiously removes the tape. A letter rests on top of a ton of packing peanuts. He opens the letter first and reads.

Dr. Laurent,

I hope you take this letter and its contents with the utmost importance and urgency. I have been working with a certain group
of people on creating anti-gravitational propulsion prototypes. I
need you to know that we have all the intel to complete a working
prototype, but our government prevented us from completing the
mission. They were blinded by power and greed and ignored
the benefits of free energy. I'm requesting that you finish the project. You will not be alone in this feat.

I have sent different specs to nine other scientists across the
globe, each with the full set of blueprints and instructions. The complete list of scientists involved is on the next page. My hope is that
you'll come together to complete a working prototype and share it
with the world.

Your efforts will change human existence forever, and I trust
you to do what's right for humanity. Change is difficult, but it's the
only way we can truly grow.

Thank you for your secrecy on the matter,

Gregory Galileo

Dr. Laurent braces himself on the wall, wondering if he should
even look under the packing foam. As he debates taking such a massive commitment, his phone rings again.

"Allo? You have? We're all in this together? Are you sure? Okay,
send me the rendezvous point. See you soon."

He bends down and grabs hold of whatever is beneath the ocean
of white peanuts. He pulls out a large piece of material and examines
it closely. Intrigued, he opens the blueprints and gasps. He runs over
to his protégé and kisses him square on the mouth.

"This will earn me a Nobel Prize!"

STELLA

"How are you?" I ask, watching Andrew pace around our living room.

"I'm fine. Just another day of torturous wonder. The fact that we sent everything out five months ago is killing me."

"Maybe no news is good news," I say optimistically.

"Or they trashed it all, not wanting to get involved."

"Andrew, you and Zain picked people you trust. People you have history with. They will take it seriously. They're probably wishing they could tell their old science buddy about their discoveries."

He laughs under his breath and stops. He holds his hand to his ear, giving me the signal Roman is communicating with him.

"The crew has already made it eighty thousand light years out. They're almost to their planet!"

"Already?"

"Since the other ships had time to explore, they've focused on getting home as soon as possible."

"And they're all holding up okay?"

Andrew tilts his head from side to side. "As well as could be expected. Physically, they are great. The gravity chambers and daily exercises have been sufficient to keep their bodies performing normally."

"And mentally?"

"There's a certain level of guilt they can't shake."

"For their families?"

"The notes they left for their families didn't give away specifics, but said that they were leaving, and safe."

I imagine how strange it must have been for them. "It would still be hard to believe."

"The FBI will never admit it, but they know what really happened."

"There's nothing they can do about it."

"Right, so they don't get involved."

"And they still haven't asked you about anything?"

"Nope. Swanson asked Scooter many times where the crew went. His only response was, 'I'm sorry, Officer Swanson. I have no idea in this entire *universe* where they could possibly be.' Eventually, Swanson got the idea. It's not Scooter's fault, so he can't be blamed."

He finally comes and sits next to me on the couch.

"It's getting harder for me to keep all these secrets. If we could just know whether the scientists are working on it, then we'd be able to make plans. We could figure something else out, you know?"

"The truth will come out. And, whenever it does, you'll be able to shout from the rooftops."

"It will be tough to decide if we admit it's alien technology, or if we take Neil's approach and take the credit."

"That should be the next step."

"Agreed. Once the world knows of the new technology and we master traveling within our atmosphere, we can begin the introduction to Cosmic Slip."

"One way or the other," I add.

He smiles, looking down at my massive belly.

I have surpassed whale status and ordered myself to be on bed rest. At eight months pregnant, I have two fully grown babies in my uterus who are fighting constantly for more legroom. I only get out of bed for the bare necessities: food, water, and bathing.

We have the house stocked with a seemingly infinite number of diapers and onesies. My mom swears we'll run out in a week.

She bought a house just five minutes away, and I'll be the first to admit that I'm relieved. She is so excited to be a grandma, and who can blame her? Besides the normal angst and worry about being a new mom to twins, I have a general sense of peace knowing we have so much family nearby.

Andrew is going to be an incredible dad, and I've never been so happy. As happy as I was with James. He's gone, and I cannot allow myself to feel guilty for loving someone new. James and I shared the most amazing years, and I will always be so thankful to him. I know he's out there spreading his light.

I'm broken from my daydream by Andrew dusting off his DSLR camera.

"How could you ever want proof that I looked like this on our wedding day?"

He blows the brush and gives the lens one more swipe. "Whether you are willing to admit it or not, you look gorgeous, and our kids will want to see pictures of our wedding day. So, for the last time, we're taking the camera."

"I'm seventy pounds overweight."

"You're pregnant with twins. Now, get in the car. We're going to be late."

I reach my arms out for help getting off the couch. My dress, which might as well be a shower curtain wrapped around my shoulders, is already wrinkled. I was fine getting married after the twins were born, but Andrew was not willing to wait. We knew it would be risky having a wedding so close to our due date, but we figured we'd have a very good excuse for the judge if we needed to reschedule.

Getting into the Bronco at eight months pregnant is not an option, so we settle for taking my car.

"Oh, shit."

"What now?" I ask.

"I forgot to send out the extra credit assignment. My students are probably panicking."

I send him inside, knowing it will only take a few minutes.

Since we sent out the materials to the scientists, he progressively became more distracted. It appeared he was losing his patience the first month, so I made him apply for a teaching job at my school. I knew it would be a good diversion for him. He couldn't keep living in a constant state of anticipation.

For a while, we were there together, and I finished out the year teaching English. But it was my decision to quit before the new school year. I want to be home with my babies.

He comes running back, apologizing.

"You don't think they could have waited a couple more hours?" I ask, half joking. I know how seriously he takes his role.

"No way. I never would have heard the end of it. They're all good now." He starts the engine and glances my way. "You ready?"

"Ready."

"Andrew and I are on our way to the courthouse. Wish you were here."

"Congratulations, Stella. You and Andrew were always meant to be. I wish I could be there too. Enjoy it."

Her response makes me feel warm and fuzzy.

We pull up to the courthouse, and Andrew opens my car door. I suddenly feel like a celebrity in a paparazzi ambush.

Sydney and Claire have taken hold of the cameras. One has the DSLR, and the other has a phone in one hand and her digital video camera in the other. My mom is patiently waiting behind them.

I haven't even gotten out of the car yet and they've taken a hundred photos. Andrew births me from the Prius, and we make our way inside. My mom holds my other hand.

"You want to make a run for it?" she whispers in my ear. She knew I'd rather wait until I lost the pregnancy weight.

"I actually am running right now. You just can't tell." We erupt with laughter. "Thanks for always having my back, Mom." I give her a big hug and waddle toward the judge with Andrew.

He looks down at me with sheer joy and excitement. He really does think I look beautiful right now. Which, in turn, makes me feel beautiful. I squeeze his hand and turn to fully face him, ignoring the constant clicking of the shutters.

"You both look so lovely tonight," the judge says, "and especially our glowing bride."

This is the first time I've ever seen Andrew blush so much. His cheeks are blotchy, his eyes soft with emotion. Seeing him so happy makes my throat tighten.

She begins, "We are gathered here today to witness the joining of Stella Frasier and Andrew Witten."

As we say our vows, we hold hands and stare into each other's eyes. Andrew surprises me with a wedding band. I had to take both my rings off from swelling, but this one fits nicely on my sausage fingers. It's gold, surrounded in diamonds, and beautiful. It will make a nice necklace when I switch back to my regular rings.

I show Andrew his ring, and his jaw drops. "It was your father's," I whisper. He closes his eyes and covers his mouth.

"You may now kiss your bride."

Andrew holds my face in his hands and kisses me, and I melt. A gush of water smashes against my feet. I look down. The judge backs away. And I'm frozen.

"Your water just broke!" Sydney yells.

My mom rushes toward me, saying, "Shit, shit, shit," under her breath.

I look at the judge in horror and apologize profusely for the mess. She smiles, hardly hiding her disgust.

"We will clean up the mess," Claire says with authority. "You get to the hospital, now." She points to the door.

Andrew and my mom hold me up as I waddle out of the building, hoping to God these babies don't fall out. The contractions come on strong, and with every one more fluid is released. In the car, I feel horrible sitting upright. It's like I'm squishing their heads. I push the seat back and lean. Thankfully, the hospital is only a couple of miles down the road. Andrew puts the hazard lights on and punches it.

"Don't you dare get in a car wreck!" I yell through a contraction.

"I've never been so alert in my life. Don't worry. Just breathe," he says calmly, knuckles white, eyes wide.

"These are your first babies, so relax, they won't come too fast. I was in labor for twelve hours after my water broke," Mom says, stroking my hair from the back seat. "Relax. You have time."

"Mom!"

I've been preparing myself for the pain for eight months, but I wasn't expecting it to be this bad. What if something is wrong?

She shushes me and lifts her gaze. "We're here," she says. "You made it."

Andrew parks at the emergency entrance, runs around, and opens my door. The hospital staff bring out a wheelchair, and they wheel me into a delivery room. They ask which doctor to call, help me change into a hospital gown, and get me on the table.

"My water broke," I whine.

"When?" the nurse asks as she puts on gloves.

"Ten minutes ago," Andrew tells her.

"Do you want an epidural?"

"Yes!" I sob with the thought of relief.

She lifts my gown. "I'm going to check your dilation."

"You are six centimeters. Let me see how fast our anesthesiologist can get one in here." She eyeballs another nurse who rushes out the door.

"I'm having twins," I manage to say. The contractions are coming back-to-back now, leaving me breathless. I focus on getting through the discomfort. Time is nonexistent to me. "Where's the epidural?"

"I'm here!" calls out Dr. Roberts.

I'm relieved for a second, but another contraction hits, and I can't acknowledge her.

She walks over to the monitor, lifts my gown, and does her inspection.

"Your babies are ready to meet you," she says with excitement. "You are strong. You are capable of incredible things. Everything is going smoothly. I'll be back to check on you in thirty minutes. You hurry up and get that epidural. You'll feel so much better."

I say nothing, and she smiles and waves at Andrew as she leaves.

He stands next to me, asking what he can do to help. My mother is pacing back and forth next to me, asking where she should stand. I can't answer either of them without yelling, so I keep my mouth shut.

These horrible contractions keep coming, and I'm desperate for relief.

"Where is my freaking epidural?" I yell. The nurse stands stunned. "I'm sorry. I'm so sorry. Can you please check on that?" I say between breaths.

She runs out and comes back in looking worried.

"He's had a complication with one of the C-sections downstairs, so he had to go back. You're next in line."

"A complication?" I yell. "You think I want to get an epidural from someone who hands out complications? Forget it. I'll go without." When I realize I won't have any relief, I cry.

"Oh, it was nothing serious. It just didn't take with her, and he had to do it again."

"Forget it, I said!" I'm full-blown crying, shaking, sweaty, exhausted. My mom comes and holds my hand, I'm too tired to reciprocate.

I grab the sheets to brace for the contraction and try to breathe through it but catch myself holding my breath. It passes, and I collapse back on the bed, sweaty and discouraged.

"I can't do it."

"Stella, you can, and you will," Andrew urges as he strokes my hair.

I feel another contraction, and I want to push. I tell the nurse, and she calls my doctor. She runs over and checks my dilation.

"I can see the baby's head," she croaks. "Cross your legs until the doctor gets here."

"Fuck! I'm not crossing my legs. Tell Dr. Roberts to run."

My yelling causes me to push the baby's head out. An on-call doctor comes in and changes positions with the nurse. "Wait for another contraction to push," she orders. Dr. Roberts enters, and the nurses put a surgery gown on her.

"You're doing great, Stella. One more push."

I follow orders and feel the release of pressure, followed by the sound of my baby crying.

"It's a boy!" she exclaims. I'm so relieved my heart explodes. "Andrew, would you like to cut the cord?"

He looks at me with pride and steps over to greet our son. He cuts the cord and smiles.

The nurses weigh the baby and wrap him in a blanket. My mom stands guard over him while Andrew stays by my side, ready.

"He's six pounds, fourteen ounces," my mom says. She holds the baby and brings him to me to hold.

He's perfect. I don't want to let go. His little face is all scrunched up like he can barely stand life outside the womb. Against my chest, his face relaxes.

"Okay, let's see if baby number two is ready," Dr. Roberts says as she feels my uterus. "Head is down. We're good to go. Whenever you're ready, Stella."

My mom takes the baby and sits in a chair. I want to scream as a contraction hits, but I don't want to scare my baby. It passes, and I breathe in and out, concentrating on getting this baby out fast. I'm ready to hold them both forever.

I bear down with another contraction. The urge to push comes, and I go all in. Andrew touches my knee and heads down south to watch. I can't blame him. I take another deep breath and push. Relief. At last. I hear my second baby cry, and I reach my arms out, begging for physical contact.

"It's a girl," Andrew cries, clipping the umbilical cord.

One nurse brings me my baby boy as the other wraps up my baby girl. I look at his precious face and feel no more pain. They bring my baby girl, and I cry at seeing their perfect faces. They both rest on my chest, and Andrew cradles us all in his arms. He kisses me, and we cry. I'm overjoyed.

"A boy and a girl. How perfect," I say, gushing over them.

"You're so amazing," he says as he stares at the babies. "Which names have you decided on? He looks like a Cooper."

"Cooper. That's precious." I smile. "And Sunny for her."

"Sunny. I love it. Sunny and Cooper."

———∿∿∿∿∿∿∿———

I didn't get much rest last night as we juggled changing diapers and nursing the twins. We are hoping to be released when the pediatrician comes in with one more test. The nurse takes the twins to get their heel prick, and I hate to see them go. I don't like that they take them away.

Andrew lies on the bed next to me and grabs the TV remote.

He flips through channels and gasps. "Dr. Laurent is giving an interview."

Behind the man on the screen is a hovering craft exhibiting all its glory. It has a slight mushroom shape to it—a wide dome on top and a slightly narrower stem section, maybe ten feet wide. It's a bright, luminescent silver craft, hovering six feet or so above the ground. The news banner reads, "Free Energy Vehicles to Save Earth!"

"Oh my God!" Andrew's hands shoot to his head.

"They did it!" I shriek.

"They did it!" Andrew jumps up and down, and we both shriek with excitement, overcome with relief.

Dr. Laurent smiles on screen as he answers the interviewer's questions, proud of his team's accomplishment. The other scientists stand by him, some watching the craft, some listening to the interview.

"This is not a hoax," he says. "We still have a lot of work to do, but this is our future. You're seeing it now as proof that it is possible. We don't need to fight over fossil fuels anymore. We need to come together, secure our future, and embrace this new technology with urgency."

"There will be a new type of Driver's Ed, I see," jokes the interviewer.

"Absolutely! And, perhaps, a new driving age limit." Dr. Laurent laughs.

"What's your greatest takeaway from this revolution?"

Dr. Laurent pauses, looks back at his team and then toward the camera. "The truth is there has been a small group of people who have known about this technology for decades. The governments would never admit to hiding such technology, but it's the truth. The governments don't trust us, the people. They don't believe in us. It needs to change now. We cannot grow as a race without taking risks. We need to work together in this transition. No more corporate greed." He holds his arm out to the side. "We have nine countries represented beside me whose governments are willing to start this journey. The truth is out. My hope is that the public will treat this new technology with the respect it deserves, so we can prove to the other governments that we are trustworthy."

"Will you be building more of these?"

"Yes, of course. The blueprints and instructions are available on my website," Dr. Laurent explains. "We have two right now, currently building two more. My fellow colleagues and I are available for businesses who wish to begin production across the globe."

"Is it safe?"

"It's physically impossible for this machine to have a collision.

They repel each other and anything, just like two opposing magnets. They are incredibly safe."

The interviewer tells the cameraman to zoom in on the craft as it flies up to its altitude limit. It produces no sound and has no exhaust. It can turn without any resistance, in any direction. The sight is breathtaking.

Andrew flips through the channels, and the same footage is on every one. It's happening. The entire world is watching. Goosebumps rise on my body, and the hair stands up on my neck.

A nurse wheels the babies into our room, and my attention snaps back to them. They are swaddled and sleeping cheek to cheek. My heart melts seeing how they comfort each other.

"Can you believe this stuff?" the nurse asks, pointing to the TV.

I hear the delight in her voice. "Wild, isn't it?"

"I'll tell you what, it's about damn time." She laughs.

"Right?"

I thank the nurse immensely for their safe return and sit down to stare at them in awe. Andrew is rummaging through my purse. He finds my phone and takes it into the hallway.

"Are you going to be this paranoid forever?" I ask when he comes back.

"No." He shrugs. "Maybe."

"Do you think they could prove we had anything to do with this?"

"There have been ships parked in waters all over the world. They have no way of disproving that someone else like Ali got in touch with Dr. Laurent."

"It's happening," I exclaim as I embrace him.

"It's finally happening . . . because of us," he says. Andrew wraps one arm around my neck, cupping my face, and one arm around the babies. "This is only the beginning."

THE NEXT DAY, AT THE FBI FACILITY

"Did everything go as planned?" Officer Swanson asks.

"Everything took nicely. His vitals are behaving. He's in good shape. He should be coming to at any moment," replies the surgeon.

Swanson peers through the one-way mirror into the surgical room with his arms crossed. The patient slowly opens his eyes. He looks around the room. His eyes get big, and the heart monitor shows his heart rate increasing. Swanson doesn't want him to panic.

He opens the door, making a point to close it loudly behind him. He slowly walks up to the bed. The chair's metal legs screech on the floor.

"Hello, Neil," he whispers. "You didn't think we were just going to let you die, now, did you?"

Neil tries to readjust his position and blinks rapidly.

"You should know you've been in a coma for quite some time. You've had multiple surgeries to fix what that gun did to you." Swanson's eyes narrow. "You can imagine our struggles in the surgical process, given your special circumstances, I'm sure."

"Congratulations," Neil says, showing no hint of fear. He seems unbothered by the officer's company and looks under the collar of his hospital gown.

Swanson leans in a little closer. "It appears you hid your secret well."

"Well, now you know." Neil grins, holding his arms out slightly.

"Tell me, are there any others here like you, Neil?"

ACKNOWLEDGMENTS

'd like to start by thanking my husband, Jason, who enthusiastically brainstormed and debated avenues for my characters throughout my writing process, and whose unwavering support and reassurance made me feel loved beyond measure. Thank you for sending me to my room to write and taking on the extra load during my absence. I could not have done this without you and your constant motivation. Next, I'm thankful to my three little ones, Jackson, Savannah, and George, who limited their call for mommy to one thousand times per day, instead of the typical ten thousand. They understand how special they are and handled my time away with grace.

Thank you to my mom for igniting my love of writing from an early age, and always supporting my dreams. You and Mike are a constant light in my life, and I'm so thankful for your unconditional love and encouragement.

Thank you to my big brother, Addison Tackaberry, who introduced me to all the wonders of the universe. I grew up listening to him talk about black holes and quantum mechanics with his best friend, Jason, my future husband. I can always depend on Addison to share the latest conspiracy theories and new scientific discoveries. He will happily listen to me ramble about space and cheesy UFO documentaries (my guilty pleasure). Don't ask him about the future of the universe, though . . . the heat death will have him talking for hours.

Thank you so much to my book club!! You all got sick of hearing me whine about wanting to write a book and demanded I take action. Thank you for the encouragement and for letting me join meetings even when I didn't have time to read the assignment. And thank you for your perpetual support through the writing process. Thank you to Diana Barefield, LuAnn Croix, and Lisa La Susa for being my first readers, my biggest cheerleaders, and lifting my spirits. Thank you to Brittney Pettigrew, Tia Kennedy, Patti Kimmel, Liz Curry, Kristiina Ouzinous, and MaryAnn Smiley for all the love.

Thank you to Kirk Fuson for my gorgeous cover design. It is everything I could have ever hoped it would be. It draws you in with its beauty, emotional pull, psychedelic accents, and sense of awe. The longer I stare, the more I love it. I hope it connects with my readers as much as it does with me!

Thank you immensely to my editors, Kristin Noland and Jeanette Smith, who helped me navigate the endless complexities of writing my first novel. You have taught me so much!

Thank you to my entire team at Greenleaf Book Group for believing in me and providing me the opportunity to share my story with the world.

ABOUT THE AUTHOR

GENNA PFISTER is a native Texan raised in Bellaire and Flower Mound. She currently resides in The Woodlands, Texas, with her husband, three children, two dogs, and bird. She graduated from the University of North Texas in 2011. When she isn't juggling after-school activities and cooking Jessica Seinfeld recipes, you can catch her at the local rock gym eyeing a 12- and settling for an 11+ route. She also enjoys her monthly book club meetings and occasional adult ballet class. Nothing makes her feel more humbled and grateful than staring into the night sky with her family to acknowledge this magnificent universe.